THE UNKNOWN HERO

By Isaac Philips

Imaginary Publications
ZELLWOOD, FLORIDA

Copyright © 2018 by Isaac Philips.

All rights reserved. No part of this publication may be reproduced, distributed, or transmitted in any form or by any means, including photocopying, recording, or other electronic or mechanical methods, without the prior written permission of the publisher, except in the case of brief quotations embodied in critical reviews and certain other noncommercial uses permitted by copyright law. For permission requests, write to the publisher, addressed "Attention: Permissions Coordinator," at the address below.

Imaginary Publications, LLC
3406 Round Lake Rd.
Zellwood, Florida 32798

Publisher's Note: This is a work of fiction. Names, characters, places, and incidents are a product of the author's imagination. Locales and public names are sometimes used for atmospheric purposes. Any resemblance to actual people, living or dead, or to businesses, companies, events, institutions, or locales is completely coincidental.

Book Layout © 2017 BookDesignTemplates.com

The Unknown Hero / Isaac Philips. -- 1st ed.
ISBN 978-1-7320645-0-8
Library of Congress Control Number: 2018904078

To Grandma,
who never let me lose heart.

Contents

Preface I
Materials IV
Measures VI

Prologue 1
A Cloudy Day 5
Midnight's Cry 19
To Survive Reality 27
Questions 39
Stories 53
Why Me 71
Between Two Points 87
The Meeting 105
Reason & Retribution 125
Picking Up the Pieces 141
Heading Home 153
Red Skies 167

Encounter	183
Surrounded	195
Revelry & Authority	209
The Makings of a Plan	223
Touching Death	235
The Petition	249
First Dark	267
Dire Happenings	285
Departure	299
Facts & Redemption	317
One Way Out	335
Den of the Alien	353
The Face of Evil	369
A Setup for Tragedy	383
The Battle of Wills	399

Preface

The Unknown Hero is a story nine years in the making. The original concepts for many of the planets and characters came when I was twelve years old. Maybe two or three of those have survived to this final draft. The plot was secondary at first, gradually developing from the setting and characters.

I was never much of a reader growing up. I wasn't good at it and couldn't find a book that really interested me in our home library. I knew what I was looking for: a science fiction adventure without the plot holes and excessive aberration that you come to expect from the genre.

An old, space series on the top shelf eventually caught my eye. I started reading it. To this day, I don't know how I made it through the first book. From my disappointment, came the aspiration to write my own book. If I couldn't find the story I wanted to read, I would write it.

Not long after I put my pen to the paper, however, I stumbled across a fantastic young adult novel, Outriders by Kathryn Mackel. That further inspired me. I saw what a good writer could do. My best friend and fellow writer, Jesse Ramsdell, then loaned me some of his favorites. He opened my eyes to the literary world.

The lack of reading in my youth was a blessing and a curse. Mostly a curse because I didn't have a clue how to write a good book or what it should sound like. The reason I still count it as a small blessing is that it forced me to develop my own writing style instead of piggybacking on a favorite author.

This book has been my school of writing. At the beginning, I was the worst of writers! I had to completely rewrite the story three times, and we're not talking about rough drafts or the countless edits in between. Each time I wrote it to the very best of my ability, for better or for worse, and each time I could see the improvement from the early chapters to the latter ones.

My advice to anyone who wants to get into story writing is to just start writing. No doubt you've heard advice like that before, if not word for word, but there's good reason for it. Writing is an art form. So much of it can only be learned by doing the work.

It doesn't matter if your story is awful at first; you're going to rewrite it anyway!

Advice aside, you wouldn't be reading this today if it wasn't for my grandma. As a former English teacher, she made the perfect editor. Bit by bit, she imparted her mastery of grammar to me. I never would have made it this far without her encouragement. That was the greatest blessing. She is always engaged with the story and always eager to explore the next chapter. I couldn't thank her enough if the 70,000+ words in this book were divided exclusively between "thank" and "you".

Materials

Precious Metals

Pazin. Brilliant yellow, like the evening sun, and extremely rare, Pazin is a symbol of power and excellence. Beyond decoration, it has many useful properties once refined.

Hazin. Hazin is a lustrous gray metal. Its smooth feel and resistance to wear and corrosion, make it the choice material for jewelry.

Kazil. On the cheaper end of precious metals, kazil is used industrially as a substitute for pazin wherever possible. Depending on how it is refined, it can range in color from pale yellow to dull orange.

Notable Ores

Gortal. Because of its strength, gortal is the base for most alloys. It possesses a dark, matte gray coloration and is immensely heavy.

Nortal. One of the hardest materials in the solar system, nortal is mined exclusively on Dasahr. In its purest form, it is perfectly black and semi-transparent.

Torrod. Torrod is a brittle, low density ore. It is a lucrative export of Orra, more valuable than pazin. When synthesized, it provides a material superior laser resistance.

Measures

Time

Moment. One wingbeat of a commodore harrier. (1.4 seconds)
Micro fragment. 50 moments. (1.17 minutes)
Time fragment. 50 micro time fragments. (About an hour)
Mega fragment. 5 time fragments. Approximately one 4th of an Allanite day or one 5th Orranian day.

Distance

Mirco unit. The length of a yelling beetle. (1 inch)
Unit. 10 Micro units. (0.85 feet)
Mega unit. 10 units. (8.5 feet)
Coordinate. 2,000 units. Approximately the width of the Straight of Rathyn. (A third of a mile)

Prologue

"Line them up!" The order echoed off the thick walls of the throne room.

Eight prisoners, handcuffed and blindfolded, were escorted in under the guard of the palace sentinels. The guards stood the prisoners side-by-side before the throne and then dropped to one knee in unison.

"As you wish, Emperor."

The grand throne rotated silently to face them. The Emperor's eyes glowed bright as he looked the eight over. Some had taken badly to the chemical treatment, large, discolored splotches strewn about their bodies.

Steepling his fingers, he addressed them sternly, "If you help us, you will live. This is your one chance. Don't try my patience! We will find your solar system—it's a matter of calculations now—so consider your service penance for the destruction you've brought here!"

The Emperor beat his fist on the armrest but then slouched back. "We will overlook your crimes. Step forward if you will lead my scout ships where they won't be detected. Your colleagues cannot see, they'll never know."

No one moved. He waited just a moment, though, and then announced, "Ah, one shows himself wise!"

The fear of being the only one was broken, and a hefty Wulvry hopped forward. He was a scientist, like most of the prisoners, and insisted on being called Dr. Kazacara.

"And another," the Emperor declared. He looked to the palace sentinels, "Escort *these* to the launch pads. Remove the restraints once aboard the scout ships. Now dispose of the others."

At the last moment, a second prisoner stepped up before the sentinels fired a blazing, blue laser through the unyielding six. The bodies collapsed like stacks of bricks.

Only when it seemed that everyone else had left did the Emperor call out, "Furygon!"

The tall figure emerged from the shadows.

"Exactly how long would it take to ready an invasion scale fleet?"

Furygon didn't respond, so the Emperor blurted irritably, "Approximately!"

This time the mechanical answer came at once, "1.7 orbits."

"Initiate preparations."

"Yes sir."

CHAPTER 1
A Cloudy Day

Caltow awoke to the howls of iiows beckoning the new day. He glanced out an open window into the soft light of dawn. The sun had barely peeked over the rolling hills. His ranch was small but serene, and its flawless, light-green grass now seemed to radiate the few rays gliding through it. Nonetheless, a gust of cool air foretold another day of heavy rain as it buffeted his tough, red skin.

He was a Sinos. A horn, distinctive of the males, extended from the back of his head. He had deep blue eyes, a short snout, and a V-shaped tail. Large legs with back-facing knees set him right at eight units in height.

The Sinos were one of the three races native to Allanoi and coexisted with Mideks under the planetary government. The Sezree, however, were a people lost in time. They remained hostile to civilization and refused to embrace the interplanetary language.

Caltow walked through the dark main room toward the kitchen. The furniture was sparse but fashionably antique, and a mounted sword acted as the only decoration. He pictured the sword beneath its dust covered scabbard, three narrow blades standing back to back with a web of bars joining them in the middle. At the bottom, the blades swirled together like a tornado into a long tapering handle.

It had been passed down through his ancestry, always escorted by a tale that had presumably been tainted over the generations. The legend spoke of Sinos settlers attempting to colonize Allanoi, battling savages and even crossing over one of the Great Chasms before finding peace among the Mideks. These stories didn't hold water anymore; the history books showed that his species had been on the planet since the beginning of time.

Too bad too, the stories had always brimmed with valor, adventures he often dreamt of and coveted. So unlike himself, his adopted younger brother never seemed to mind the monotony of the ranch. Why should he? The hard times that had followed their parents' tragic death in a transport accident were finally behind them. The bills were paid, and for the last two orbits they'd turned a handsome profit. Indeed, things were good now yet apparently not good enough to quell his yearning for excitement.

A long sigh brought him back to his dull reality. He rummaged through the kitchen cabinets for flour and elleal nectar. *There's just enough left for sweet cakes.* He pulled the other ingredients from the cold storage, measured them out and then whipped them together. The mere aroma of sweet cakes never failed to rouse his brother from even the deepest sleep, and he soon had two stacks piled on the table.

A moment later, Kiiyeepo waddled in, his giant eyes struggling to stay open. He was average for a Midek, almost two units shorter than Caltow with towering, pointed ears that equalized them. He was covered in thick fur, dark gray except for a lighter patch on the front of his chubby body. His giant arms and hands could nearly touch the floor, because of his short, squat legs.

Kiiyeepo sniffed the air once more before exclaiming. "Oh, my favorite!"

"I figured we deserved it, and I was up anyway."

"Yeah, it's a good thing iiow birthing season is over, I don't know how much longer I can go on with such little sleep."

"Tonight's not going to be any better I'm afraid. More rain is on the way, and I heard another baby coming last night."

"Rain treatment again!" Kiiyeepo muttered. "But the iiows sounded so happy?"

"You know they can't predict the weather any better than the forecaster!"

"Another long day. Better eat up, we'll have to get out there early," Kiiyeepo replied and then buried his broad snout in a stack of sweet cakes.

As soon as they stepped outside, they were smacked by a strong gust. Two iiows stood on the covered porch, a mother and child. The baby had gone through what every iiow on their ranch had to, rain treatment. In the wild, these creatures traveled the planet in a herd, never being caught by the rain.

When tied beneath a covering during a storm, the newborn would come to believe that rain couldn't touch it, and its natural fear would be driven out.

Taming these creatures is probably the most heroic thing I've ever done! The thought disgusted Caltow as he untied the pair. Nonetheless, it was true.

They specialized in raising the purest breed of iiows. However, to maintain highest quality animals, they had to limit the size of their herd. This made their iiows very valuable, coveted by breeders and racers alike.

Kiiyeepo had hurried ahead to the stable to let the other iiows into the pasture. They needed plenty of time to run and graze before the rain, especially the young ones.

He found the newborn already standing. When Caltow arrived, they checked its vitals and then injected it with a fortification tonic. They also tagged its ear, labeling the youngster 31D.

After leading it out to join the others, they set about the worst part of the job, cleaning the stalls. The stench was an effective motivator. They hastily shoveled out the manure to be used as fertilizer in the garden and then laid down fresh bedding.

The garden was thriving with the recent rain. They grew three crops, all nutritious for the herd and not too bad to eat themselves. By the time they finished weeding and gathering the ripest fruit, storm clouds had obscured the sun.

They tethered the newborn on the porch with its mother, which meant another night of blocking out screams until the baby finally accepted the lie. The ranchers mounted their preferred steeds. The large, mature iiows carried them at high speeds on powerful hind legs. Caltow worked in memorized rhythm with his brother, rallying the rest of their herd and then slowly guiding them into the stable.

Kiiyeepo kept watching the sky as the looming clouds darkened. They'd cut it close. Much to his naiveté, far beyond those clouds, another darkness was rushing in.

Furygon studied a holographic map of this new solar system. The planets danced in the air before him, slowly rotating on their axes. They were exceedingly close-knit, orbiting the sun as a single entity and maintaining a constant relationship from one to the next.

Moving in from the edge of the map, an armada of gargantuan space cruisers was shown in perfect detail. It was inside the flagship of this fleet, Sovereignty, that he now stood.

This was the control room, the crux of the strategy and war departments. At this rare moment it contained the four highest ranked officers and their assistants: Kallor, high general of the army; Rekiph, aerospace commodore; and Hajrius, chief of intelligence. Together these three made up the First Council, and Furygon was their only superior on this fleet. He was the Supreme Operating Officer, or S.O.O., and was second only to the emperor of their own solar system.

With his command, this moment would mark their first action in this system and no doubt war. It had been simulated again and again, but now everyone was hesitant, checking their calculations one last time.

Rekiph finally turned away from the data interface. "All landing ships are ready for your command, sir."

"Launch!" Furygon spoke like a computer spitting out words, as though he had no voice of his own.

There was a nod and a button pushed before tiny specks began streaming out of the holographic fleet. The landing ships. Each was headed to one of the eight planets that exhibited some signs of life.

On board were two drones and a team of spies, which would be left on the planet to gather information, as well as two agents tasked with collecting specimens of any sentient species. By analysis and interrogation, those captives would be the key to understanding these faintly familiar worlds. Familiar because two hundred and ninety-six orbits ago, they'd shared a solar system.

Everyone stood around the map for another micro time fragment or two, some uttering silent prayers that all would go as planned. They were of the same species, Deurtex. Most were very tall and very lean. Their long limbs ended at small, two-toed feet and spidery, five-fingered hands.

Their natural appearance mattered little, however, for they were covered in dense, gray suits that fit like a second skin. It shielded them from the air, which would burn their flesh, even wrapping into their mouths to a one-way exhale valve. Inhaling pulled air directly into their tracheas through modifiers that filtered and treated it.

Affixed to each suit were innumerable black, metallic panels, forming an armored shell. The suit itself could only be seen through the gaps between the panels that allowed the wearer to move freely. That is, with the help of many small motors to counteract the extra weight. Though this artificial exoskeleton made them rather indistinct from one another, it had become who they were over the orbits.

The crowd soon disseminated, leaving Hajrius standing inert beside the holographic map, seemingly oblivious. He was in deep thought, with his knife-like ears laid back and eyes dimmed.

Although Furygon hadn't moved from his place either, he questioned, "Have you nothing to do?"

"Too many things," Hajrius replied, his ears returning to their usual vertical position and his orbs regaining their pale-green glow, "and thinking is one of them."

Standing eye to eye, Furygon inspected the Chief of Intelligence. Hajrius's long face was typical for a Deurtex yet so unlike the large, black sphere he'd learned to call his own head. It had been twenty-six orbits since Furygon saw his true face, twenty-six orbits of seeing through bright yellow slits and speaking through a metal face-plate. Everyone knew about the combat injury, a terrible blow to the head, that had given him this sphere. It was said that without it he would die.

"Is something wrong, sir?" Hajrius asked, still tracking the progress of the landing ships.

"No." The answer was cold and abrupt. A second pause would not ensue, however, as the room's doors slid open and Myeerp rushed in.

"Forgive me if I'm disturbing you, sir, but—"

"Forgiven. What do you want?"

"Your audience is required on the teleconscious."

"Who is it?"

"The Emperor, Exavyir, he wishes to speak with you at once."

Furygon said no more, quickly following his secretary into the hallway network. The main corridor dead ended at his office, a dark, plain, and respectively humble room. He took a seat in front of the teleconscious, through which he could both see and speak to the emperor. He shooed Myeerp out and then stared blankly at the digital screen. Exavyir was seated on his throne, back home on Pazarin.

Impatiently, the Emperor demanded, "Explain current location."

"We are entering the lost system. We are passing one of its outer worlds. Rapid deceleration is active."

"Explain the present state of the landing ships."

"They were launched fifteen micro fragments ago. They will reach their destinations simultaneously in eleven point seventy-nine time fragments."

"Good," Exavyir muttered to himself before ordering, "I want images of every captive and any information about them sent to me as soon as possible."

"Yes sir."

"Try to make allies with some of the leaders there, on our terms of course." The Emperor considered for a moment if there was anything else to add but then switched off the teleconscious without even the slightest conclusion. Though abrupt, a series of demands followed by an explanation or a 'Yes sir', this was how all their conversations were.

After an evening meal of roast meigoo and ololie berries, Caltow was finally able to relax in the main room. He switched on the broadcast receiver. A female news anchor appeared on its digital screen seated behind a wide desk. The name of the channel,

News 77, covered the wall behind her along with the company slogan, "See the big picture."

"...Breaking news from Chriyoss!" she announced. "Only one week after the heartrending assassination of Decider Arkash, the First Prince has been found guilty. Following Chrion royal tradition, he will be banished to one of the uninhabitable worlds. An image was leaked earlier today of the capsule that will make the terminal voyage positioned for launch. It's possible that justice may already have been served.

"Prince Phendrou, Arkash's younger son and soon-to-be Decider, said in a speech earlier this morning, and I quote, 'In one week I have lost the two dearest to me and Chriyoss its greatest leader. I am inadequate to take my father's place, but together, Chrions, we can right this atrocity'. Now to our colleague on Chriyoss for more information."

The scene changed to a reporter standing in front of a huge triangular structure. "I'm outside the Royal Gathering where Phendrou made his speech, half of which in tears. This will also be the site of his formal inauguration in just a few days. Despite how dark these times are for the people here, most of all for the new Decider, he has already shown leadership by renegotiating the Chriyoss-Xonero Pact with Arch Duke Uryiten, effectively strengthening the alliance.

"As you may know, however, only the First Prince is given access to his planet's deepest secrets. This means many long days are ahead for Phendrou as he assumes the role of—"

The receiver cut out as the rain intensified, pounding the house. Caltow rose and peeked into Kiiyeepo's room. He'd been reading, but now, with the screams of the baby iiow, he just begged for sleep.

"Good night," Caltow said and headed to his own room. Small, wooden sculptures were perched on a high shelf encircling the space. He sat down at his desk and drew out his latest piece. It was a carving of himself leading Kiiyeepo over a grassy hill, a tribute to the day he'd brought the Midek home from the orphanage. *Almost done.* He pulled out his chisel and started carving.

CHAPTER 2
Midnight's Cry

Kiiyeepo's eyes shot open. A fleeting screech, like glass scraping against metal, had pierced his sleep. Had it been the baby iiow? A squeaky door? The crack of lightning? Had he dreamt it? He shrugged it off and tried to go back to sleep, only to have a sudden click jerk him bolt upright.

Darkness poured in through the windows. Neither of Allanoi's moons shown outside, yet the surroundings couldn't be concealed from his huge Midek eyes. He looked at the time keeper on the wall. *A quarter past midnight. What would Caltow be doing up at this time?*

He focused, blocking out the iiow's screams and the patter of water drops. A series of barely audible thuds sounded from his brother's room. *Footsteps,* he concluded, *but not Caltow's.*

He slipped out of bed and crept to the other bedroom, as quietly as he could. He pressed one ear to the door. Not a sound came from within. Pushing inside, he found the covers thrown off the bed, a single window open, and a small black object sitting atop the desk.

He picked it up, a smooth bag with a long drawstring containing something odd shaped and hard. He shoved his massive hand through the loop made by the drawstring and let the bag hang from his wrist as his mind raced with possibilities. *Maybe Caltow's outside. Maybe he's just checking on the iiows. Those could have been his footsteps, couldn't they?*

It was a reasonable scenario, yet it didn't keep his legs from shaking as he advanced toward the front door or keep him from glancing out every window on the way. He stepped out between the two iiows, the baby now thrashing against its restraints.

"Caltow..." he called but instantly silenced. Something had flinched in the darkness. He scanned the scene, his eyes straining to penetrate the walls of rain and mist. Then he saw it, a giant form as pitch black as the night. It turned and ran, melting into the distance.

Kiiyeepo put his hands on his head. His jaw hung open in disbelief. Every likely cause of the strange noises dissolved, his mind stitching them together into one horrifying incident. That creature, whatever it was and for whatever reason, had abducted Caltow.

He's not gone. Not yet. He pulled himself onto the mother iiow and loosed the rope. *Not if I can help it!*

"Go! Go!" he yelled. His mount reared back, almost bucking him off, and then leapt from the porch. It galloped forward, its feet plunging into the saturated soil and mud flying up behind it. It was relying on its rider to steer it clear of rocks and holes, for iiows had very limited night vision. Mercifully, the terrain was a soft carpet of grass for many coordinates around the ranch.

One obstacle stood in the way, the fence. Approaching the edge of the pasture, however, Kiiyeepo saw that a section of the fence had been smashed. He knew he was on the right track now and gunned for the opening.

Less than a micro fragment later, he caught sight of the black monster. A fourth of a coordinate separated them. He spurred his iiow faster with a slap on the tail, but, as if in retort, it ground to a near halt. It howled and thrashed, trying to shake the water out of its soaked fur. One water drop taken to the eye had washed away everything rain treatment had taught it.

Kiiyeepo fought to keep hold with one hand, while reaching up and pushing the iiow's ears down over its eyes. No longer seeing or hearing the rain, and with the Midek's warm arm around it, it settled down after a few moments.

He steered back toward the target, but the monster had disappeared into the hills. Undeterred, he made a guess and trotted onward, his hand still clamped in place. Eventually, the rain broke, and his mount accelerated to its top speed.

At the crest of the first hill, he could see but a thousand more grassy knolls stretching to the starry horizon. A sinking feeling began to weigh on his frenzied heart. His gaze fell. That's when he noticed the wide indentations left by the monster's heavy footfalls.

"Go!" He slapped the iiow's tail. The tracks flew beneath him, as he sped over a second hill. Summiting a third brought the monster into view again.

His wits flew the coop at the glimpse of his goal, and he was changed at once into a mad hunter. The next hill halved the monster's lead. No longer did the undulations block his line of sight, so Kiiyeepo took in every detail of his foe.

This was no beast, rather a mighty machine. Pneumatic pistons hissed, shooting in and out with every step. He estimated that it was eighteen units tall and at least ten wide. There was good sense in running from it, but all his sense had already fled.

Two huge cylindrical tanks were attached to its back, both full of murky, green fluid. Hazy silhouettes appeared suspended in the dark substance, unmoving. One looked to be a Midek; the other had to be Caltow.

What has it done to you? He felt nauseous but assured himself, *He's alive. He has to be!*

A plan to rip off the tubes or to shatter them and lift his brother out churned in his mind. The daydream was soon upset, however, by the scent of pumping engines. He was close, really close.

Up on the iiow's back like a jockey, he charged down the left flank of the monster. Its body swiveled toward him, and it quickly took aim with the arsenal of weaponry mounted to its right arm. Without a moment's thought, Kiiyeepo jumped straight at it, arching his body to avoid the shot. He felt a large projectile graze his hide, and then an explosion erupted behind him. Iiow blood splattered him in midair, and the shockwave slammed him against the front of the black monster.

He found himself clinging to a glass cockpit of sorts. Peering through its tint, he saw a more reasonably sized being inside. A grin formed on the pilot's face as he drew his arm inward, as if to beat his chest. Kiiyeepo got the picture in time and swung to the side before the mech could mash him.

A surge of adrenaline heaved him up between the mech's huge, metal shoulders. Its arms flailed to bat him off, since, not having been designed to shoot itself, its guns couldn't hit him. He dodged and ducked, and then he climbed down onto its back.

Wrapping his arms around Caltow's tube, he set his feet to push off. The chance never came, as the mech's body began to rotate. It spun faster and faster until centripetal force sucked Kiiyeepo's legs out behind him. In a moment, he was whirling horizontally, but his grip held firm. *I... Must... Hold... On... for Caltow!*

This thought alone permeated his mind, as the hard claw-like tips of his fingers dug into the tube's every imperfection. It all turned futile when the rotation suddenly reversed. The strength of a hundred couldn't have resisted the inertia. He flew off, tumbling to the ground.

Darkness closed in on him. He had to fight for his grasp of reality. Something huge and metallic began to materialize on the nearest hill. *A cloaked space ship...* The thought drowned in the darkness, when he finally blacked out.

CHAPTER 3

To Survive Reality

Kiiyeepo groaned at the blinding light and squinted. The midday sun beat down on him from a cloudless sky. *Where am I?*

He gradually sat up, every muscle screaming in protest. He never knew a person could ache in so many places. Big bruises covered his back, and he was sure his head had been hit with a sledgehammer. His arms felt like they couldn't even lift themselves. He grumbled and moaned, and that seemed to help a little.

Picking at the blood caked onto his fur, he wondered, *What happened?* It was as though his memories were obscured by thick fog. There yet indecipherable.

He started to scan the area, though it was a struggle just to bring the blurry world into focus. He was on a hillside. Further down, a shredded iiow was scattered across the embankment. He looked away gagging, and his gaze fell upon a small black bag to his right.

He scooped it up, moaned again at the pain, and dumped its contents out in front of him. There were two pieces of carved wood that had evidently once been connected. Turning one around in his hands, he stared straight into the eyes of a wooden Caltow.

"No, no, no!" His mind became clear in an instant, the events of the previous day flashing to the forefront. Nonetheless, it all felt wrong. *Senseless evil.*

"Why would it take him? Why Caltow? Why!" He yelled at both everything and nothing, which only served to bring reality crashing down on him. The tears began to flow unabated. His brother was gone.

He grabbed the other piece of wood and squeezed it mercilessly in his fist. He didn't need to look at it to know it was a carving of himself. *I should have gone when I heard the screech. I could have stopped the abductor! I'm a pathetic excuse for a brother!*

Up on his feet, he threw the carving with all the strength he could muster, even though doing so sent pain rippling to his toes. He watched the tiny wooden Kiiyeepo shatter upon a rock and shatter his anger.

Only sorrow remained. He dropped to his knees beneath the weight of grief and wept. He would cry until the tears ran out.

Prodek stood amidst the cold cosmos itself. Magnets in his feet held him at the very edge of the launch deck, which extended out from Sovereignty's front hangar. Most of the fleet could be seen from here: two invasion cruisers, one battle cruiser, two landing frigates, and two destroyers were at the front. Though out of sight, he knew that an identical formation headed up the rear.

Parallel to Sovereignty was Ascendancy, an immense dreadnaught that eclipsed the four coordinate long size of the mighty flagship. Both capital ships had an additional landing frigate and an orbiter docked to their undercarriages. Lastly, floating between them was a pair of blocky freighters.

Prodek gazed down at the beautiful, green globe the fleet was parked beside. He couldn't help but imagine it as a young planet, unsullied. *Vibrant, tranquil... innocent. Will we have to bring destruction and war even here?*

They'd received its name, Allanoi, before they lost contact with the scouts. Soon enough, sentient specimens would give personality to the planet. *Very soon*, he thought, picking up on the fast approaching landing ship he'd been waiting for.

He pushed off and floated back into the hangar. None of the hangars or storage areas across the fleet were equipped with gravity fields, but, normally office-bound, the experience still enthralled him. He was a high administrative officer of the Intelligence Department, Hajrius's right hand, and the go-to for gossip.

The activity in the hangar was much more subdued than one might expect. A team of workers stood with hover-carts at the ready, and a few others milled about, yet they all sprang to life when the first landing ship alighted upon its rail.

Electromagnets rapidly decelerated the ship as it coasted in. The rail could also be used to launch the ships at up to five thousand coordinates per time fragment. For this reason, the landing ship's return trip had actually been significantly longer, even though the distance was shorter.

It was directed to a spot on the far right side of the hangar, leaving plenty of room for the others to line up beside it as they came in. The doors of its storage bay folded down like ramps, allowing the workers to rush inside.

Come on. Those specimens can't stay in their tubes forever! Tubes big enough to hold a small Dragon streamed out, riding on the hover carts. Already the transfixing syrup had become mostly clear.

Prodek walked over and inspected the first one, particularly the being inside, before instructing, "Research area zero, bed one."

The worker hurried away without a word, and the next tube was brought up to him. Distinctly red in coloration, the being had an avian figure, including a long parted tail and no noticeable ears. *Now this is a new lifeform, different from any of the species back home.*

Though intrigued, he didn't delay. "Research area zero, cell fifteen."

The mood was very serious here, not one cheer like those that had rung through the intelligence division of the control room when data started pouring in from the drones. Nonetheless, it gave him a sense of authority that he never had around Hajrius, and he relished it.

Six tubes came and went. There were multiples of the same race, in addition to some that they would no doubt find on other planets. It was information that they were after, though, and the more the merrier.

When they finally emerged from the landing ship, he motioned to the two agents. They came promptly and stood at attention before him. They were in high spirits, so he asked a question he knew they wouldn't anticipate, "How was it?"

It was a moment or two before they replied, their unlike answers merging into unintelligible noise. One thing was certain: both concluded in a clear 'sir', and that was enough for him.

"Continue to the debriefing area. Agent XR2, I will be expecting you at my office tomorrow, by the seventh time fragment. We shall discuss your run in with that native," he ordered abruptly, when he noticed Myeerp enter the hangar.

"What's up? Are you in charge of this whole operation?" Myeerp questioned, looking around at the workers preparing for the next landing ship. His tone was happy and excited, but Prodek heard the sharp message hidden beneath, *What do you think you're doing calling me out here? Remember who's in charge!*

Brushing it off, he answered, "It's a great opportunity to get out of the office while I still can. I'll practically be strapped to my desk for next seven days or so."

He was thinking, *It's the perfect opportunity. We probably won't be able to meet again for at least seven days.*

Myeerp shrugged. He didn't have any news on his end.

"What time is it?" Prodek asked. The inquiry would have been a shock to those who knew him personally, who knew that he was a walking timetable. He watched Myeerp mull over the true meaning of the question and then try to formulate a natural sounding response.

"I believe we're in the fourteenth time fragment. I was keeping tabs on the landing ships; it looks like you'll be here a while. It might get pretty busy for you, though."

Prodek heard only the essence of the communication, *It's not time to make our move. It won't be for a while. I'm watching for the right moment, but we need to wait for things to get going first.* He indicated that he understood with a sigh. Speaking in code was arguably overkill, but he knew better than most the full scope of Sovereignty's surveillance.

"Any interesting beings?" Myeerp meant nothing more, just trying to make small talk. They were friends after all or perhaps used to be. The stress of their scheme seemed to have reduced them to mere colleagues.

"Look in cell fifteen of research area zero," Prodek shouted above the roar of engines and the zing of the rail as the next landing ship entered the hangar.

The sun was setting over Allanoi, but that was little relief. It had done its damage. Heat exhaustion had set in, bringing on waves of dizziness and nausea. Kiiyeepo would have thrown up a hundred times if he'd had something to heave.

He stroked his hands through his fur, trying to release the heat trapped against his baked flesh, as he managed another step forward. It felt as though all of his brainpower was required just to put one foot in front of the other. He would have preferred it that way, at least, since he had nothing pleasant to think about.

More than four time fragments had lapsed, spent persistently slogging along, and there was still no sight of anything. He could tell he wasn't walking in circles by the position of the sun, which was something, but in the back of his mind he knew he'd chosen the wrong direction. He was too sad, though, and too desperate to accept it.

The rolling hills seemed to transform into sand dunes in the orangey, evening light. *How fitting.* His mind transported him to the never ending deserts that he once read covered the planet Orra.

It took him a whole micro fragment to perceive that something had blocked the last sliver of the sun but less than a moment to recognize what. Caltow stood on the next hill with open arms. *It can't be. It's just a mirage like all the others. It's not real, there is no Caltow anymore!* He reluctantly tried to convince himself, but he ran to it anyway, and Caltow ran toward him. As Kiiyeepo stepped into his brother's shadow, it became apparent that this was no mirage.

"I thought you were..." he threw arms around his brother, but they passed through, and grief surged into his tone, "...dead."

The image melted away, and he beat the ground with his fists in frustration. The tears would have come again if he'd had any left. *No... That's the third mirage so far, and it was so real too. I must be losing my mind.*

He climbed to the hilltop and then turned in a circle, searching for any sign of hope. The sight of a lone ololie berry bush not far ahead would have to do. He touched its branches just to make sure it was real and then gulped down the first berry he saw. He instantly vomited. Steadying himself with deep breaths, the next berry stayed down, as well as every other on the bush.

Night had fallen before he continued on. Allanoi's smaller moon shined from the zenith of the sky. The Tracer it was called, because it always followed the sunset by a few time fragments. The ololies did more than replenish his fluid. They also indicated that there was a farm nearby or perhaps a woodland, for the bush couldn't pollinate itself.

Long before his theory could be tested, though, he was shocked to find a road. With weeds shooting up through every crack and whole chunks of it buried or missing, he'd stepped on it before noticing it was there. He couldn't guess how old it must have been to have deteriorated to such a wretched state. One thing he was certain of was that no one used it anymore. He would have bet his black bag on it. That is, if there hadn't been a transport coming his way.

CHAPTER 4
Questions

"So, what are ya doing out in this here nothingness? You look awful!"

What am I supposed to say? That I was chasing a mechanical monster? He'll think I'm crazy! Kiiyeepo thought, hesitant to answer. In truth, he merely didn't want to relive the experience. "It's a long story."

He was sitting on the passenger side of the old transport he'd seen. The driver, a Midek in his mid forties, had generously offered him a ride. He spoke with a heavy accent stereotypical of eastern Allanoi.

"If ya don't wanna tell me 'bout it, that's fine. I do need'a know where you live, though. Somewhere around here?"

"I... don't know actually," Kiiyeepo said, glancing out the window. He didn't want to impose any further on the Midek's kindness. "Just take me to whatever town you're heading to. I'll stay at a hotel and then catch a people carrier home in the morning."

"Alright, there's still a ways to go," the driver replied, giving the transport's speed dial almost a half turn. "The name's Fradoo by the way."

"I'm Kiiyeepo—" His breath was short as the old transport's hover jets bounced them over a large rock. They were going three times faster than what he would have considered safe. There was long pause and another jolting bump before he probed skeptically. "Do you drive this road often?"

"I'd say! I'm on it most every day."

"Wow," Kiiyeepo exclaimed, halfheartedly. "Well, what do you do? Where does it go?"

"I, uh, can't exactly... tell ya that. Ya see, it's kind'a a government thing," Fradoo stammered, shifting uneasily in his seat. He quickly changed the subject. "You heard 'bout the invaders?"

"Invaders! Someone's attacking Allanoi?" Kiiyeepo's giant eyes flared with panic. "Who? Where? Why!"

"Calm down! Ain't nobody attacking nothing... yet." Fradoo took a long breath before explaining, "A mid-space buoy picked up on an incoming fleet of space cruisers only yesterday. Not far outside the atmosphere they are now. People are go'in nuts, some say it's the end'a the galaxy. They might be right too, them ships are huge, could take on the whole solar system."

"But why would they do that?"

"It's hard to say. They might not do anything. They might'a been explore'in the galaxy and happened to find us. Who knows! It's all speculation. They haven't tried to make contact nohow. Several nations have sent 'em transmissions at bunches of different frequencies. No response."

They took Caltow. It's too much of a coincidence. The being in the black monster was of no race I've ever seen! Kiiyeepo realized yet questioned further to confirm his suspicion, "Do we at least know what they are or where they came from?"

"Nope. My guess is that they came from the other side of the solar system. Ya know, the lost worlds."

"I thought those planets became uninhabitable after the Separation, like Grekin, or were completely destroyed."

The Separation was the first bit of history a person learned. It was what set history's present course and shaped the modern age. Nearly three hundred orbits ago, the solar system was torn in two by an approaching star, now the binary of the sun.

Twenty planets met their demise during the Separation, many of which were inhabited. Numerous ill-fated species were wiped out, civilizations were entirely obliterated, and knowledge and technology were set back by a century. Millions of people fled their homelands to planets that astronomers had predicted would survive.

"So did I," Fradoo replied. "But has anyone gone find 'em and checked? Nope."

"I guess you're right," Kiiyeepo said, though his thoughts were elsewhere. *I should tell him. I saw an invader! If no one knows what they are, then any information could be important. I should probably tell him about the mech too.*

Fradoo was saying something or other, but he interjected, "I—I think I saw one of the invaders."

"What?" It was impossible to discern if Fradoo was surprised or legitimately didn't hear.

"I ought to explain from the beginning," Kiiyeepo said, a tad louder. He recounted his chase, describing as best he could the details of the mech and its pilot. He couldn't bear to make any mention of Caltow.

"An eighteen unit tall, drivable robot and a space ship that can become invisible, that's *really* something." Cynicism saturated Fradoo's tone. "Why in the galaxy would ya chase such a machine?"

When Kiiyeepo kept quiet, he continued, "I heard a story 'bout a Nilose living on Orra who might'a fought an invader. He claimed he'd fought it 'cause it was try'in to abduct his father." He looked straight at Kiiyeepo, suddenly stern. "Is that what happen'a you?"

"My brother," was all Kiiyeepo could choke out in response.

"Oh, I see. I'm real sorry 'bout that."

Each drifted into his own thoughts. The transport plowed through a field of flowers then out onto a modern road. Plentiful traffic greeted them, even at this time fragment. Most of the shops they passed were still open and would probably never close. Since most of the population had perfect night vision, Allanoi's cities truly never slept.

"Them abduction stories are true then," Fradoo mentioned, as if to himself.

"Stories? There are more?"

"There've been people vanish'in all over the solar system. That Nilose I told you 'bout is the only person who *saw* the abductor, though, other than you that is."

His voice fell so low as to be barely audible. "I don't think you'll be get'in home any time soon."

"Why's that?" Before Kiiyeepo could get an answer, a small hotel caught his eye. "How about there?"

"Alright, that'll do you nicely. The carrier depot's just a block further. I'm sure that they'll have maps and such," Fradoo said, bringing them to a jarring stop. "Maybe I'll see you 'round one of these days."

"Maybe so." Kiiyeepo hopped out onto the sidewalk. "Thanks for everything. Why don't you think—"

"See ya!"

Kiiyeepo watched the transport speed off, feeling quite unsettled by their final exchange. Several people bustled past him, some glancing at him sideways. He felt humiliated. He realized that he must have looked and smelled vile, covered in blood and sweat. *Shouldn't that be all the more reason to help? Instead, they turn their noses up at me like I'm trash.* He glared back with contempt.

Turning to the hotel, he was startled by an old Midek who'd stopped right in front of him. He was a short fellow with an unyielding stare, his eyes narrowed in suspicion. In one hand, he carried a couple of grocery bags. With the other, he leaned forward on a wooden cane, elaborately carved, as if straining to see. "You've been in a fight, have you, son?"

"Well, um..." *Kind of. What does he want? He must think I'm some hooligan up to no good. He looks ready to call law enforcement!* "I... fell down a hill... a steep one," Kiiyeepo fumbled for a reply. His half lie seemed to melt in this Midek's piercing gaze. He promptly added, as politely as he could, "Thank you for your concern, though!"

He made haste to the hotel before the interrogation could persist. After Fradoo's disturbing comment, the last thing he wanted was rumor going around that he'd chased an invader. He placed a hand on the lobby door, ready to go inside, when he was hit by a sickening realization. He had no money.

You idiot! He rested his head heavily on the glass door, as to punish himself. Usually it was his satchel that he felt hanging at his side, but now it was just the small, black bag. *Can't you do anything right? Anything—*

"I take it you do not have a place to stay for the night?" A subtle, raspy voice called from behind. Kiiyeepo turned to face the old Midek, who was still standing in the same spot on the sidewalk. He answered with a reluctant nod.

"You do not have any money, yet you have a money bag." The Midek walked up to him, and his penetrating stare returned. "Did it fall out on that oh-so-steep hill?"

"Oh, that's... nothing," Kiiyeepo said, unconsciously grabbing the bag. *He knows I lied about the hill. There's no way I can talk myself out of this now.* He sensed a need to explain everything, absolutely everything, hoping that maybe then this Midek would be convinced he wasn't a troublemaker and simply needed a little help. For some reason, he was comfortable doing so, entrusting a secret to a total stranger. Though he didn't know why, he felt certain that the elderly gentlemen would handle the information wisely.

"This, I can tell, is the truth, strange though it may be. It is good to properly meet you, Kiiyeepo. I am called Veellee," the old Midek said. He circled around him once, attempting to be inconspicuous but obviously inspecting him. "You could stay at my place tonight."

Kiiyeepo was shocked. *I guess a few* are *willing to help!* He stumbled over his words, trying to express his gratitude, "I don't know what to say... Thank you! You're too kind!"

"I am." Veellee seemed to be reconsidering, his fingers drumming on the head of his cane. He held out the groceries and instructed anyway, "Now come along, son, and do carry these for me."

Kiiyeepo took them gladly, though he got the impression that it was a test of sorts. As he trailed after his new friend, he mentioned, "I feel like I know you from somewhere."

"Is that so. You wouldn't happen to frequent these parts?"

"No, not at all." Then Kiiyeepo thought about it. "Actually, I'm not sure. I don't even know where I am."

"Why you're in the suburbs of Diishan. The Pazin Reach is fourteen coordinates to our rear."

Kiiyeepo's mouth opened and closed a few times. His dreams had taken him here on numerous occasions, letting him gaze down from the Pazin Reach with all the tourists. A bridge over six thousand units long, about three coordinates, the Pazin Reach was the pride of Allanite engineering, a marvel to the rest of the solar system, and a symbol of Allanoi's strength. It spanned one of the Great Chasms, and from its ends rose the metropolis of Diishan. If his eyes hadn't been glued to the road as Fradoo narrowly missed pot holes, he would have seen the towering skyline and the ceaseless flow of air and space traffic.

"Wow." The words finally came out. "I've always wanted to come here."

"I suppose the circumstances affect the mood of coming, but you should see the bridge before you leave, nonetheless," Veellee commented and then returned to their previous topic. "You have visited Chriyoss, perhaps? We could have met there."

"No, I've never been off the planet or done any traveling really. Do you go to Chriyoss often? What do you think of the new Decider?"

"I have a house there. I have not yet made my mind up about Phendrou. He is certainly not his father. Arkash was a solemn individual, willing to make hard, even controversial, decisions. He possessed an erstwhile view that the executive is a slave to the welfare of his people. I do not see this in Phendrou."

They continued back and forth in an effort to find where they could have met but were still at a loss as they stepped through Veellee's front door. It was a sizable house, three times larger than the tiny structure Kiiyeepo called home, and very elegant. The decor was old-fashioned yet exotic. The wood furnishings, engraved with flowing symbols, displayed the work of master craftsmen. Carved figurines and mounted, ornamental pieces rounded out the layout. All retained the natural, unfinished beauty of their ruddy wood. *Caltow would love this!*

"Welcome to my humble abode. There is food in the cabinets. Help yourself. You must be famished." Veellee said, as he stooped down to one of the lower compartments. He dug out two little jars. "Use these ointments on your wounds. They will facilitate the healing process. I suggest you get cleaned up before applying them of course. Down that hall you'll find a wash room. You will have to pardon me. I have a couple of business transmissions to attend to."

Kiiyeepo gratefully took him up on every offer. First things first, cobbling together a meal. He ate almost as fast as he could put the food on his plate. Nothing lifted a Midek's spirits like a full stomach.

Eventually, he got to the bath. As he lowered himself into the warm waters of the wash pool, he discovered that it was quite an advanced apparatus. It even had a waterproof remote control for adjusting the temperature and detergent concentration and for operating the built-in jets.

It's like in the fancy resorts! he marveled. Turning up the pressure, he let the jets massage his sore body. *So soothing...* He very nearly fell asleep but held off the drowsiness to lather on the ointments.

Veellee briskly showed him to one of the guest bedrooms. The transmissions had left him visibly stressed, but he didn't talk about it. On his way out, though, he stopped to bid, "Good night."

Say something else, just one more word! Kiiyeepo begged. Those same words had been Caltow's last. *No, not last! He's still out there...* The door gently closed. Other than the invader's footsteps and the iiow's screams, a thick silence blanketed the room. *No! That's only Veellee walking, and those are transport signals...* The darkness grew static, for there wasn't a moon in the night sky. He tried to evoke pleasant memories, but his mind kept on recreating the horrible scene. The tears came anew; then came the nightmares.

CHAPTER 5
Stories

By the time morning rolled around, Kiiyeepo was winded. Sweat dampened his fur, and his heart raced. He sat at the edge of the bed and placed his hands on the sides of his head, as if to keep it from falling off.

Every gruesome fate that the invaders could have inflicted upon his brother had played out before him. From Caltow being experimented on in a laboratory to being brainwashed until all that was left was a mindless drone, the nightmares knew no bounds. In the last one he'd thought he was right there, watching helplessly, as an invader dissected him.

A shiver ran up his spine, the images were unbearable. Nevertheless, he didn't bother telling himself that they were only dreams, for any of them could have been true. He would never accept that his brother was dead, but he now realized that he would probably never see him again. As much as he didn't want to, he fled back to the memories.

"You are crying, son." Veellee stepped into the room and sat beside him. "It has really hit you now?"

Kiiyeepo hadn't noticed but now wiped his eyes. Between sniffles, he spoke in a faraway tone. "They're all gone. First my parents, then his, and now he's gone too."

"Your brother had different parents?"

"He's a Sinos. They adopted me. I don't even remember my real parents. It's the orphanage as far back as I can recall."

"I see."

"Then my new parents died in a transport accident, and..."

"I know how you feel," Veellee said but then paused. The look on his face suggested that he had a story just as grim but hated to remember. Sometimes reopening an old wound was the cost of healing someone else's. "It has been so many orbits, but still I see her face as clearly as yesterday. She was my better half. I had been away on business, the norm then, when the horrible disease reared its ugly head. Or, as they say now, 'went virulent'. Of course, this happened before the cure and before they could detect the disease in its dormant form. The same day that the contagious monster erupted in my wife's body, it infected my son as he tried to help. He, in turn, passed it to his wife..."

Kiiyeepo watched the water build in his eyes. Veellee looked away, rubbing his hands together until composed enough to continue. "They died within a couple of days. Even my dear grandson was taken from me. He was only two orbits old. Life often begins at the bottom."

"What do you mean?"

"When you are down in the valley you never come up in the same place you went in. The valley forces you to make a choice. You can become bitter and depressed in the shambles of your former life, or you can use that opportunity to lay a stronger foundation and rebuild as a better person. You have to make that choice."

It was so easy to be bitter. *How am I supposed to rebuild? I can't run the ranch without Caltow,* Kiiyeepo thought. "What did you do?"

"Come along, son. I will tell you over breakfast. How does a cup of tea sound, to warm your soul?"

It sounded wonderful to Kiiyeepo. The problem was choosing a flavor. Veellee had almost fifty different teas from every corner of the solar system. The collection brought the old Midek obvious delight. Not surprisingly, quite a few originated on the glacial world Rodeous.

However, he recommended a Prax favorite, dordy berry tea, imported straight from Dasahr. Kiiyeepo blew into the steaming mug and then took a tentative sip. The herby taste of the tea leaves counterbalanced the potently sweet berries, creating a tangy but smooth amalgamation. Never before had he experienced such a flavor. *Maybe I should consider traveling!* In his heart, though, he knew it would take a miracle to get him off the planet.

The mood lightened a great deal after a warm morning meal. They leaned back from the table, sipping their teas, as Veellee continued his story. "In that deep valley, I became a miserable person, full of hate and regret. It plagued me that if I would have gone home the moment she said there was a problem, I could have said goodbye. Instead, I returned to cry over corpses. My emotions took over. I had let them and quite nearly lost the company to foolhardy decisions.

"It was the wise counsel of a Dragon by the name Yonan that pushed aside the dark veil. I have viewed the world differently since then. The company used to be the idol to which I devoted all of my energy, yet it is now that it most prospers. I try to appreciate people more and be a blessing to them by offering my home and my many things."

Kiiyeepo didn't like being one of 'them', but at least he would soon be out of his way. "What company do you run?"

"I founded CosmoCon thirty orbits ago, when I invented the modern space lane. From there, it has grown beyond my wildest hopes. We now manufacture the majority of flight navigation equipment for personal spacecrafts. Of course, we also operate space stations orbiting most of the inhabitable worlds. The empire is incomplete without a space station in Nieyowpon's orbit, though. Its location in the middle of the planetary cluster makes it a precious jewel for regulating space travel, but Chriyoss and Xonero have the gaseous orb blockaded. They refused even the largest sums of money... but I digress, forgive me."

He hadn't needed to say more than the name. Before CosmoCon, space lanes were simply interplanetary flight paths that accounted for the planets' rotation and the movement of space stations around them. Now they were constant and everywhere. They adjusted automatically for the range and speed of one's vessel, as well as for the space traffic already on a specific route. People could choose a lane and be sure that it was the most efficient way to their destination. This was one of the most powerful companies Kiiyeepo knew of. He would have expected its founder to live in some moon-sized mansion.

He was shocked, but one question sprang to the end of his tongue. "Why'd you move? Layoff all those workers and leave to Orra?"

Veellee's countenance darkened; frustration tinted his eyes. He must have been asked that question a thousand times. Over the past two decades, many of Allanoi's leading corporations had transferred their operations to facilities on other planets. As one of the biggest, there was a major uproar when CosmoCon made the move, leaving a small army of Allanites jobless.

"That was the worst decision I've had to make," Veellee began. "The wrong people have been in our government, son. Selfish, stubborn fools who drive on their petty agendas no matter what the cost is to others. Do not misunderstand me. The current administration is a good one, I believe, but it seems to be too late to mend the damage. Regulations and taxes have burgeoned, markedly in the manufacturing and mining industries. Furthermore, Allanite workers want more for their labor than it is worth.

"The point came when I had to move production to Orranian factories for the low tax burden. For other companies the all but nonexistent regulations on Krashad and cheap labor were a better bargain. It probably would have been for CosmoCon as well, but I refuse to support that regime."

"You're saying Allanoi brought it upon itself?"

"Yes, but I fear rival nations may also have had a hand in the matter. Without those businesses, our planet is weak. If war should come again, our assembly of war machines will be protracted to put it lightly." Veellee spoke in fear-filled words. Both of them immediately thought of the looming alien fleet. "Enough of the heavy talk. Do you like to read, son?"

"I enjoy a good book when I can find one."

"Good, then come along."

They ambled through the main room to a pair of thick doors, patterned with windows that gave away the spacious library they protected. It took a firm heave to get the doors open, and they closed behind them with a satisfying thud.

Veellee disappeared behind a tall shelf. Although he spoke normally, his voice reached Kiiyeepo as a measly whisper. "Go ahead, browse the shelves. Take whatever interests you. I have read them all."

The room was cleverly designed to dampen sound, so much so that Kiiyeepo could barely hear his own footsteps. He perused the first section in awe. "All of them! But there must be a thousand books here!"

His jaw was agape as he scanned the other shelves. There were more than just books. Chrion scrolls, tomes from Dasahr, and even olden manuscripts were spread throughout the library. Veellee had quite a diverse palette for literature.

"I read with haste, and I am old," the reply struggled to make it across the room. "I implore you take at least one tome. None have been produced in several orbits, at least not a proper one. I fear their time has come to an end."

To be deemed an authentic tome, a work had to be of Dragon or Prax, native Dasahrian, authorship and had to be written to the standards of the planet's ancient scribal order. Kiiyeepo had heard that each one was a masterpiece and asked, "Why? What would stop people from writing them?"

"The Krashad-Praxus War. The Prax are too busy rebuilding their nation and preparing for when the king of Krashad, Vorrnum, puts action to his threats and strikes again. Vorrnum has turned his own country into a monstrous sweatshop. The Dragons are slaves to his bidding with no will, incentive, or education to write a tome," Veellee explained. "That Vorrnum is an evil fiend, seeking only to rule all of Dasahr. He would have overrun Praxus already had our planet and Thirasmasoaric's empire on Zanquin not come to their aid, purchasing their ore and placing tariffs on Dragon goods."

The tomes stuck out like stars in the night, shiny metal rings binding together the thick pages. Each ring was engraved with a snippet of information, like the author's name, the title, and all the lackluster, legal stuff. Kiiyeepo pulled a tome from the shelf, examining it before reading its synopsis. Engraved in its title ring was The Unknown Hero. He chuckled inwardly, the two species that struggled most with the use of a writing stick were the two with the writing renowned.

"That is a good one, son, even among tomes... for fiction that is." Veellee appeared at his side. "It was authored by a recent tome writer. Some of his works were thought to be prophetic, as well as his death on the very day Vorrnum hatched."

"Could I?"

"Yes, do take it," Veellee pushed a small book into his hand, "and take this too. It's a pocket guide to the planets and peoples of our solar system. It will come in handy when you do decide to travel."

"Thanks," Kiiyeepo said faintly. He hesitated for a thoughtful moment. "I can't keep these. You've already given me so much. I don't know what I would have done if you didn't—"

"Shhh!" Veellee interrupted. "Everyone needs help sometimes. I did. One day it will be your turn to help someone. Besides, what are two books to me? I could buy a hundred more if I wished. Take them and gather your things. We might be able to get to the Pazin Reach before the tourists."

Kiiyeepo retrieved his bag and slipped the books inside. *Veellee sure knows how to pull a person up from the valley! I should hope to be like him when it's my turn.*

Hajrius walked toward the council chamber, annoyance quickening his steps. He was busy and saw little point in the meeting. Yes, there were a few matters that needed an audience, but they would be approved or declined without debate. A few transmissions could have done the job. Unfortunately, it made no difference to Furygon. If a council session was scheduled, then a council session there would be.

He never questions the rules; never gets bored; never tries to change anything. He has detached himself from his own will! That's why Exavyir trusts him... I can't help but think that the injury damaged his brain in more ways than one. Hajrius knew the S.O.O. very well but never feigned friendship like Kallor did. Then again, if he'd been hand appointed to his position by the S.O.O., like Kallor had, he would be a bit friendlier too.

Only Rekiph occupied the chamber. He was an anomaly, with twice the shoulder span of most Deurtex and a wide face to match. The burly figure promptly rose from his seat when Hajrius entered. It was a protocol show of respect to his superior. After the untimely death of the former commodore, he'd been fast-tracked to his position, yet his rank hadn't caught up.

Hajrius mouthed the words 'at ease' and took a seat, a familiar conversation echoing from down the hall. If one could even call it a conversation. Kallor would say a few things, and then Furygon would give an emotionless, single-word reply. Hajrius imagined a jester talking to a rock and grinned at the picture.

No one stood as the S.O.O. plodded in. He cared nothing for the formalities, a fact he'd made quite clear by ignoring them himself. There wasn't the slightest pause before Furygon commenced, "Status report, Rekiph."

"All landing ships have returned. Some were detected but successfully avoided confrontation. Our fleet is set to form the blockade. Should I begin intercepting suspicious vessels? Chances are that armaments are already being delivered to Allanoi."

"Not yet," Hajrius said. "We know, thanks to Phendrou, that the solar system's leaders are planning a meeting, undoubtedly concerning our presence. As long as we have only abducted a few beings, they will be guessing at our true intentions. Blockading a planet leaves little room for confusion."

Kallor agreed with a nod, and then Furygon ordered, "Space vessel interception will begin after the native's meeting. Status report, Hajrius."

"We are closely monitoring the first deployment of reconnaissance agents. We maintain regular correspondence with one agent on each planet. So far, the natives do not seem to detect our signal. More spies will be sent out as we have opportunity.

"I wish to concentrate efforts on infiltrating that meeting in order to pinpoint who is responsible for the epidemic. Should conquest be verified necessary, the agent will eliminate the heads of the opposition—"

"No," Furygon cut him off. "You cannot kill those who are not party with the epidemic or that will join us. Exavyir wants additional allies."

"Very well, I shall have the agent be alert for dissention among them. If a strong enough signal can be established, we should be able to oversee the operation from the control room."

"That will suffice. Status report, Kallor."

"The strategists are all working off basic outlines for now, updating them as we get better information. I'm thinking it'll be about ten days to get through the preliminary phases. After that, we'll have a good vision for the complete battle plan." Kallor looked imploringly to the Chief of Intelligence and added, "Once the interrogations begin, we might get some insight into what we're up against."

"Tomorrow," Hajrius promised. "Tomorrow night at the latest. We had to catalog the captives first and ensure that none of them were carrying diseases."

Apparently satisfied, Furygon rose from the long table. "Adjourned."

Kiiyeepo stepped down from the people carrier onto a broad, sun-warmed sidewalk. Tourists lined the walkway. Most were crammed against one side, as if trying to get as far away from the road as they could. Cables, over two units in diameter, were anchored between the crowd and the road, reaching up to three metal towers, one at each end and a slightly less mountainous one in the middle.

"Welcome to the Pazin Reach," Veellee declared.

Kiiyeepo turned in a circle with his eyes bulging, wonderstruck. An identical sidewalk ran the bridge's length on the opposite side of the roaring, six lane highway. The vehicles hovered onto the bridge as tiny specks in the distance, grew until they finally passed him, and then slowly shrank back to specks before getting off.

"Let me hold your things, son, so that you can shoulder your way through and have a look."

Kiiyeepo didn't wait, releasing his bag and wedging himself into the crowd. Cool, wet air greeted him when he finally stepped up to the railing. He gazed straight down into the Great Chasm; the clouded abyss encompassed his whole view. Coupled with the reduced gravity from having so little ground beneath his feet, an overwhelming feeling of free-fall impaled him. He tensed, seizing the rail on impulse.

Most of the Great Chasms thinned out at some point, allowing people to build bridges across with relative ease, but this one's narrowest point was here. That amazed Kiiyeepo as he traced it out to the horizon. Along either side, woods, fields, hills, and even the concrete jungle of Diishan came right up to the brink, like a giant had sliced the region in two and carefully slidden the halves apart.

He could see the layers of the world: greenery on the surface, and then black soil, and then rock. Each one had been a habitat for Allanoi's three native races. Long before any united planetary government, the Sinos had held only tiny, isolated bits of territory. Entrances were all they were, entrances to their vast labyrinths of tunnels. Down there was where most of them had once dwelt. Some still did.

A Nilose standing beside him withdrew a light stick and tossed it over the railing. Though its brilliant light beamed into Kiiyeepo's eyes, he couldn't help but watch as it plummeted into the dense fog that permeated the Chasm. The light dimmed rapidly and eventually gave in to the fog. He strained his ears to hear the crack of it hitting the bottom, but it never came.

"Wow..." he began to exclaim when a strong hand grasped his shoulder and spun him around. A big, brawny Midek stood over him. His blue sash held a shining, law enforcement badge squarely on his chest and a hefty handgun at his side. "Are you Kiiyeepo?"

"Oh, uh, um..." Too startled to form words, Kiiyeepo answered with a gulp and a quick nod.

The officer's firmer-than-stone voice rumbled in his ear, "You're coming with us."

CHAPTER 6
Why Me

"I got him," the officer said into a transmitter clipped to his sash. He shoved Kiiyeepo toward a law enforcement transport that had pulled up onto the sidewalk. "Get in the vehicle."

"What is going on?" Veellee hustled over to them. He set his piecing gaze on the officer. "Where are you taking him?"

"We have orders to bring him down to the station. Step out of the way, sir."

Veellee did just the opposite, slipping his cane between the officer and Kiiyeepo. "Here's your bag, son. It was good to meet you."

The officer snatched the bag first. He rummaged through its contents before passing it on to Kiiyeepo with a sour look on his face.

"If you need anything," Veellee continued, "my private transmission code is ten, forty-seven, three hundred ninety-four. I hope we meet again soon!"

Kiiyeepo intended to say something polite and thoughtful in response, but "Bye!" was all he could shout before the officer stuffed him into the backseat of the transport. The door slammed closed, its extra tinted window obscuring his view of Veellee.

He was about to wave anyway, out of defiance, but the vehicle bounded forward, throttling him into his seat. Dread hit harder than the headrest. *What am I doing in a law enforcement transport? I haven't done anything wrong! It's kind of hard to break the law on your own ranch. Did something happen here? What if Veellee was being nice to me so he could use me as a scapegoat for some devious scheme!* Kiiyeepo shook his head at the outlandish conjecture.

He waited for a break in the dialog between the driver and office and then piped up, "Did I do something wrong?" He regretted opening his mouth as soon as he heard the fright in his own tone.

"You tell me," the officer demanded. "What were you doing on the Pazin Reach?"

"I was just looking at the Great Chasm."

"Is that all?"

"Um, yes, same as everyone else."

"Trying to blend in with crowd then, huh?"

"No..." *Rude, blockheaded oaf,* Kiiyeepo seethed. He hated having everything he said turned against him. Then he got to thinking. *How did they find me?*

I don't think you'll be get'in home any time soon. The furtive words of Fradoo now rang clear. *Did he tell them? He certainly knew they would come for me, and he did say that he worked for the government. Fradoo seemed nice enough. If he's behind this, then there must be a good reason for it.*

Nonetheless, he kept quiet for the rest of the trip. His nerves got the better of him as they walked into the station. The two officers kept him between them like he was a prisoner about to run. *Did they mistake me for a dangerous criminal?*

The receptionist looked up at him with a comforting yet automatic smile. She was a female Midek, slightly smaller, with brownish fur instead of the gray and a more rounded snout. She glanced at her data interface a few times and then exclaimed,

"Yup, that's the one. What did you do to him? He looks worried sick."

Her girlish voice revealed her age. She must have known someone to get a job here. The waiting list was probably outrageous. When no answer came, she sighed. "Some fellow from higher up is waiting for him in the interview room. Go ahead and take him back."

The burly officer muttered something under his breath that caused the receptionist to shrink down in her chair, but he led Kiiyeepo down the corridor all the same. A Midek was already seated at the table in the interview room, with a sleek, black carry case angled so that he alone could see inside. He showed his badge, bigger and shinier than those representing law enforcement, and then dismissed the officer, "Thank you. I'll take it from here."

He motioned subtly to the chair across from him. Kiiyeepo sat in it leerily.

"Hello Kiiyeepo. You may call me Agent Taatus. I apologize for the brusque transit. I'll get right to the point." His speech was devoid of stutter or hesitation, unnaturally so. "We were recently informed that your brother, Caltow, was abducted—we sympathize with your loss—and that you had prolonged interaction with the guilty party. Information about these beings is very rare and important, as they pose a potential threat to the peace and harmony of every planet.

"The most powerful leaders in the solar system will soon assemble on Orra to determine the best course of action. Should you agree to help this great nation and civilized people everywhere, you will travel with the presidential convoy to Orra. There you will work with a team of bioengineers to construct an accurate model of the being. This will be an asset to our leaders as they address the threat. Are you willing to lend a hand?"

Of course Kiiyeepo would help, yet the thought of going to another planet gave him the fantods. His eyes darted about for an escape route, even though he would never use it. Something in Agent Taatus's tone said that he didn't truly have a choice, but he still asked, "Okay, but do I really have to go to Orra? I have a ranch—"

"I'm afraid so. Don't fret; we have made arrangements for your ranch."

Well, that's just great. What does he expect me to say? Am I supposed to be excited? Kiiyeepo probed crossly, "So what now?"

"We appreciate your decision. Let's get going." Agent Taatus scaled the carry case without a sound and started for the door. A small hand gesture commanded Kiiyeepo to follow.

He obeyed, though it took great effort to maintain Taatus's hurried pace. His legs were agonizingly sore from the previous day. They went out the back door of the station, cutting through alleys and dodging across busy streets.

He didn't complain, for they were in downtown Diishan now, weaving through the masses of shoppers and office workers. Tremendous sky skyscrapers surrounded them, shooting up side by side by side, yet each one was special in its own right. He craned his neck to see where they met the sky. *How can the bottom floor hold the countless others stacked on top of it?*

After several micro fragments, however, Kiiyeepo asked in bewilderment, "Where's your transport?"

"I... don't have one." Taatus's seemingly unbreakable confidence faltered. "I'm working on it. I have bills to pay."

So it was no surprise when they arrived at a people carrier depot. They rushed brazenly past the ticket counter and baggage check-in. It wasn't long before security approached them and requested to see their tickets. Instead, they got an eyeful of Agent Taatus's badge.

"Official business," he said with authority, not even slowing down. For his part, Kiiyeepo did his best to look serious.

When they got to the terminal, however, the carrier was nowhere in sight. Many people were already waiting, but there was space on the benches for two more. Taatus preferred to pace back and forth, checking his timekeeper every other moment.

"It's late!"

"How much time do we have?" Kiiyeepo asked, glad to be able to rest his legs. It was a selfish thought, but half of him hoped the carrier wouldn't come.

"It's a tight schedule. I was told to have you at the capital by morning tomorrow. This is an unwelcomed setback." Though his tone was still cool and collected, his words painted a very different picture. As the carrier finally hovered up to the terminal, he stated, "I'm going to have a little chat with the driver."

The passengers disembarked from the opposite side of the carrier before the gate opened to let them on. Everyone in the waiting area mobbed the boarding ramp at once, elbowing and shoving to get the best seats. Kiiyeepo was sucked into the chaotic stream and deposited in the very last row.

Agent Taatus had somehow avoided it all, showing off his badge to the driver. Kiiyeepo couldn't hear their "chat" amidst the other clamor, so he imagined the words, *I'm on official business. If you don't make up the lost time, completely, it will be bad for you. I think you understand.*

The huge vehicle lurched into motion. Those who weren't seated properly toppled into each other, except for Taatus. He sauntered down the aisle with a roguish grin and took a seat beside Kiiyeepo. "I think we'll make it on time."

Kiiyeepo sighed. The last glimmer of hope that he wouldn't have to go and the excitement of the previous time fragments evaporated in that short moment, yet the day dragged on and on. He would have liked to look out the windows, but his seat afforded him almost no view at all. The agent let him use his mobile vocal transmitter, on the conditions that he kept it brief and didn't give away their location or travel arrangements. Kiiyeepo agreed, simply leaving a message for Veellee to explain what had happened and that he was alright.

He'd read up on Orra in the pocket guide by the time they reached their first stop, where people could buy food and relieve themselves. Lunch was an artificial tasting meal from a package that made him beg to be home. The stop did provide him the opportunity to snag a better pair of seats.

As the sun set over the small town they were passing through, he dove into The Unknown Hero. The story was set in a vast empire, split amongst power-hungry dukes. The technology resembled that of the eighth era, pre-space travel. After reading steadily through several chapters, rumors of a civil war began to take center stage.

"You should get some sleep," Agent Taatus suggested, pulling the lever to recline his chair. It only moved a micro unit.

Kiiyeepo heeded the advice, but trying to get comfortable proved futile. He couldn't shake his anxiety. *I'm just going to give them the information they want and then go home. Everything will return to normal.* Something deep inside told him that many things could never return to normal, however, and he waged a mental war to block it out. Sleep eluded him for the longest time.

When he awoke, large buildings rose in the town's place. They'd made it to the capital, early. *The driver must have continued straight through the night!*

Disembarking was slow, as everyone trudged down the ramp half rested and stiff legged, in stark contrast to the manner in which they'd boarded. Agent Taatus led him through the depot to a black transport awaiting them outside.

Again the windows were tinted to opacity, but, this time, Kiiyeepo dared to lower his to witness the beauty of the city. He expected to be scolded, but the agents kept quiet, and he grinned. The majority of the capital was under historic designation, off limits to new development. The same cobblestones that had been laid so long ago now bustled with all sorts of people and species.

The transport glided along the narrow, convoluted streets. The layout of the city was inscrutable from the surface, corresponding to its subterranean structures. This was typical of all Midek communities from past eras. Mideks had a natural aptitude for digging, with their big hands and ability to see in the dark, which made it a convenient way to construct rudimentary villages. It was after decades of trade and cross settlement with the rest of the inhabited planets that skyscrapers seeped into their society.

In other sectors of the capital, the old edifices of brick and stone intermingled with the modern of glass and metal. The further they went the more government buildings he recognized from news broadcasts: the National Mint, Promissory Court, Constitutional Court, and the fourth house of the legislature.

The road crossed a quaint, little bridge and then curved alongside a weathered yet stately, brick wall. People were clustered at each gate, reaching up with their cameras to capture an image of the President's Mansion.

The executive spaceport, used exclusively by government officials, was hardly a coordinate away. As they pulled into the inspection chamber, thick doors sealed them in on both sides. One guard examined Agent Taatus's conveyance forms, while two others guided scanners around the vehicle. Kiiyeepo was then ordered to get out. He was personally scanned, and his bag was searched once more, before he was permitted into the lobby.

Smooth, white carpet caressed his feet. The large room had an unmistakably modern flair, lavish yet sharp. The ambiance seemed blemished, however, by an extraordinarily thick window in its interior wall. Beyond the glass was a charred, utilitarian launch chamber, the absolute opposite of the lobby, but the contrast was stunning.

A sleek space jet was already parked on the launch pad. Kiiyeepo gawked at its massive engines. The ship was huge, his entire house and stable could fit inside. It was hard for him to fathom that it was on the smaller side among spacecrafts. Whenever the president went on a diplomatic voyage, the news always showed him descending from this very vessel. *Or at least one like it.*

That's when it occurred to him. "Am I going to Orra in that?" He turned to face Taatus, who was leaning against the wall. "With the president?"

"In the same ship, at any rate." The agent looked up from his mobile transmitter. "He's a nice guy. I'm sure he'll greet you. Politicians do that. It's good for their P.R. Just don't get your hopes up too high."

Kiiyeepo was still thrilled, and dreadfully unnerved, by the prospect of flying in the president's space jet. He was drawn to the sound of more vehicles entering the complex but nearly jumped out of his skin when he turned face to face with a presidential bodyguard. The guard didn't budge, so he peered around him. Four elite guards, armored in black, emerged from the motorcade, encircling a tall, austere Midek.

It's President Haazon! He sees me! He's coming this way!

"Stand down," Haazon commanded. The guards blocking off Kiiyeepo immediately withdrew, and then he extended his hand to the young Midek. "It's a pleasure to meet you, Kiiyeepo. I want to thank you personally for your cooperation and offer my sincerest condolences."

"Um... yes... Thank you! It's an honor to meet you too, Mr. President."

"Please, call me Haazon."

"Okay, sir." Kiiyeepo felt so awkward, tripping over his words, but, for that fleeting moment, excitement suppressed his fear. He'd met the leader of his planet, the most famous person he could think of, and was now walking next to him.

Anxiety quickly surged back as they passed through a heavy blast door into the launch chamber. From beneath its wings, the space jet took on an intimidating, even ferocious, appearance, like a leviathan crouched to strike. Ascending the long, narrow boarding ramp, they entered a room directly behind the cockpit. It contained nothing but a row of seats and a compartment in which to stow loose items.

Everyone strapped themselves in. No sooner had Kiiyeepo clipped his restraints in place than his fear welled. He'd never flown before, not even within the atmosphere. *This is insane! What does it take to power those ginormous engines? This thing is practically a bomb!*

He tried to see through the tiny porthole in the door as the launch chamber's roof retracted and the space jet was tilted skyward. By the time it reached its near vertical takeoff trajectory, he was sick with fright. The resonating roar of the engines sent his heart racing out of control. Fire filled the chamber, consuming the ship in a burning cloud before it finally rocketed out.

He was flattened against that back of his seat with such force that it was like having a Buladuk landwhale sitting on his chest. He was wheezing hard, already feeling lightheaded, but couldn't get the air into his lungs. His hands clung to the armrests. He closed his eyes tight and begged, *Space, come already!*

CHAPTER 7
Between Two Points

The atmosphere gave way at last. The engines powered down, there was a pause, and then the hyper cell kicked in. The passengers were slammed back again but only for a moment. The velocity of the space jet soon plateaued, and the crushing inertia let up. They wouldn't have to use another booster until they reached Orra's atmosphere.

Kiiyeepo came to with a whiff of harsh smelling salts, gasping and sneezing. He immediately reached for a barf bag. The medic, an elderly Sinos, already had one out. She checked his pulse languidly.

"You're fine," she said, as she disposed of the bag. "How do you feel?"

"Dizzy but okay." Kiiyeepo unstrapped himself and stood. The inside gravity was active, but he could feel a slight difference from being on Allanoi. *Stronger perhaps.* Everyone else had cleared out of the narrow chamber, so he retrieved his bag from the compartment and followed the Sinos to the main living area.

"My God." He heard Haazon mutter to himself. The president was gazing out one of the windows in the port side of the space jet. "It's so hard to get perspective from the pictures."

Kiiyeepo rushed to a porthole of his own and gazed beyond the stars into the endless nothingness. A chill ran up his spine. He'd lost his bearings. *There are no borders, no bottom or top. We're nowhere in particular, just between two points.*

It was the strangest sensation, like being outside reality and looking in. He felt so tiny and so, so detached. However, that, he now realized, was not a new feeling. For the past two days, he'd been adrift in the tumultuous current of events. *Dragged along, unable to influence my own existence. Each day has been a new crazy dream.* Some part of him still expected to wake up on his ranch to the life he'd always known.

He pulled away to clear his head. When he turned back, he simply admired the splendor of the cosmos. Zanquin took center stage. The oceanic sphere glowed a radiant blue. It was the closest planet to Allanoi, visible from the surface a few time fragments before dawn. At the right edge of his field of vision were the swirling red and yellow gases of Nieyowpon. He shifted his gaze left, where Rodeous shined in the distance.

When he tried to look backward at his own planet, his eyes locked onto what Haazon had no doubt been referring to. The invader's fleet. It looked like a splatter of combustion oil on the green backdrop that was Allanoi. He noticed one puny speck that didn't belong. *That's a space station! Those ships are huge... and Caltow is in one of them.*

"First time in space?" Haazon walked over. "You didn't look so good back there."

"Yeah. I mean, yes, Mr. President—Haazon."

"No need to get self-conscious. I'm nothing more than anyone else. I just have a very uncommon job."

It was spot on reassurance and spoken with such humility. Kiiyeepo was astonished. Glancing back at the window, he admitted, "Sorry, I get pretty nervous sometimes."

"Who could fault you?" Haazon followed Kiiyeepo's jumpy gaze to the fleet. "Daunting, isn't it? That which has come to destroy parked at our doorstep."

"How do you know that they're going to invade?" Kiiyeepo questioned, remembering his talk with Fradoo. "I mean, they could've come for some other reason. Maybe they were exploring."

"Not with a fleet like that. We've sent drones to get a better look at it. It's outfitted for war. The expense of building it must have been astronomical. Exploration fleets are small, because there is no guarantee that they'll find anything, and have life support systems designed to last decades away from any planetary base. I can't imagine the invader's fleet would last much longer than two to four orbits. Moreover, if they were seeking peace they wouldn't be blowing up our drones or ignoring our every transmission."

"But why abduct... all those people? And why wait to attack?"

"I know, it doesn't make sense. It would seem that they're gathering information about our solar system, but why would they invade without knowing what they were up against? That would be like going into battle blindfolded. Nonetheless, we must prepare for the worst, especially since it's also the most probable scenario.

"On that thought, I was informed about your experience, but I would like to hear it from you. Are you up for a late breakfast?"

Honestly he wasn't, still queasy, but it was a chance to talk to the honorable ruler, and he wouldn't miss it. "Um, sure."

They strolled toward the stern of the ship. The rooms resembled a small, modern home and, though sterile, had a lived-in feeling about them. With the flight now rock-solid, it was easy to forget that they were blasting through the heavens. They'd brought a pocket of Allanoi, with gravity and air, into the black void of space.

The table was already set for two in the dining chamber. They dug in—the cuisine was high-class and fresh—before Kiiyeepo began his tale. Haazon paid uncanny attention. He rested his head on his hand, evaluating each statement, but remained silent even well after Kiiyeepo had finished.

It was Kiiyeepo who eventually ended the awkward pause, when he probed, "So, what do you expect of this meeting?"

"Longwinded squabbling. The goal, of course, is to unite the solar system. It may be the only way we can fend off an invasion."

"You don't sound very confident," Kiiyeepo murmured, fidgeting in anxiety, yet he held out hope. "Surely a whole solar system can defeat one fleet, even if some of their ships are bigger than space stations."

"It's not that, though we can't underestimate what they might have aboard those cruisers. The numbers are soundly in our favor. What troubles me is finding unity with the other nations. I often doubt its feasibility."

"But with such an obvious threat, I would think—"

"You don't understand. You see a solar system that hasn't faced war in a decade—or any real combat apart from the scrimmages on Zanquin, when Thirasmasoaric exacts tribute from his satellite nations, and the constant little battles on Dasahr—but I know the political back-stabbing and sabotage that has festered behind the curtains."

"Like what?"

"Most of it is classified. Let's see what I can say without further endangering you."

"Am I in danger?"

"I should hope not. Information can be a dangerous thing, Kiiyeepo. We must be careful of where we look for truth." Haazon got right back on topic. "I trust you've heard about the Chriyoss-Xonero Pact or the Krashad tariff?"

Kiiyeepo nodded.

"Take the tariff for example. Zras, Prime Minister of Praxus, has fought to preserve his republic and liberty for his people. Nevertheless, Prax ore cannot yet compete with the price of Krashad's, because the mining firms there effectively have access to free labor. Allanoi and the empire of Thirasmasoaric placed the tariff on Dragon goods to support the last hope of freedom on Dasahr." Haazon sighed.

He checked the time before he continued, speaking slightly faster, "This is where it gets tricky. We need Vorrnum's military strength, but he won't stand with us unless we bring down the tariff. To do so, however, would leave Praxus in a precarious situation."

"I'm guessing Zras won't join if that happens, right?"

"Zras knows what must be done, but I fear that Vorrnum would go back on his word and exploit the opportunity to finish his conquest. I have to leave you now. Please, excuse me."

Kiiyeepo didn't see Haazon again for the rest of the day, not even for meals. Their conversation had answered one question for him, yet it begged so many more. It was a ray of light shined into the dark cellar of interplanetary politics, and the solar system suddenly seemed ten times as complicated. *I'm glad I'm not the one who has to sort it out!*

Completely alone, he wandered about for a time fragment, exploring the nooks and crannies of the space jet. Aside from the main room and kitchen, though, he had access only to his personal quarters. From the layout of the floor, he deduced that the president had a sizeable office area. The lower deck was exclusively for the staff and guards. Occasionally, he heard them taunting each other and laughing about some sort of game.

He was slightly jealous. After the hair-raising takeoff, he expected the voyage to be exciting, but he had never been so bored in his life. Plopping down in front of the broadcast receiver, he started cycling through the channels. They were dominated, without exception, by talk of the "aliens".

No results from the last major tournament in iiow racing? Or update from The M&D Chasm Speeder Enduro. Come on, the world still goes around! I want to know who won! In truth, he would have been happy with anything that could take his mind off the invaders. He eventually resigned himself to the panels of supposed experts spewing every conceivable speculation about the reason for their coming.

He settled on a program where five such analysts were gathered to evaluate the facts. At this point, however, it had devolved into a head-to-head debate between their personal theories. No two members of the panel were arguing from remotely similar rationales. Both the reasons he was familiar with, conquest and exploration, were vociferously opposed by a theorist who claimed that there was a conspiracy between the invaders and the Chriyoss-Xonero Pact.

Another was more creative, suggesting that the newcomers had lost their home world to war or calamity. Naturally, they would use whatever fleet they had to escape. If they had foreknowledge, it would make sense that they would build colonization ships, as big as possible, to save themselves. The cost wouldn't matter in a survival situation of that scale, since the resources would be lost anyway. He further explained that it isn't strange for the fleet to be equipped for war when they're looking for somewhere to live by any means necessary.

The rest of the panel tore the fairytale apart, calling it a wild speculation without any basis in reality. That couldn't be denied. A historian was the last to present his case, starting off with "a description given by a local Midek".

Wait... A local Midek? He's talking about me! Kiiyeepo listened with sudden interest, "...recovered pre-separation records tell of people on Kallamada 3 already using robotic enhancements to make up for their lack of skeletal structure. Should one of the Kallamadas have endured the separation, we could very well be seeing the result of that continued evolution. In this scenario, we may conclude that they have returned in search of their brethren on Kallamada 1, not knowing that it's little more than an oversized asteroid now."

Kiiyeepo quickly switched off the broadcast receiver. The other theorists would attack the idea on the grounds that it didn't make sense of the threatening war fleet. If the leaders of the solar system were divided amongst conjectures as diverse as these, then he could imagine how heated the discussion would get at the Orra meeting.

The sun never set in space. He decided to turn in when he simply could bear the boredom no longer. The single porthole in what would be his room for the trip looked out the starboard side of the ship at the fiery heart of the solar system, the sun. How strange it was to see a light so intense surrounded by a blackness so deep.

He pressed his face to the glass trying to see behind the space jet. Allanoi had shrunk enough to fit entirely in view. It seemed to glow vibrant green, though mottled with blue seas. The long, jagged lines of the Great Chasms were unmistakable, try as the clouds might to obscure them. His ability to comprehend the beauty of the scene was stunted, however, by his own pessimistic thoughts. *Now I know what it's like to travel a million coordinates and feel like you've gone nowhere. Home has only gotten further away.*

When he awoke, a much smaller Allanoi floated outside the porthole. *I wonder if that means I slept in. What time it is? Or what day it is? Is it a day if we're not on a planet? More like a period of wakefulness.*

It proved to be a better one at any rate. Haazon wasn't so aloof. Over lunch he explained the problem of the Chriyoss-Xonero Pact, more venting his frustration than teaching. "We don't know what stance they will take against the invaders. If they throw their weight behind a particular policy with another powerful nation, like Orra or Krashad, it will instantly have half the political power of the solar system backing it. The remaining four inhabited planets would all have to unite for another policy to contend."

"Is that possible?" Kiiyeepo asked. "What would happen if they didn't unite?"

"If it came to that, it would hinge almost entirely on what course of action the Pact endorsed. Let's hope it's a good one," Haazon said, his attempt to sound positive failing horribly. He did manage to end on a lighter note, offering, "Allow me to show you around the rest of the ship."

The guards leapt from their seats at the sound of the president descending the stairs. In a flash, they had scooped their game pieces into a small metal box, which they now stood guiltily in front of. Haazon pretended not to notice their antics, pointing out the three bunk rooms to Kiiyeepo. The lower deck was expectedly functional with several tables, long couches, and an armory.

The bridge went a step beyond mere practicality. A broad windshield begirded the room, made up of long, transparent slats with strong metal beams between them. It angled back over the front half of the room from the sharp, cone-like nose of the space jet, creating the illusion that they could walk right off into space.

In comparison, the portholes were like trying to see through a crack in a fence. Here there was no fence. Orra, though one of the smallest planets, now appeared as a giant orb. With the sun directly to their right, the planet was perfectly bisected between night and day. The day side was a featureless beige beneath the streaky, smoke gray atmosphere. The darkness, on the other hand, revealed Orra's sprawling cities, a hundred scattered spots shimmering like molten pazin.

Looking up, Kiiyeepo finally noticed the escort fighters. Two were optimized for space with powerful laser canons and heavy armor and would have to dock at a space station. The last one could go airborne and would continue to the surface with the presidential jet.

"I'm going to rest up," Haazon declared. "It'll be morning where we land, and the meeting won't be until late. The pilot will gladly teach you the instruments, though." He cast a stern glance toward the Sinos, who nodded assuringly.

Kiiyeepo grinned. He eagerly examined the plethora of screens and controls. Six meters were featured prominently, labeled fuel, engine heat, surface heat, efficiency, power, and life support. Below them, a digital screen displayed a diagram of the space jet with sections highlighted in various shades of green.

"That shows strain and tension," the pilot explained. "Sensors throughout the body of the vessel monitor its structural integrity."

He briefly went over the other instruments. Most of the screens showed the live map. They could see every vessel within one million coordinates around them moving in real-time. It relied on CosmoCon's space traffic data, collected from space stations and scanners onboard the spacecrafts themselves.

"In reality, the ship flies itself, controlled by our space lane. I only have to take over once we hit the atmosphere or in case of an emergency," the pilot said. He looked at the trip status. "You'll see, we're only 1.8 time fragments out."

They waited a short while before the space lane commanded the ship to initiate deceleration. Automatically, the engines reversed thrust direction and then rumbled back to life. Kiiyeepo watched their speed gradually fall in accordance with their lane. They dipped below 150,000 coordinates per time fragment as they made the final approach.

The trip log flashed, and a message popped up on the screen. "Two thousand coordinates to trajectory correction." The pilot immediately picked up the ship's intercom. "All hear. Rotating to entry alignment in one micro fragment."

Kiiyeepo didn't know what that entailed, but the Sinos was certainly unperturbed. Then the ship pitched sideways, the stars and planets swirling ninety degrees around them. His body instinctively leaned to counteract the movement. Of course, without a corresponding shift in gravity, he simply toppled over. Genuine laughter erupted from the pilot.

Eventually, he was able to suppress his amusement long enough to pick up the intercom again. At the push of a button, a siren blared through the ship. "All hear! We are approaching Orra's atmosphere. Secure all loose items and strap into a g-force seat. Prepare for gravitational deceleration."

He offered Kiiyeepo the copilot's seat, as he strapped into his own. Kiiyeepo quickly sat down. At this point Orra filled their entire field of vision. When it was confirmed that everyone was secure, they disabled the gravity fields.

Moments later, they were plummeting toward the planet's surface. Spearing into the atmosphere, the front panels of the ship in the diagram changed from green to blue. The pilot brought up the nose as the desert unfolded before them, increasing the air resistance until the wings were highlighted in orange.

Still, they were descending fast, but the pilot held firm. Bit by bit the curvature of planet gave way, sloping parallel to their course. Kiiyeepo gritted his teeth and gripped the armrests of the chair with all his might. Despite the altitude gauge, it looked like they were skimming across the desert.

Then he saw the city on the horizon, and his jaw went limp. Skyscrapers of an unthinkable scale rose without any median from the unvaryingly flat sands. The towers of Diishan were no comparison.

"How do they build them so tall?" Kiiyeepo wondered aloud. They were flying, normally now, through the capital city. Many levels of roads intertwined amidst the immense structures, so much so that they couldn't see the ground. The buildings themselves were each fashioned from a compilation of geometric figures. *It's like we time traveled into the future!*

"It's a smaller world so the gravity is a bit less. That and better technology," the pilot admitted. "Quite a sight, isn't it? It never gets old to me."

"It certainly is! Do you come here often?"

"You could say that. Cueyo III, the president of Orra, is a friend of Haazon's. He doesn't know what he's doing—I'd go as far as to call him clueless—and Haazon has had to help him run his planet more than once. Sometimes it's like Haazon runs both planets and has an Orranian secretary."

"But why would our president do that? He should worry about Allanoi first and last!"

"It's a good thing to control Orra. Industrially, it's the most powerful world, which makes it key in a battle against the invaders. There's our stop, the Orranian administrative tower."

Sunlight glistened off the skyscraper's glass façade, as though it was hewn from pure hazin. It tapered, crescent-shaped ledges cutting in incrementally, up to a huge quarter circle crest. An extensive hangar occupied a large section in the upper half of the tower, and they adjusted altitude for landing. Clearance came through at once.

CHAPTER 8
The Meeting

Soft, placid music played in the level interchanger. Kiiyeepo stood in the corner beside his guide, twiddling his thumbs. One of the express interchangers had been reserved for the arriving dignitaries, and the guide had led him right past the second to a basic interchanger.

It stopped every few floors as people got on and off, mostly Orranians floating on their hover discs. Some would stare at him but never say a word. Then again, it always looked like an Orranian was staring, having a single gigantic eye for a face.

He faced his guide rather than stare back. The being's diminutive, feeble body toiled to hold up his oversized, cyclopean head. It was easy to see why they didn't leave home without their hover discs.

130... 114... 97... 68... Once in awhile, Kiiyeepo glanced at the screen above the door as the numbers ticked down. He was seated on the floor with his head resting on the wall by the time they'd reached their stop, level 21.

Silent, lifeless hallways awaited them. Only the path to their destination was illuminated, leaving shadowy offshoots. The guide stopped where the lights ended and faced a door. It retracted in the blink of an eye.

There were ten Orranians inside, four at data interfaces and the rest gathered around a Nilose, who, telling by the exaggerated hand gestures, was trying to describe something to limited avail. He was young, with robust, dark green flesh, and skinny, yet he carried himself with immense poise. *That's the being Fradoo told me about! The one who fought the abductor.*

One of the Orranians broke away, plodding over to the door. He released the guide and then ushered

Kiiyeepo in. "We are glad for your *choice* in coming. I am the supervisor of this department. Follow me."

Data interfaces lined the walls. Long, metal tables were arranged in a zigzag down the middle of the room. Above them, curious equipment in great quantities hung from tracks in the ceiling. Despite it all, it was impossible to get a good idea of what they normally did here, especially since the side rooms were sealed off.

"This team of engineers will be working with you to translate your memories of the alien being into an accurate rendering," the supervisor said, introducing Kiiyeepo to the group. "The Nilose is Valexs, also a witness to an abduction. I hope you two will prove competent in recall."

Valexs extended his hand. "I've heard of you. It's Kiiyeepo, aye?" His smile was small and friendly on his round face, but the black sockets of his dull gray eyes were a bit dispiriting.

"That's right," Kiiyeepo answered. The green hand looked so little within his Midek grasp.

"What do you think?" Valexs pointed toward one of the screens. The figure on it was rough but undeniable; it was the same kind of being as the mech pilot.

"It's certainly coming along."

They took seats, and the whole team set about the task again. Four engineers worked to recreate specific details as Kiiyeepo and Valexs described them, while a fifth compiled the various elements on the main model. There were constant questions, most of which Valexs had to answer. His knowledge of the invader was much more complete, particularly in regards to proportions and textures. There were details that he had inevitably missed in the midst of battle, and Kiiyeepo racked his brain to fill them in.

Although they differed acutely in personality, they worked together with the cooperation of old friends. Their recollections synthesized within the image, sharpening it unremittingly. Nonetheless, they could hardly have been more grateful for the break when lunch was brought in.

"Ugh..." Kiiyeepo instantly silenced himself. He didn't want to offend the Orranians, but the food certainly deserved the exclamation. Upon his plate was a gelatinous cube that tasted like ground up writing sheets and several thin, brittle strips with diverse yet mostly hostile flavors. However, no one else seemed to be affected in the least.

The team split up after the meal. Kiiyeepo was pulled away to develop a model of the mech. Amazingly, they already had a partially shaped blob of almost the exact height and breadth. *How could they know? Had to be Fradoo.*

He was timid about ordering around the engineers, though he could picture the black monster clearly. The memories were etched in his mind. When he concentrated on the details, however, the instructions flowed forth naturally, and the black monster began taking shape from the ground up.

Time droned on to the sounds of punching buttons and constant elucidation. The tedious work grew only more exasperating. Kiiyeepo felt mentally exhausted, yet he persevered until the general form was adequately reconstructed.

To release his own vexation, Valexs paced up and down the length of the room, his long, heavy tail swaying rapidly. The engineers had switched their focus to articulation, and he was doing his best to recreate the battle in his mind.

"Are you sure you cannot think of any other particulars?" the supervisor questioned Kiiyeepo. At this point, though, he cared less about the minutiae of the mech's appearance and more about how it worked.

Kiiyeepo was little help in that department. Rubbing his temples, he answered, "No, nothing."

"Are you confident in the details you have given?"

"Yeah... I mean... I guess so."

"Perhaps the animation will help."

Kiiyeepo looked back at the screen. His eyes widened. He could feel his heart rate rising. The pistons of the black monster came to life as its heavy steps propelled it forward. The body rotated toward him, lining up its arsenal for the shot.

Screech! He slid his chair away from the screen. "That's it, that's the monster."

Everyone stopped and stared, until the supervisor squinted slightly, disapprovingly. He checked the work of Valexs's team and then addressed both witnesses, "Very well. I will send for a guide. These digital constructs may prove to be valuable aids for testing and research." It was the closest thing to a "thank you" one could get from the Orranian.

Kiiyeepo took the moment to view the results of Valexs's efforts. The model of the invader surpassed his best memories in accuracy as well as wholeness. He shivered. Two images that had haunted his dreams were now captured outside himself for everyone to see.

A different guide floated in the hall when the door swished away. "Follow me. Our endowed president, Cueyo III, will have you in attendance for the commencement of tonight's meeting. In the meantime, I will show you each to a suite. Sustenance will be provided at your request."

The hallway lights formed a new route, this one leading to an express interchanger.

I can't believe they want me to speak before the solar system's greatest leaders. Stay calm. Breathe idiot! Kiiyeepo wrung his hands, sweating under his fur. He was riding a level interchanger up from the food court.

Rather than ordering room service in his suite, he'd requested a guide and gone in search of a more palatable, preferably non-Orranian, evening meal. One stall, called The Green Hill, tried to imitate Allanite cuisine. They did a good job of it too, he had to admit, but the prices were outrageous. Of course, he wasn't the one paying.

Floor 192. We're here. He stepped out onto polished stone floor, ornately patterned. There was no way to guess what would lie outside the interchanger doors in this building. He'd gone from a hanger to a suspicious research center, from a hotel to a restaurant, and now to a palace.

The wide passage quickly narrowed to a dead end at a wall with thin lines branching out from the center like cracks. A small device to one side scanned his guide's eyeball, and then the wall retracted in every direction, allowing them a little bit further. It reclosed firmly behind them before the opposite side opened up to the vast foyer of the meeting chamber.

There's Uryiten, Arch Duke of Xonero! And he's talking to Decider Phendrou from Chryioss! Kiiyeepo could feel himself shrinking in the presence of such huge names.

The small Prax entourage looked almost out of place meandering through the scattered clusters of people. They walked on all fours, their broad tails kept low, like predators stalking prey. They were a powerful species, large and muscular, with a dense carapace like armor plating. *They have to be to survive their battles against the Dragons.*

The leader of the pack drew himself up on his hind legs, his tail acting as a support to hold him upright, and then addressed the others. *That's Zras!*

"I will show you to your seat," the guide declared, but Kiiyeepo asserted himself.

"Just a moment." He sidled along the wall as he sought out Haazon.

"Let's play it by ear, if we don't have to suspend the tariff we won't." Haazon was in conversation with a tall blue character wearing a pressed red cape.

The webbed feet and hands meant that this was a Zanquinite. Although Zanquin was home to several races, only two could live out of water, and the amphibious Velphan had controlled the planet since the advent of space travel. Based on their discussion, the being could only be Thirasmasoaric.

"Truly it is a dark day if the best of us should even consider an alliance with that vulgar Dragon. Be it far from me to doubt justice in the face of danger! If I capitulate, I do it for your sake alone. You remember that." Thirasmasoaric's tone was audible pride. How Haazon didn't roll his eyes, Kiiyeepo would never know. The Zanquinite ended the conversation there and turned away dramatically, his cape twirling behind him.

Kiiyeepo waited a moment before approaching. "So... What's been going on?"

"Strategizing. You have to test the waters to know when to compromise and when to hold your ground. In fact, Decider Phendrou arrived early yesterday to negotiate some sort of deal with Cueyo," Haazon answered. "What are you doing up here? Did you finish the construct or whatever they call it?"

"Yeah, but it was the most boring thing I've ever done! They only gave us one break for... I guess that would be lunch here. Anyway, I think I'm supposed to give an account of the abduction. It seems like that's all anyone wants to hear out of me."

"I see." Haazon didn't sound excited. As he turned to his advisors, Kiiyeepo beckoned his guide.

The Orranian led him briskly into the vast, elliptic meeting chamber. The glass shell of the skyscraper comprised the far wall and ceiling, long panels arching high overhead, and allowed hazy stars to shine through. *We're inside the curved crest of the tower, nearly at the top!*

An expansive ring of eleven chairs, each one like a throne in magnitude, encompassed the room's center. Kiiyeepo grinned as his guide gestured to a seat right next to Haazon's. It was designed for

Mideks, down to a step to help his short legs get him up.

Already, people had begun to trickle in. Valexs waved from across the room. The queen of Rodeous, Nighdra, was planted upon her assigned throne, her blue and silver gown glittering as she bobbed to an unheard melody.

She was short and stocky. Indeed, all her features were bulky but also pronounced, like chiseled stone. Most astounding, however, was her super long hair, every unit of which was dyed a different color. It wrapped three times around her shoulders, acting as a shawl, and then cascaded almost to the floor.

The official start time of the event came and went, yet one place remained empty. The chatter around the room petered out, and glaring gazes shifted toward the door as it was flung wide. The figure that strolled in was great and imposing. A crown of bejeweled pazin flowed rearward with the frill of long, pearly horns on the back of his head.

"That would be Vorrnum, late as ever," Haazon whispered to Kiiyeepo. Scaled in a deep orange and auburn with two rows of sharp spines running down his long neck to the end of his tail, the Dragon was still a sight to behold.

Immediately, Cueyo III stood up atop his chair. He waited for the attention of the assembly and then commenced, "Greetings friends and fellow leaders. Thank you for being here tonight on such short notice; however, is it not fear that has gathered us? A space fleet so formidable as to rival our every world has come out of nowhere, challenging our understanding of the galaxy and our wisdom to act rightly.

"It entered our solar system all but five days ago, yet already innocent people have been stolen away from each of our lands. The two beings who witnessed the abduction of their loved ones have worked to form a rendering of the alien. I would like to commence our meeting by hearing their sobering accounts. I hope a sense of urgency takes root in this place."

As he spoke, the floor began to glow at the epicenter of the room, and then a hologram was projected up. It was the model of the invader, life-size and even further refined. Gasps and murmurs rippled around the room.

When Cueyo took a seat, Valexs spoke up, "It was shortly after midday. I stepped inside and knew something was wrong. Aye, a huge robotic arm was reaching in through the window, holding a long cylinder, and that creature," he pointed to the hologram, "was loading my father into it! I charged; tackled the being to the ground, but I couldn't dent the armor. It kicked me off, aye, across the room, and then dropped a silvery ball. Some sort of invisible gas must have been released, because I was out in a whiff."

Whispers stirred the air. People fidgeted, unnerved, but hushed as Kiiyeepo summarized his brother's abduction, struggling to mimic Valexs's confidence. Quite the opposite of Veellee's library, here his words carried with ease.

As soon as he concluded, Cueyo III rose again. "We cannot let these offenses go unpunished, yet senseless war would be a far greater atrocity."

He looked at Kiiyeepo, then Valexs, and then the door. Before he could send them off, however, Phendrou promptly seconded, "I concur entirely! We must endeavor for peace at all costs."

Desertion marred Haazon's countenance. He seemed acutely disappointed and aimed his words at Cueyo, as if they'd gone over the issue before. "The hard facts are that they've taken our people, destroyed our drones, and ignored our transmissions.

Their plans have no place for peace. Are the stories we just heard not proof enough of that? We have to unite our forces and prepare for the worst!"

He had to raise his voice to get in the last line, as Uryiten retorted crossly, "You don't know their plans!"

It was to be expected that he would take Phendrou's side, more than ever with the new, stronger Chriyoss-Xonero Pact. "It is an undue extrapolation of the scant facts we have to infer hostility, let alone intent for war. Until we understand their motives for taking our people, it isn't proof of anything. Secondly, we destroyed their drones as well. What right do we have to say that they shouldn't do the same to ours?"

"Theirs were on *our* land," Zras reminded.

"And ours were encroaching on their fleet," Uryiten instantly countered, though the argument was weak. He turned right back to Haazon. "By saying that they ignored our transmissions, you're claiming to know that they received and understood them. None of it would get through if they use an incompatible communication technology. They may be trying to make contact even now."

"We've picked up on transmitter frequencies between their ships, much the same as our own," Haazon explained, unconvinced.

"Have you intercepted a message?"

"No. That will take—"

"Then there's no telling what those frequencies are for! Perhaps controlling machines remotely or synchronizing their ships. These alien beings may yet conduct communication by other means."

"That's fool's talk, Uryiten," Zras proclaimed. "We must base our actions on whatever is most probable, not on faint possibilities. That's a basic rule of logic. They brought a warfleet, so we must reinforce our defenses."

"The nature of their fleet should not be presumed," Phendrou said coolly, supporting his ally. "We see only the outside and do not know what sort of life support systems these beings require."

Everyone slumped a little in their seats as Nighdra chimed in. She spoke in a slow, steady stream and never paused, not to change topics or even to take a breath. "I do not mean to cut anyone off, please excuse me if I have, but I would be grateful if all—or any—in attendance would give heed and am already thankful to Cueyo for his forthright invitations to dialog here together, even though I become more concerned each moment about the timing as it would appear, unless we are not being truly open with one another, that we have yet to attain the proper insight into our circumstances to definitively set a course, which is why I must say now that I believe an important point, how these aliens operate their fleet—battle ready as it is—in that they haven't shown an aspiration to attack, has not up to this point been addressed, despite giving clear indication that they are seeking an end other than invasion, that they are willing to engage in total war to obtain if extreme force bears out necessary."

For a silent moment, everyone was left trying to sort the influx of ideas. Phendrou was the first to seize the opportunity. "Nighdra is right. Invasion is not their goal. The armaments that incite our dread might very well be to defend them from us. They fear us. We sent transmissions in every recorded, pre-separation language and with what we thought were recognizable pictographs, but these could easily have been misunderstood. If we mobilize our militaries now, they might think we want to wipe them out. That would instigate a war."

"We have to assume that they are rational and competent—a glance at their fleet proves that they are—and they must expect the same of us." Zras contested the Decider's claim, "It is only reasonable to reinforce our armed forces. If logical behavior is enough to trigger an attack, then they're craving a stimulus and could find it anywhere."

The next leader to jump into the debate was Thirasmasoaric, booming, "We must do both! Mobilize yet continue to appear peaceful and diplomatic. To counter a fleet as powerful as this, no matter the method chosen, we must become all the more powerful. That power can only be had in oneness.

"I speak from experience. I united Zanquin, and it has grown mightier than ever in history. Through mutual alliances—"

"And bloodshed," interjected Borgu, the leader of the second most powerful nation on Zanquin. Regardless of the title, his country existed in Thirasmasoaric's shadow.

He was completely ignored, as Thirasmasoaric continued without a stutter, "...and compromise I rallied the Thousand Clans behind my steadfast principles. The benefits of unification that they gained under my government can be realized on the grander scale of our solar system—"

"Put a cork in it already, you quintessence of arrogance!" Vorrnum roared loud enough to make anyone shudder. "War has been preordained by the invaders. It cannot be avoided, at least not in totality. If you weren't so insular, Phendrou and Uryiten, you'd see that! Divided we *will* be crushed one by one, but I won't stand with *you*. You that want to control me by placing tariffs on my goods and funding insurgency!"

Thirasmasoaric slammed his fists down on the armrests of his chair and pushed himself to his feet. "We wouldn't need a tariff if you treated your people even half decently, but you insist on squeezing out every iota of their energy and channeling it toward the obliteration of Praxus. My people love me because I've improved living conditions with each orbit of my rule. I bestow freedom, and my nation becomes greater. Not one word of that can be said for *you*. I—"

"Oh, shut up, no one wants to hear your self-propaganda." Abominable though this Dragon was, it was nice to have someone keeping a handle on the Zanquinite's overactive mouth.

"You've purchased your people's love with their own taxes and blinded them to the tactics you employ in your governance. My people hate me because they know me. Never have I hidden myself behind a veil of deceit as you do. I've chosen my ways for reasons you're clearly unable to comprehend!" Vorrnum rose. Light flashed in his mouth like arcing electricity, but only words poured forth. "Krashad maintains the largest army in our solar system. If you want it on your side, I suggest you don't tell me how to run my country again!"

Haazon stood before another word could be uttered. "We will concede the tariff. We should all be grateful to have your forces fighting with us."

A decision, finally, Kiiyeepo thought but cringed on the inside as he remembered what losing the tariff meant for Praxus. More small concessions were made in this way, the results of the ever-shifting debate and undoubtedly the manifestation of plans crafted well beforehand.

At the same time, hard lines were also being drawn. Haazon and Zras stood on the side of meeting firepower with firepower, appealing for full-blown defense production. It was direct opposition to Chriyoss and Xonero's petition to remain passive until the aliens' motives could be ascertained. The other five leaders took up discrete positions ranging between these poles.

To Kiiyeepo, no argument was without merit. He found himself modifying his own stance after each speaker. Indeed, he was engrossed in the negotiations from the very onset. Little by little, however, his thoughts began to stray. *How long will we be here? I wonder what Valexs thinks of all this.*

Halfway through Nighdra's next monolog her words disintegrated into gibberish. Kiiyeepo gazed up at the stars competing against the city smog. Eventually, his eyes focused in on a pair of large pallid stars set in a blackness darker than the night.

CHAPTER 9

Reason & Retribution

"There!" A shout and a scream combined, Kiiyeepo's terror-stricken voice rattled the chamber. "An invader!"

No one moved, stilled by fear, as they traced his line of sight. The quiet tension was the fuse of a bomb, and the meeting exploded into pandemonium. The unseen occupants of the room, the bodyguards, sprang into action. Most surrounded their respective leaders, rushing them to safety, while the rest opened fire.

Blinding shafts of light punched through the glass. The invader sprang up to evade the barrage and then hurled a silvery ball through the fresh, gaping hole. It rolled to the feet of the bodyguards, erupting black fog that flashed like lightning in a storm cloud.

BANG! The ground quaked. With nowhere to land, the invader itself had crashed down, concealed in the impenetrable cloud.

The scene suddenly spun away, as Kiiyeepo was jerked down behind the huge chair. Valexs dropped to the floor next to him. "What do you think you're doing? Trying to get killed, aye?"

The Midek couldn't conjure a reply, too startled even to draw a breath. Only then did he realize the peril he was in. Though he was still getting his bearings, the weight of this incident was not lost on him. *That invader got through a first-rate security network to spy on our meeting. Our best chance was unity, but what hope is there for that in this chaos? Would it even be enough when they know our weaknesses?*

As the smokescreen faded a firefight began, lasers beaming across the room. The aim of the guards swept to the right, suggesting that the spy was making a run for it. Kiiyeepo peeked out just in time to watch it roll through a side doorway.

"We have to contain it!"

"Circle around and block it off."

"You two are with me." The guards formed a quick strategy and then split up, three giving chase directly into the building's web of halls.

A moment of calm ensued. Kiiyeepo composed himself and then looked to Valexs. "What do we do now—"

His voice was overwhelmed by a protracted shriek, like a shrill siren, that blared from the corridor. Cracks appeared around the doorway, gradually spreading over the wall. The noise culminated with the sound of rocket engine igniting, except short and concentrated.

Immediately, the fractured wall burst inward, bombarding the meeting chamber with a mixture of shrapnel and the three bodyguards. One landed limply beside them, but a groan revealed a spark of life. It was as if a monstrous, invisible fist had throttled down the hallway. Kiiyeepo wagered that, had there not been so much dust, the path of destruction would have led straight back to the invader.

Valexs jumped to his feet with the guard's gun in hand and finally answered, "We get revenge!"

Yes, revenge. Revenge for Caltow. For everything that has happened since that fateful night! Kiiyeepo thought, picking up a gun of his own from an inert Midek. It was one of Haazon's bodyguards, now with blood pooling underneath him. Before his eyes met the unblinking stare, however, Kiiyeepo launched after Valexs. There was a part of his brain that begged him to stop and warned of the danger, but he ran in spite of it. He had to do something to combat this villainy; something for himself, off anybody's leash.

After passing through the jagged opening where the doorway had once been, though, he slowed. The walls on both sides bulged outward. Long gashes had been ripped by the force, even in the floor and ceiling, and many places had been scrapped dangerously thin. The corridor was effectively booby-trapped.

Valexs dodged the hazards so nimbly, disappearing into the dust ahead in no time. For a while, Kiiyeepo could only crawl after the light, quick footsteps. Thankfully, solid ground soon came beneath him, and a long hallway on his left put the invader in view. It was almost at the end of the passage, hobbling slightly. Evidently, the guards had dealt some damage.

Not far behind, Valexs charged after it unwavering and fired off a salvo. The invader threw itself to the side, smashing through the glass as the lasers sizzled by. It flipped midair and landed squarely on its feet on the wide crescent-shaped ledge outside.

It was exchanging shots with Valexs by the time Kiiyeepo caught up. He hastily climbed out into the warm, sooty air that gusted past the building and then scrambled for cover behind a scanning tower. Communication antennae and large electrical boxes crammed the ledge, plenty of barriers for the combatants to hide behind.

It had always looked simple enough, but now, as he raised his blaster to aim down the sights, the whole device seemed much more complicated. He found the safety, a small lever that his thumb had to hold down before the trigger would slide. Through the scope, the world was shown digitally with a bright green dot at the center. The dot hovered over the invader's barrier, a surge box, but he hesitated.

What if I kill it? That's the goal, isn't it? Kiiyeepo's guts churned at the thought of having blood on his hands. *What if Phendrou is right and the invaders aren't bad? They took Caltow. It's trying to kill Valexs! Shoot now!* He fired. The scope flickered to black, so that he wouldn't be blinded by the laser, and then there was a hole through the corner of the box.

Outgunned, the invader retreated, spraying the ledge with suppressive fire until it slipped between a pair of immense temperature control units. Valexs sprinted up to the first unit and waved Kiiyeepo over. He communicated his plan in just a few hand signals. While Kiiyeepo took up a position on one side of the gap where the invader had hidden, he rolled across to the other.

He raised four fingers, but the countdown ended before it ever began as a clear, youthful voice scoffed from the passage, "Mad simpletons! You chase me though your meeting has been ruined all the same and you with it. You will never be able to continue your epidemic. Our vindication will be absolute!"

The shrieking recommenced, so much closer this time, and intensified so fast. A force like solid wind gushed from the opening. All Kiiyeepo wanted to do was plug his ears, but, even though the box was taking the brunt of the torrent, he had to hold on. He strained against the force, heaving his blaster up to the gap. It was impossible to hold it steady, to get off a shot; metal shards were now being scraped off and propelled at lethal speeds.

He still didn't budge, but then came the invisible fist. The temperature control units crunched like beverage cans. They snapped free from their fasteners, skidding away from the blast in a stream of sparks. The unit that had been Kiiyeepo's anchor now slammed into him and knocked him barreling backward.

Time seemed to slow as the ground was pulled out from under him like a rug. He tumbled helplessly over the building's edge, his gaze falling to the tangled highways over a hundred levels below. Even the largest vehicles were indecipherable.

Is this how I am to die? A splat on a highway—No! He rebuked the paralyzing clutch of death that was fear and thrust his arms forward. His fingers curled around the rim of the ledge.

Immediately, the redirected momentum slapped him against the side of the tower. Aches scourged the front of his body; the impact to his head left him dazed. One hand had slidden off before the high-pitched scream of an Orranian on the other side of the glass jolted him from his stupor.

His grip was failing, yet he swallowed his terror long enough to analyze his predicament. Then he forced his tense muscles to swing him to one side, his feet scrambling for traction to push him higher. His hand slipped free—his heart nearly skipped a beat—but the other caught hold.

Don't give in, it's only fear. It did little to calm his frantic breathes. He swung again, in the opposite direction, and seized the rim there too. He grunted heartily as he clambered up at last.

Rolling onto the cool ledge, Kiiyeepo flopped to his back, exhausted. He laughed and cried and gasped for air, all at the same time. "I'm alive! Oh, God... I thought I was done for. What was I thinking to chase the invader?"

He wiped away the tears, the overflow of his emotions. The stars offered but a dim greeting, however, compared to the heavy lasers that blazed seemingly within reach. Two warships, larger than Haazon's space jet by three fold, parried overhead. Each one had its full arsenal aimed at the other. Shells burst in air, shot down before they could hit their mark.

His eyes locked onto a smaller craft descending from the fray, oddly recognizable. *The cloaked spaceship! That's the ship I saw appear on the hill.*

It turned straight toward him. Kiiyeepo immediately started scooting backward. Then he saw the twin rapid guns on the front of the ship shift, and a chill rushed up his spine. He pushed himself to his feet, stumbling as he tried desperately to run. Not a moment later, lasers barraged the ledge.

He dove as a ray flashed above him, close enough to feel its heat. He glanced every which way for some sign of Valexs, but what he saw were shots beaming back at the ship. More guards had finally come.

One micro fragment too late, Kiiyeepo complained, as the invader jumped off the ledge and into the hovering landing craft. The ship swiftly descended out of view before rocketing up again toward the warships. As soon as it had docked inside the larger vessel, the warship pulled away from the aerial combat. It turned spaceward, knowing its opponent was too damaged to give chase.

A feeling of defeat infected all who watched it recede into the starry host. The battle was lost, and there wasn't one less foe to show for it. Kiiyeepo's hands curled into fists. However, the flames of his anger were doused by relief as a small, green hand landed on his shoulder.

"I guess revenge will have to wait for another day."

"We lost. You heard the spy, we're ruined! They know our weaknesses now."

"Since when do we believe the enemy? This was a minor skirmish, not the war. Aye, nothing happened here that can't be fixed."

Kiiyeepo pursed his lips. He didn't believe that last statement. Something had happened; a wedge had been driven between the nations of their solar system.

Counterintuitive though it seemed, he knew this would strengthen the petition to make peace with the aliens. The invader could have easily picked off at least a couple of the leaders, but he only listened. Why shouldn't he have tried if conquest was indeed their goal? In fact, when he did fire, it was in self defense. Kiiyeepo could almost hear Phendrou presenting the argument. Conversely, to the likes of Haazon and Zras, this audacious act of espionage would undoubtedly be a declaration of war.

One of the guards, a Gredwol, strode up to them. "You're both very brave. I'll admit, I doubted your stories, but now I am certain of every word." He escorted them back inside. "Medics have arrived. They will tend to your injuries."

Kiiyeepo's mind was far from his aches and pains, as they backtracked through the hallways. *How could the invader speak the interplanetary language when it wasn't established until decades after the Separation? No one could have learned it that fast! And what it said was even more disturbing. What did it mean by 'continue your epidemic'? What epidemic? How will they exact their 'vindication'?*

He and Valexs were told to wait in the anteroom of the meeting chamber, and they eagerly slumped into the cushy seats. Two of the guards who had so gallantly faced the invader in the corridor limped, bandaged and bloodied, toward the level interchanger, accompanied by a legion of medics. A cart occupied with a body bag trailed the procession.

Kiiyeepo had to gulp back his nausea. There was no disguising the Midek form inside the bag. Was this the price of bravery, a looming destiny for all the real heroes, so unlike the happily-ever-after endings of the stories?

I came a micro unit from paying it. He sank into gloomy contemplation, even as several Orranians quietly medicated and wrapped his cuts and bruises. *I have to get out of here. I can't take this anymore: not knowing what will happen to me in a time fragment and not having any say over it.*

It was, to him, only a moment before the medics had finished and a voice cut off his inaudible plea, "Hey, are you okay?"

He gave no more than a mental reply. *No, I'm fighting aliens and worrying about interplanetary politics! I'm not okay. I want to go home to the things I understand, like iiows and sweet cakes and rain treatment...*

Valex probed louder, "Kiiyeepo, talk to me. What's wrong? Was it the body? Or something that happened outside?"

This time the Midek forced himself to speak, "Both... and then some."

His vague answer warranted an onslaught of questions, but he immediately switched topics. "You live here on Orra, right?"

"Aye, we came from Xonero over nine orbits ago."

"Why'd you move? I mean... It's a desert here."

"My father worked for a real estate development company and readily accepted the position of chief surveyor at their first branch here on Orra. It was our chance to get away from certain... family problems. The company gave us a little, old spaceship, and we left with whatever we could carry in our laps."

"And then what? It must have been weird for you, adjusting to such a different environment and culture."

"Aye, it sure was, especially for my sister since she went into the school here. The academic requirements are brutal. I became a surveyor as soon as I was old enough to take responsibility for the equipment." Valexs sighed wistfully. "Orra's no climate for Xonerites. Aye, the plan was to eventually move to Allanoi. Father got a job offer from a company out there, and we even bought some land."

"Well, what happened!"

"The surveying robot. We knew it was coming, but, like fools, we didn't adapt. Aye, pretty prideful of us to think that no one could devise a machine capable of doing our job. We were laid off before we knew it, and the job offer was rescinded. My family has been struggling ever since. Now that... father's gone..." Memories arrested the Nilose, but he stayed composed. It was a few moments, though, before he could speak again. "I'm going to Allanoi as soon as possible to see if there are any opportunities there. If not, I'll sell the land and... I don't even know."

"Where's your property at?"

"I don't remember the coordinates. Near a town called Nol if that helps."

"My brother and I used to sell our iiows there! Your land probably isn't too far from my ranch. I'd be happy to help you guys if you do decide to move."

"You mean it? What if I flew you home? It would be nice to have a copilot. Is there anything I could do for you on the ranch in exchange for maybe spending a few nights? What a small solar system, aye!"

"Yeah, actually that would be great!" Kiiyeepo exclaimed, picturing his verdant home world. Agent Taatus had said the ranch would be maintained, but he anticipated a lot of work when he got back. *I guess I'll be needing an extra hand now.*

"Then it's a plan! We can leave tomorrow if they drive us out early!"

More time elapsed. It was almost midnight now. They were beginning to wonder if they'd been forgotten when the doors of the level interchanger slid apart and a cluster of guards marched toward them. Haazon stepped out in front of them and addressed Kiiyeepo, "I'm very sorry about what happened. My guards should have gotten you to safety with the rest of us."

"That's okay. They're *your* guards, their job is to protect *you*. I'm nobody."

"Your understanding is undeserved. Unfortunately, our stay will have to be prolonged a few days in order to salvage whatever we can from this meeting. How long exactly is not set. You—"

"Excuse me, sir. Would it be alright if Valexs takes me home?"

"Oh, yes, of course, that would be ideal."

Haazon lingered, unsure what else to say, so Kiiyeepo seized the opportunity. "May I ask you a question, sir?"

"Go ahead."

"Does 'the epidemic' mean anything to you?"

A troubled look darkened Haazon's countenance. He hesitated. "No, I can't say it does... Why do you ask?"

"The invader said 'You will never be able to continue your epidemic'."

"It spoke to you in intergalactic, fluently?"

Kiiyeepo nodded. "I was wondering about that, too."

"That means they had contact with our solar system well beforehand." Haazon's gaze drifted as his focus turned cerebral. No doubt the news had generated a plethora of new scenarios to scrutinize. "Did it say anything else?"

"'Our vindication will be absolute.'"

"Thank you for telling me this."

A voice squeaked, and everyone jerked to face the Orranian guide that had silently hovered up beside them. "President Haazon of Allanoi, Cueyo III will see you now."

"This is farewell then, Kiiyeepo, you're a good lad."

"And farewell to you. If anyone can stop the invaders, it's you!"

Haazon smiled weakly, too weakly, and then turned to follow the guide.

CHAPTER 10

Picking Up the Pieces

"What in the galaxy was that, Cueyo?" Haazon's tone was as sharp as knives. "How did that thing infiltrate your government tower?"

"I don't know... and that means it could happen again! I'm afraid, Haazon," Cueyo whimpered. "I just spoke with the head of security and with the Central Information Bureau. They're reanalyzing their recent findings. One thing is certain: the spy was in the building well before the meeting began."

Haazon tipped his head to the side. There had to be more, as Cueyo unconsciously wrung his hands.

Eventually, the Orranian relented and went on. "Our best guess is that he stowed aboard one of the ships that landed in the hangar. Which means the mystery really is, how did he get on an approved vessel?"

That changed things; it brought another party into the equation, the owners of the ship. Then the implications dawned on Haazon. *The meeting attendees themselves are all suspects. I'm a suspect.*

"The fact that it remained undetected inside a space ship and then somewhere in this building speaks to their capabilities," Cueyo mentioned. "Maybe Phendrou is right about their life support systems and it's not a warfleet after all."

"Don't tell me you're arguing for fairy-tales too now. What if they consider it a colonization fleet? That doesn't make it any less of a threat!"

"Phendrou told me you'd say that, but—"

"Ah, yes, Phendrou. He comes a day early, and suddenly you don't know what to believe. You said nothing of value during your own meeting."

"You can't just ignore his points! How do you explain why an invasion fleet seems to be merely gathering information? No one would seek conquest without already knowing the opposition or without a specific goal worthy of the effort. So, why abduct random people? There has to be some motive or justification for their actions."

Especially if they already had contact. They must have known the exact location of our solar system to send that fleet before any exploration or scouting parties, yet none of our explorers have been able to find their system. Perhaps they knew enough to have such a goal. Trying yet again to reconcile his own position with the facts, Haazon delayed answering. "Those were the Decider's exact words to you, weren't they?"

Cueyo's sheepish voice barely drifted across his oversized executive desk. "Mostly."

"Well, I don't have an answer. I never claimed to have it all figured out. That being said, my people are checking out a new discovery that will, hopefully, unravel this baneful paradox." Haazon didn't share what Kiiyeepo had told him. He trusted Cueyo, but not to keep a secret. The Orranian was his friend, maybe his best. *I can't allow that information to fall into the wrong hands.*

"We were at the intruder's mercy, Haazon! He fled rather than strike. That must mean something."

"Their toying with us, don't you see? They clearly understand our language. How else would they have known about tonight's event? They probably intercepted a transmission. Now we know that they're intentionally ignoring our attempts at communication." Haazon leaned forward, pointing at Cueyo with his huge Midek hand for emphasis. "Whatever they're after, they intend to get their way, and I'm afraid of what that could be. Obviously, it's not negotiation. They will take advantage of any leniency we give them."

"Oh, it makes so much sense when you explain it, but it made sense the other way when he was here. If what you say is true, then why does Phendrou believe in peace?"

"Don't we all want to believe that nothing has to change and that nothing bad will ever happen? We're lazy cowards. Your right, though, he seems too smart for that or too arrogant. He ascended the throne only a week ago! Perhaps he's just following Uryiten's lead. I'm sure they have something up their sleeve," Haazon replied, gradual and pensive. "The problem is your sleeves are empty. Should you accept his rhetoric, you'll be stuck with the short straw somehow."

One could almost see the thoughts swimming about Cueyo's head as he struggled to determine a course of action. "What are you going do?"

"There's already a bill being batted around the legislature to push funds to defense and authorize all war expenditures. If I declare a state of emergency, it will pass with a simple majority in the Common House and the Commerce House," Haazon explained. "I may be able to use this to cut off or suspend certain subsides and pension payments. I'll need the support of the House of Conscience to do it, though."

Cueyo nodded, gravely. He had to think along those lines as well, though the method would be quite different in the Orranian government system. "I will propose a temporary amendment to the Cueyo II doctrine of war to make provision for our current situation."

"Good! Do you think that would be approved?"

"I'm not presently favored by most of the lords. My party does, however, control the assembly in coalition with the Reds."

Haazon scratched his chin, unimpressed. After a moment, Cueyo requested, "Do you think you could stay a couple of days to help me sort things out? I don't know of anyone I can trust in my government."

"I'll stay as long as I can," Haazon answered. He'd already planned on it. "Is Queen Nighdra still on the planet, do you know?"

"She mentioned she would be taking a short holiday before leaving, or I believe that's what it amounted to." As his aid hovered into the office, Cueyo concluded, "I better go now. I'll have someone escort you to your quarters. We'll talk tomorrow."

It was like seeing the natives' meeting in a shattered mirror. Bits and pieces of the event were strewn across the umpteen, digital screens in the intelligence division of the control room. At each station, agents picked apart the words of the native leaders. After filtering through the lies, any potentially valuable statements were categorized and sent to Prodek. The officer then set classification levels, distributed the data, or assigned agents to verify it.

Furygon and Hajrius stood in the very middle room, overseeing the operation. The S.O.O. would not wait for the report. "What have we learned?"

"Much to our good fortune, the leaders were quite clear about what they thought of us. Phendrou did the work for us, inciting them to voice their beliefs and intentions," Hajrius answered, with his eyes fixed on a large, central screen. He used a handheld remote to pan through the newest information.

"No evidence has been found related to who is responsible for the epidemic. As of yet, Haazon is our prime candidate. Even if he is not the perpetrator, his adamance about strengthening militarily still makes him a threat. Thirasmasoaric, Zras, and Cueyo are also suspects. Cueyo didn't posit or support any position, which suggests that he's either hiding something or is politically submissive. If the latter is true, we may be able to usurp him through his own government, leaving the public unaware."

"It is most probable that a coalition of several nations brought about the epidemic." Every word came through Furygon's face-plate utterly deadpan. "Remember Exavyir's orders: total takeover unless they raise their folly."

"Or we're able to nail down exactly who's behind it," Hajrius added. His enthusiasm was immediately quenched when Furygon continued, as though nothing had been said at all.

"Will any of them join us?"

"Uryiten will follow his ally steadfastly if we extend to him the promise we gave Phendrou. I advise sending him a private message, worded to cement his faith in the Decider's claims. Prodek..." Hajrius spoke the name a touch louder, and his second-in-command promptly swiveled his chair to receive the instruction. "...will contact Phendrou to apologize for endangering his life and to tell him that we are pleased with his performance at the meeting.

"We don't know which of the other leaders are involved in the epidemic or to what extent. However, Vorrnum, king of Krashad on Dasahr, seems concerned only with his own gain and has the largest standing army. An alliance with him would vastly weaken the resistance and would provide an inroad into Praxus. Our offer will have to be good, though, for Vorrnum to accept."

"Focus your efforts there."

Hajrius merely nodded to show his concurrence, as Myeerp sped up to the S.O.O. "Sir, destroyer 3 is in position. Rekiph is ready to commence the Allanoi blockade."

Before following his secretary down to the heart of the control room, Furygon left Hajrius with a warning. "See to it that you substantiate your claims,

Chief of Intelligence. Our plans will not be built on the discharges of your imagination."

You have to know what you're looking for if you want any chance of finding it. It's a matter of connecting the dots... One step at a time, Hajrius reminded himself. He strode over to Prodek's station. "What is the status of agent RI1."

"According to the infirmary, he suffered a superficial wound. He will make a full recovery, probably before his suit does. The recon infiltrator's breach of protocol in speaking undirected has been addressed, and he has submitted to reconditioning."

Hajrius seemed appeased, so Prodek asked, "What do we do about the leaked information?"

"What can we do? Hope the two natives didn't spread the information. As long as the chain of communication died off quickly, there shouldn't be a problem. If leaders who have no part in the epidemic find out about it, they will have a choice to make. They could either help us or watch the backs of our enemies. Exavyir didn't want to take that risk."

"They must value justice. Why then would they stand with the perpetrators of the epidemic?" Prodek's tone was oddly indifferent, like that of a teacher testing a student.

The unknown scares people. We're the aliens; we always have been, Hajrius thought. "You know our history. Before the separation we were despised, considered less than the other races. That's what the historical documents here say about us! Once they realize what we are, they will look again to those records, records with a hatred for our people written into them."

"Understood."

Hajrius took over an empty station, swiping his authorization card on the data interface. He worked in silence for quite some time. Many agents had finished and returned to their private offices or quarters before he gathered the head officers.

"I have reprioritized our objectives. Many agents will be reassigned according to these changes, so be sure to double check your mission outlines. Outgoing agents to Dasahr have priority, since we are seeking an alliance with Vorrnum, King of Krashad. I want a detailed analysis of his military and technological strength as soon as possible."

"Imkar." He gestured for the officer to step forward. "I have assigned you to the Allanoi team. You are to look into the enhanced interrogation and disposal of President Haazon. As of this moment, you have overriding authority over the infiltrators and assassins who are already on the planet or that arrive hereafter."

"Yes, sir!" Imkar responded with more than a hint of excitement.

Hajrius addressed the full group again, "Have I made myself clear?"

They replied in unison, "Yes sir!"

"Dismissed!"

CHAPTER 11
Heading Home

Kiiyeepo yawned to life. The tinted glass of the high-end transport could no longer hold back the sun's bright rays. He raised his seat from its reclined position just enough to see out of the windows. Beyond the awe of the city, Orra wasn't worth pictures. A flat sea of sand with an occasional rock or dried up shrub, it appeared that they were continually passing the same plot of land. He looked over the driver's shoulder at the road ahead. It was a perfectly straight, perfectly black line tapering into the horizon.

"How much longer?" he asked quietly, so as not to rouse Valexs.

"A time fragment and a half, at most."

Kiiyeepo would enjoy this ride, serenaded by the peaceful hum of hover drives and cradled in luxury. He pulled The Unknown Hero from his black bag and settled in.

He identified with the protagonist whose family had been slain by an insurgent. Hunting down the killer soon led him to the assembly of the dukes. Time blurred as Kiiyeepo read the dukes' comical bickerings. Each one had a scheme to both combat the eminent revolution and come out ahead of the others. It was a wonderful mockery of the squabbling he had just witnessed. Right under the dukes' noses, the rebels managed to set the building on fire!

"Here's fine. Thank you," Valexs said, and the transport gently stopped. A town, average in size but derelict, had materialized around them. Kiiyeepo gathered his things and reluctantly hopped out onto the sandy curb.

"It's no tourist destination, aye." Valexs led the Midek between two deserted, industrial plants. An old apartment complex was sequestered behind them, and the shortcut was usually faster than driving around on the narrow streets.

They got long stares from the residents, all Orranians sitting idly on their balconies. When they rounded the corner to the front of the complex, however, a teenage Nilose girl came running out to meet them. She wrapped her arms around Valexs's neck, and he returned the embrace.

The family resemblance was unmistakable. She had the same willowy figure and hairless, green skin, only lacking her brother's tan. The same vivacious spirit ran through them both. Nevertheless, her tired, reddened eyes were windows into the stress and hurt that she held inside.

"We got so worried when we heard what happened. Are you well?"

"Aye, I'm all right," Valexs answered. He waved over his new friend. "Meet Kiiyeepo, aye, the bravest Midek I know! He lives near our property on Allanoi, so I'm going to take him home. He said he might be able to help us."

"How do you do? I'm Linotra, Valexs's sister." She curtsied. "You two have impeccable timing; lunch is just about ready."

As they rode the level interchanger up to the fifth floor, Valexs recounted the wild events of the previous night. Linotra was enthralled. There was no end to her questions about the invader and the bioengineers.

"How cool! It sounds like you were in a rapid mutation lab. I would love to work in a place like that!" she exclaimed, startlingly fast, and then skipped up the corridor. The door to their apartment was adorned with a handmade wreath, the only decoration in the whole dreary complex. She went in and called, "Mother, he's here! And he brought a guest."

"Oh! Let me throw some extra food in the pot," Kiiyeepo heard the older Nilose reply as he stepped into the living room. Altogether, the apartment was two bedrooms larger than his house and immaculately well-kept. Though lightly furnished, the layout displayed the care of a skilled homemaker.

His mouth watered at one whiff of the ambrosial aroma wafting from the kitchen. The source was a steaming, metal pot, which Valexs's mother set in the center of the table. She then introduced herself to Kiiyeepo, wiping her hands on her apron before shaking his. Banya was her name.

"Please, make yourself at home. I do hope you like the stew. Aye, it's a family recipe."

"Thank you. It smells incredible!"

The aroma hadn't lied. He savored each spoonful of the stew. In fact, he was so fascinated by the intricate flavor imparted by a fusion of zesty herbs and spices that he had a hard time keeping up with the table talk. That was his excuse, anyway.

He was watching the family interact: how they knew what each other's gestures meant and referenced shared memories. They were so close. Try as they might, they couldn't completely conceal the pain from the loss of their father or husband.

At least they still have each other. His heart ached. *Why'd I have to be left so alone?*

"Yeah, Valexs can stay at my house to save some money." Kiiyeepo jumped back into the conversation, putting on a happy façade. They were discussing the travel arrangements and determining what to pack.

"Do you imagine there are any job opportunities? Or are we being desperately optimistic?" Banya asked. "I heard there was serious unemployment on Allanoi."

"There is in the cities, but it's not as bad in the country. Nol is kind of in between the two, so there is a chance to find something... if you're willing to be paid under the table for awhile," Kiiyeepo explained. Prudently, he declined to mention that he would be looking to hire someone. He didn't want to get their hopes up until he saw that Valexs could actually do the job.

"That's better than nothing. When are you two planning to leave?" She knew the answer just from the look on Valexs's face and wasn't happy. "I don't think so. You're not flying that thing when you can hardly stay awake! Leave tomorrow, aye, that'll give me plenty of time to pack up some food for the trip."

Valexs was visibly upset, but he didn't argue.

The icy night had dissolved at the first sign of morning. Warm, dry air was already blowing in when Valexs and Kiiyeepo set out from the apartment complex. Linotra and Banya walked them all the way to the doors, helping them carry down the baggage.

As the family embraced again and prayed for safe travels, Kiiyeepo had to gulp back his own sadness. *Does anyone care about me like that? I have no one left that I can even claim to be related to, not by blood or adoption.*

"Let's go. The dock is five blocks from here," Valexs said as he slung an air sail over each shoulder. Kiiyeepo took the food sack from Linotra, careful not to crush its contents, and trudged after him. They shouted their final good-byes before turning down one of the dusty streets.

Five blocks in this town proved to be quite a hike. After two blocks, the buildings became noticeably better maintained, by no means scenic but functional and up-to-date. It was evident that the town had once been a developing industrial and mining area.

"What will you do if you don't find a job on Allanoi?" Kiiyeepo asked and then coughed because of the sand in the air. "Why not sell the apartment anyway and get off Orra?"

"Who would buy it?" Valexs threw his arms in the air. "Look at this town! It's gone downhill badly.

"Like I said, I'm not sure what we would do. Probably send Linotra to get her certification in chemical psychology and hope someone will hire an inexperienced Nilose. It's costly, though, and Orranians are not what you would call an accepting people."

In the five days since the abduction of his father, he must have considered his family's dilemma a thousand times. Nonetheless, he considered it again and then continued more confidently, "We have to give her a chance. Aye! She's worked so hard! Besides, our other option would be to go back to Xonero and hope our relatives don't hate us anymore. That's a one in a million!"

"Why? What's their problem... if you don't mind me asking?"

"It's stupid. Most Nilose have hair on their head, like Uryiten with his long braids, and some think that means they're somehow superior to the rest of us. You've seen my family. We're all bald. My father wasn't. He went against his family to marry my mom, like in the old stories. They do have a way of repeating themselves. Since my sister and I took after my mom, we were seen as a disgrace to the family. As for my mother's side, the few left are complete strangers to us."

"But that's so silly!"

"Aye! Clans and their feuds are a thing of the past, but there's still animosity between certain bloodlines. If you're bald, it's obvious what line you descended from."

"Oh..."

Valexs pointed a half block up the road. "We're almost there."

When the Nilose had said dock, Kiiyeepo had envisioned a rudimentary version of Haazon's spaceport. What awaited them wasn't a dock at all but an expansive airfield. Large, metal hangars were scattered across the flat sands near the outskirts of the town. Between them, runways, some almost a half coordinate wide, and circular launch pads blanketed the sand. The airfield also had launch towers and other facilities to service spacecrafts of various kinds and classes.

Valexs stopped at the aerospace traffic control kiosk to register their flight plans and spaceship. He looked to Kiiyeepo for the destination, who then spoke the coordinates of his house rehearsedly as he punched them in, "Allanoi, two point one two one two P, section twenty-seven dash two hundred forty-three." The automated system then printed out three documents: a code for their approved space lane, a narrow launch window, and directions to the proper runway.

"The head of the Orranian division of my father and I's old company lets us keep our ship in his hangar. He knew my father. Aye, it's his way of helping after the layoff," the Nilose explained as they walked straight toward a hangar over three stories tall. He crouched by the side door and picked through the rocks there, stacked decoratively in a pyramid, until he recovered the hidden key.

Entering, he slapped a button mounted to the inside wall. Motors revved high above and then the huge roll door began to open with the cacophonous noise of a hundred metal wheels sliding in their tracks. As it rose, sunlight sluiced in, gleaming off the chrome hide of a monolithic shuttle.

It looked to be the same class as Haazon's, though significantly wider and flatter. A row of eight advanced engines with hyper cell capability filled the backend of the ship. It was a shame to walk past it.

In a dark corner of the hangar, sat its antithesis, small, antiquated, and rickety. Worries infected Kiiyeepo's thoughts at the sight of the contraption. "This thing still works?"

Valexs grinned, "I told you it was old, aye. I've done some work on it here and there, so it should be okay."

Kiiyeepo didn't like the "should be" part of that assessment. However, it was strong motivation as he helped Valexs tighten bolts and refuel the ship. Another key let the cockpit hinge open to reveal four cramped seats. Kiiyeepo passed the luggage up to Valexs, who then strapped it into the back seats with the safety belts.

"We might have to give it a push to get it going. The tug wheel's a bit weak," the Nilose warned, fiddling with levers and punching stuck gauges on the control console.

Kiiyeepo doubted a push would make a difference. It may have been minuscule for a spacecraft, but the ship was still bigger than most transports. They set their hands on the back of the ship and planted their feet all the same, and then they shoved with everything they could muster. The tug wheel mercifully started to pull.

"Keep pushing!" Valexs commanded as he sprinted forward and dove into the cockpit to steer.

Kiiyeepo had to keep the effort up for the landing gear's single powered wheel to slowly tow the ship. They were already halfway through their launch window when they reached the runway.

Valexs dragged the exhausted Midek aboard and then slammed the cockpit closed over them. Making the chamber airtight proved to be a reassuringly involved process, with three progressively stronger locks and multiple layers of seals.

"Ready?" Valexs asked, going through the final checklist. Kiiyeepo didn't answer, frantically strapping himself in as the thrusters right behind them ignited. There was nothing to dampen their roar. The whole ship trembled and surged down the runway

Valexs upped the throttle, smooth but quick, to full blast. Sweat beaded on his brow as he strained to hold the ship steady. The acceleration was so much more intense in the tiny vessel.

He flipped a switch and then eased back the joystick. The ailerons angled to increase lift, and the nose tipped upward. The next moment they were off the airstrip, gliding over low sand dunes.

Valexs quickly retracted the landing gear and then gradually pulled away from the ground. He maintained an even curve until vertical. He then flipped several other switches, setting the ship for atmospheric penetration.

"Hang on!" he said, though he couldn't even hear himself. Beside him, Kiiyeepo sat wide eyed and stiff as a board.

Violent oscillations rippled through the ship. Valexs grabbed hold of anything he could, as if trying to hold the vehicle together. When they broke through, however, he was grinning and almost laughing. "You should see your face!"

"You didn't... warn me!" Kiiyeepo retorted, panting and clutching his stomach.

Valexs only grinned wider. After adjusting the settings for space travel, he pushed the CosmoCon logo on the control console and typed in the code for their space lane. The system immediately took over the ship's controls, correcting their course.

The one small screen in the center of the console displayed the space lane with the key points of speed and trajectory alteration. They were set to refuel at one of the Nieyowpon space stations, since the ship didn't hold enough for both take off and landing.

All that was left to do was sit around for almost two days.

CHAPTER 12
Red Skies

Beep. Beep. BEEP! Valexs and Kiiyeepo snapped awake at the noise. A sensation of falling struck them at once. Without gravity, they'd drifted up to the roof of the cockpit in their sleep. When the shock had passed, they reoriented themselves over their seats.

Nieyowpon was so close now. No doubt the alert had been signaling their approach to the midway point on their voyage. They could see several space stations clearly, busy with traffic. Thankfully, their space lane would ensure that there was a place waiting for them.

They watched the flow of spacecrafts, amazed by the variety. From a ring-shaped vessel to an almost perfect cube, they pointed out the coolest and the most bizarre. Of course, they also fantasized about which one each of them wanted.

As they passed one station, another came orbiting around Nieyowpon. It was a larger station, a coordinate in diameter by their guess, yet no ships flew to or fro. Only one long freighter floated idly behind it.

Like most space stations it was built on a disc, several levels thick. Two massive parking towers occupied the majority of its surface. The few smaller structures jutting up around them gave the station the appearance of a shadowy city block. Every detail, however, was perfectly mirrored on the reverse side of the round platform.

For a moment Valexs's gaze alternated between the displayed space lane and the windshield. "That's *our* space station."

"CosmoCon would have alerted us if something was wrong, right?" Kiiyeepo asked anxiously.

"Aye, but they may already have." Valexs checked the trip log. There were two urgent notifications. He read the first aloud, "Station C.D.N. 3 has gone dark.

Reconnection has been unsuccessful. Please confirm your new space lane, code: 34877. We're sorry for the inconvenience."

"Well, put in the code."

"There's another message, aye, a newer one," Valexs said gravely. It was marked with the highest level of urgency. This was the alert that had broken their slumber, and that they had ignored.

"Stations C.D.N. 3 and X.C.N. 2 are under hostile control. All ships are warned not to come within one thousand coordinates. Offenders will be shown no mercy. Immediately confirm your new space lane, code: 34877, or manually divert your ship."

Their jaws went limp in horror. They couldn't have been more than a hundred coordinates out.

Kiiyeepo took a second look at the parked freighter knowing now that he was seeing another angle of the invader warship from Orra. A shadow caught his eye as it passed beneath them. It was a black space ship over twice the size of theirs and formidably armed. *A fighter.*

"Hold on!" Valexs yelled. He hit the retrorockets and jerked the joystick to the side. The ship yawed sharply to the right, putting the space station at their backs in a moment. He immediately punched the throttle forward again.

"We should have enough fuel to get to another station," the Nilose said dryly. His emotion had died away, and resolve like stone shown in his eyes.

"If it lets us." Kiiyeepo's eyes were glued to the glass, trying to track the fighter. It appeared on their port side. "Go down!"

Valexs firmed his grip on his chair and then shoved the joystick as far as it would go. The upper, rear engines and lower retrorockets both fired, flipping the vessel end-over-end just as a laser skimmed across the back of the ship.

After a complete loop, they leveled out, but the fighter was on their tail before they could blink. It easily matched their maneuvers yet its guns were dormant. Apparently, the pilot wasn't looking to destroy them but to land a debilitating blow. Its next shot didn't miss. The laser pierced both of the main boosters and the fuel tank in between. In the void of space, the devastation was silent and flameless.

KABOOM! To Valexs and Kiiyeepo it was like thunder had cracked inside their cockpit. Bolts rattled, everything rattled, but they had only an instant to brace themselves. The blast, mangled boosters, and imbalanced thrust combined to whirl the tiny ship in a vicious corkscrew, careening toward Nieyowpon. There was no way to hold on.

Roof, chair, wall... Thrashed from one side of the cockpit to the other, Kiiyeepo could only reach out his arms to break his next impact. His fear spiked higher with each blow, to the verge of fainting. Valexs's flaccid body crashed onto him, proving the Nilose had already succumbed.

Windshield... Kiiyeepo's head bashed against the glass, and reality was gone.

"What has come of the amendment to the Cueyo II doctrine of war? Does it have enough support to pass?" Haazon queried. He was hastening down the lengthy halls of Orra's government building toward the hangar. Cueyo III kept pace, hovering at his side.

"No. The lords don't want to declare war. Even with the amendment we would have to declare war for the Cueyo II doctrine to take effect. Instead my party has proposed the Cueyo III doctrine of defense, which stipulates that a hostile show of force should be met with equivalent defensive strength. The result is similar, military augmentation and development, but it's not proactive," the Orranian explained.

"Hmm..." Haazon's pace slowed as he considered the potential implications, but he didn't reply.

"What of Nighdra?" Cueyo asked. "What did she say when you spoke to her?"

"Three earfuls, as usual. To sum it up, she agreed to the wartime trade alliance. You can count on Rodeous's fuel, but she's focusing on Allanoi while there's a chance to get supplies in." Cueyo looked relieved. "So that's Orra, Allanoi—temporarily thanks to the blockade—Rodeous, and Praxus. Zanquin is considering the trade alliance, but I'd say that's fifty-fifty."

"The blockade is setting up fast. Are you sure you'll make it back safe?"

"I'm positive, but there's no time to waste. My space forces can only stall them. I'm sorry I couldn't stay longer.

"On the bright side, the blockade has scared the majority over to my side, even in the House of Conscience. The reappropriation bill passed easily. I was able to cut funding to two major subsidy programs."

They rounded a corner. The door to the hangar was at the end of the next, much shorter, hall.

"Speaking of the blockade, the invaders just took over two of the Nicyowpon space stations, one Chrion and one Xonerite. Phendrou didn't flinch, but Uryiten has to be questioning his notion of peace."

"I wish I could believe you..." Cueyo stopped. He held up one fist and turned it in the air, opening it in the same motion. A moment later the guards had moved out of earshot. Quietly, he explained, "This is all confidential, but we picked up on a transmission from that space station soon after the takeover. It was sent to the Xonerite capital, but Uryiten hasn't come forward about receiving anything."

"Thank you for telling me." Haazon glanced over his shoulder before continuing, "Also confidential, I authorized an espionage operation on Xonero. Now we know what we're after, that transmission."

Cueyo nodded approvingly. "Just today, Xonero lowered the export quota on many food products. Once your planet is bottled up, they will have a near food monopoly for as long as Thirasmasoaric persists in stockpiling. What will I do? Orra scarcely grows weeds."

"You might be able to get more from Thirasmasoaric than you think. After tomorrow, Allanoi won't be getting any of Zanquin's exports."

They called for the guards and resumed walking or hovering.

"Then there's money to worry over," Cueyo complained, putting a hand on either side of his aching head. "Orra's already running a big deficit. The national debt will burgeon in this crisis!"

"You have to cut back on the subsidies. We already talked about this." Haazon tried unsuccessfully to mask his frustration. "That's how your family has sustained its power through the decades, by always enticing your voters with new programs. It's about time someone cut the chains."

"The people will riot. They count on those benefit checks. They'll hate me, Haazon!"

"I could name which of your advisers you last spoke to." Haazon sighed. Without slowing his pace, he fixed a hard stare on the Orranian. "Who're you going to listen to? The people crying for protection from these invaders or those so selfish for their neighbors' money that they won't give it up to save their own planet?"

A murmur fizzled but no real reply.

The guards moved ahead to hold the door for them. It was bright and hot in the hangar. A breeze blew in sooty air. On the main launch track, the space jet was already primed for takeoff. They had reached the boarding ramp before Cueyo finally answered tersely, "Oh, I'll do it! Why does everything have to be so hard?"

"When you find the answer to that, tell me!" Haazon stepped onto the ramp, but the Orranian hovered ahead of him and blocked his path.

Cueyo's mouth opened and then immediately shut. How could he express his feelings? His only friend, the one person he knew he could trust, was flying right into hands of the aliens. Worst case scenarios flashed through his mind.

Haazon read the emotion on his face but replied coolly, "I'll try to keep in touch."

Cueyo nodded solemnly. A great tear dropped from his eye as he withdrew. "So long."

Kiiyeepo... Kiiyeepo... A voice called to him in his mind. He started to feel his body being shoved about. Then the voice became loud and audible, "Kiiyeepo, wake up!"

His eyes snapped open but immediately fell back to a squint. Bright orange painted the windows. Valexs stopped shaking him and breathed a sigh of relief as Kiiyeepo looked around. They were firmly belted into their chairs now and the flight interface blinked red. *The cockpit... still.*

Pain blasted from the side of his head. He reached up and rubbed the swollen bump, even though the fur was wet with blood. He then gestured to the windshield, "Nieyowpon?"

"Aye." Valexs slapped the ship's controls. "The retrorockets are fried, but somehow the stabilizers worked."

Forgetting the blood, Kiiyeepo covered his face with his hands and then dragged them down his cheeks in frustration. "You woke me up just so I can watch myself die? That gas ball will suck us right to its core, and we'll burn to death. Eject us now, and we won't have to suffer!"

There has to be a solution, aye. What am I missing? Valexs wondered. The situation rested in his hands since his copilot clearly wasn't thinking straight. He processed his thoughts out loud.

"If I try to fly us out, we'll spin out-of-control... unless we can recalibrate the engines to produce uneven thrust that will account for the damage!"

"We don't have any fuel," Kiiyeepo reminded.

"It's possible that the lower chamber wasn't lost. Perhaps the fuel can be channeled to the engines without going through the main chamber."

"Yeah right. We're doomed!"

"The manual might be in here, somewhere." Valexs ignored him, still talking to himself. He wouldn't go down without a fight. He tore off a panel below the control console. "Not there anymore..."

The planet's gravity reeled them in ever faster. Intense heat buffeted the ship. It was like sinking into a pool of magma, though the orange gas that enveloped them was fading rapidly. The ship's insulation and coolant could hold back only so much, sweat breaking out on their foreheads.

The temperature continued to climb but not enough to roast them in their seats before cool liquid slashed over the vessel. Once the mist cleared, they could see a great distance in all directions.

The next layer, composed of rich greens, sped towards them. Unlike the reds and yellows that had blended into the beautiful oranges they'd woken up to, these colors were static. Had Valexs not been preoccupied with finding the manual, he would have noticed the inconsistency immediately. Instead it charged ever closer, its details becoming ever more obvious.

Kiiyeepo's dying words suddenly cut off. He leaned forward. "Land?"

Valexs couldn't believe his eyes, but the planet's surface was unmistakable now and closing in much too quickly. He reached for the air sails, thrusting one into Kiiyeepo's arms.

"The atmosphere is probably toxic!" Kiiyeepo whined, even while frantically strapping on the air sail. He heaved the food sack and his black bag onto his lap and then firmed himself for the blast.

"If a forest can survive here, why not us!" Valexs slammed the eject button. He hit it a second time then again, almost at his wits' end when the roof finally peeled off. Their seats discharged with a crushing jolt.

Falling at terminal velocity, the air whipped around them, loud and cold. Their security belts automatically disengaged, releasing them to the wind. Kiiyeepo screamed, swinging his legs to right himself. As soon as he was top-side-up, he pulled the pin on his air sail.

Two oval sails billowed out from the pack, joined to his harness by a network of cords. They caught the air and extended like vast wings. His speed was dashed by such a margin that it felt like he was yanked backward.

Momentum tore the luggage free from his grip, but, by sheer willpower, he kicked his black bag back into his arms. It was agonizing to watch their food go. His gaze jumped to their tiny ship, however, as it cratered the terrain. He covered his ears and shuddered at the reverberating crunch.

With their ship in shambles, Kiiyeepo finally accepted his fate, drawing a long, potentially toxic breath. Air so refreshing inundated his lungs. Hope and relief bubbled up inside him. It was as if his heart hadn't beaten since they were shot down and now life returned.

"We're alive!" Valexs exclaimed and pumped both fists. He glided past the Midek, riding a cool zephyr.

Kiiyeepo smiled and then laughed, leaves tickling his feet. He descended through the treetops and was left hanging a few units off the ground with his air sail caught in the branches. Valexs, on the other hand, landed competently in a small clearing. When they met up, neither uttered a word, for they were rapt by their surroundings.

The grass was lush and soft. Large flowers, as clear as crystal, blossomed hither and thither and released a fragrance like fine perfume. Leafage of various greens and blues shrouded the trees. Wherever the canopy was too dense to see Nieyowpon's orange, yellow, and red skies, vase-shaped plants grew in the same swirling colors.

Unlike a painter's masterpiece, however, silence seemed to be anathema here. Music flowed from the milieu. Distant waterfalls with their eternal roar and the trickle of myriad creeks generated the chorus. Birds sang the verse and refrain in a thousand diverse tones. Every so often, the howls of creatures they hoped not to meet brought the song to a climax.

As though afraid to interrupt, Valexs was whispering when he finally voiced the obvious question, "How can anyone say that *this* is just a gas ball?"

No one would ever know if Kiiyeepo heard him or not. He'd taken one of the air sail's straps and now tied it onto the drawstring of his black bag so that he could carry his belongings over his shoulder.

They looked at each other and then up the nearest rivulet. Without uttering a word, they understood and agreed upon a plan of exploration. They would stick to the riverbank in case they needed to find their way back to the air sails or to the crumpled heap that had been their ship. Before starting upstream, though, they cleansed their scrapes in the cold, clear water and let it the run over their bruises.

Could there be a place more exotic and mystifying than a planet they hadn't known existed? Their imaginations buzzed with excitement, wonder, and not nearly enough fear. The great unknown had welcomed them, singing its peaceful ballad and sharpening its claws.

CHAPTER 13

Encounter

Following the rivulet was a task unto itself. Narrow streams crisscrossed through this region like a web. Whenever the wandering waters forked, fed from two directions, Valexs and Kiiyeepo kept to the right. They also planted a stick in the ground by each downstream offshoot to mark the return path.

The ground was never quite flat, gradually undulating between lumps and depressions. Smooth rock formations, some over fifteen units high, added their matte hues to the scenery. Wildlife could be heard but rarely seen scampering through the tree limbs overhead.

Periodically, Valexs would mention something about scientists that had supposedly conducted tests in Nieyowpon's atmosphere but had found nothing or about explorers that were never heard from again. Kiiyeepo never responded, though a theory was brewing in his mind.

"The big governments have to know, aye, so why have they propagated the lie?" the Nilose asked, thinking aloud again. "Unless you can't get out. No one would ever return to tell the tale."

Beautiful as it was here, that was still a dismal thought. There was little chance of it being true, fortunately. They got in after all; what would stop a ship from leaving? Or what would block transmissions from people here? Nieyowpon's atmosphere was strange, but that seemed impossible.

"The fighter wasn't looking to kill us," Kiiyeepo said, seemingly out of the blue.

"It almost did."

"Because our ship was so old," Kiiyeepo corrected. "The invaders seem committed to playing coy. I'd bet money that they took those space stations without any bloodshed. Why then would they blast us into a gas ball? The result would be the same as blowing us up."

"What are you driving at?"

"It's like the pilot knew Nieyowpon is habitable and assumed we did as well." He paused, considering the ramifications of what he'd just said. "We weren't miraculously saved by an unknown planet. This was the intended outcome."

"Most people will think they killed us, though... if this gets to the news. Aye, their attempt to appear civil will backfire on them." Valexs liked the idea, that somehow their crash could strike a blow at the enemy. Nonetheless, he said no more, stooping to drive another stick into the riverbank.

Kiiyeepo's stomach grumbled as they skipped over the offshoot. They passed bushes dappled with large, white berries. Fruit trees abounded, as assorted and peculiar as the produce that stocked their branches. Some looked questionable, but most of the fruits were tantalizing. Any one of them, however, could have been poisonous. They considered turning back. The food they'd brought was indubitably mush now, but at least it was safe to eat.

A giant, maroon bird jetted past them. They felt the wind off its four-wings and decided to press on a bit further, eager to explore.

"Shush!" Kiiyeepo hissed. His huge ears picked out faint but heavy clomps from the ambient noise, and they were getting closer. It was a large biped, but in this strange land he wouldn't assume it was a person. He quickly pulled Valexs behind a cluster of billowy shrubs.

Not far ahead, a muscular Gredwol jumped the stream. He was fully clad in armor and walked vigilantly. Solid pazin inlaid both front and back of his body armor to form an elaborate, circular emblem.

"That's an ancient Xonerite symbol," Valexs whispered. "Aye, those are only used ceremonially nowadays, since the interplanetary language. Some are still taught in school, but I can't say I paid much attention. I do know that the gun he's carrying is an early Xonerite model from when lasers were first being weaponized. Shows where my academic priorities were growing up."

"So there must be an old, Xonerite colony here, probably a whole civilization!" Kiiyeepo declared optimistically. *Maybe we* won't *be stranded here forever.*

"Aye, let's go see where he came from."

Valexs took the lead once the warrior was long past, going in the opposite direction. They'd crossed over another creek or two before their advance slowed to a creep. They could hear soft humming, occasionally accentuated by whispered lyrics.

The tune arose from a Nilose woman sitting on a large rock. She appeared to be painting a stalk from one of the vase-shaped plants. Unlike Valexs's bald family, she had straight, silky black hair, cut squarely at her jaw line. A delicate chain of glistening hazin ringed her head, with precious gemstones dangling from it.

Too close to speak without being overheard, Kiiyeepo had to read the expression on Valexs's face. *He wants to talk to her! This can't go well. We shouldn't be here.* He shook his head ardently, but his partner grinned, undeterred.

Valexs winked and then strolled out from trees they had hidden behind. "Hello there!"

The hum stopped dead. The jewels fanned out then jingled like a wind chime as she spun to face him. Despite the fright, she giggled when she saw him, as though she were trying to suppress a laugh but some got out anyway. Ten bracelets of the finest materials adorned her arms, yet she looked to be only his age or younger, eighteen orbits perhaps.

"I'm Valexs, how do you do." He extended his hand. She almost laughed again.

"I am fine thank you, this weather is a delight, and how are you?" Her voice was singsong and sweet.

"Um, I've been better," Valexs answered honestly. He went right to the point. "Are there any towns or stuff like that around here?"

"Naturally, I never go far." Her big eyes lit up. "I must know about that fluffy creature you have with you."

Kiiyeepo's cheeks turned bright red beneath his fur. He stepped forward, quite flustered. "I'm a Midek, not an animal. My name's Kiiyeepo."

"My apologies sincerely. You must forgive me; I have on no account seen any person like you before, a Midek as you say." Everything she said was accompanied by gentle, flowing gestures. Her voice became rueful. "I am afraid you two must go. My guards won't take kindly to your being in my presence."

"We didn't get your name," Valexs said quickly.

She looked at him sideways and then answered as if he should have known, "It is Nieyowsue, derived from that of our planet. Now move swift and be careful. I hear regalltees have been prowling these parts, those terrible beasts."

They nodded and retreated. Once they were well out of earshot, Valexs glanced back through the flora. A guard with the same armor as the Gredwol had approached Nieyowsue. Whatever he said, the girl was visibly disheartened, her whole body drooping a little. Valexs hoped it wasn't because of him.

He and Kiiyeepo headed downstream along what they guessed was their original rivulet. They wouldn't be sure until they found one of their sticks. Nonetheless, mystery and discussion kept their worries at bay.

"Did you hear her answer when I asked if there are any towns? Very strange, aye? At least we know that there is one nearby."

"Yeah. A direction would have been nice," Kiiyeepo grumbled. "She must be pretty important, though, to have her own guards."

"Aye, she was wearing more wealth than I could earn in an orbit! She certainly was..." Valexs let the statement go unfinished. He doubted his Midek friend would understand. Their two races probably had very different perceptions of beauty.

He returned to his main question. "I still can't fathom how this can be an inhabitable planet and we didn't know it."

"Here's what I've been thinking," Kiiyeepo began. "The only ones who could even try to keep this place a secret are Chriyoss and Xonero. They control all the space stations around Nieyowpon and have refused CosmoCon's biggest offers to buy one. However, they don't seem to use their monopoly, allowing traffic from other nations to pass at next to no cost."

"So you think that's the deal: free passage in exchange for not spilling the beans? Aye, it does make sense of a lot," Valexs resentfully admitted. He hated the notion that not having to pay a toll could be more valuable than the truth. He did realize that, if the Pact abused their ability to determine which ships could move through the center of the planetary cluster, it would lead to open warfare. Protecting this secret was a crucial incentive for them not to use that power. Who knows how many people were keeping quiet in order to avoid conflict.

"Perhaps this is why the Chriyoss-Xonero Pact was established in the first place," he theorized. "That *was* in the same period as the original laser blasters."

"They probably sent those scientists you mentioned or bribed them to say nothing."

"They're not going to silence me!"

"They will if we starve to death." Kiiyeepo's stomach grumbled louder. "Are we anywhere near the ship?"

"We're on the right track." Valexs pointed to one of their sticks. "We could always risk one of these fruits. They can't all be poisonous, aye?"

"Ha! You first."

Once they'd spotted Kiiyeepo's air sail, it didn't take long to locate the food sack. They could tell it was a mess at first glance. Most of the containers inside were utterly smashed. They fished out the few that were left intact for lunch, or at least it felt like lunch to them.

"How are we going to find that town?" Kiiyeepo asked and then poured more stew into his mouth.

"My guess is that it's past where we found Nieyowsue. We could follow the same stream but go left at the forks." Then Valexs remembered, "I saw a hill while gliding in, not far from where the ship went down. Maybe we could see something from the top."

The hill was covered in sparse foliage and rose above the majority of the trees. From its height, they could see the lay of the land. A plateau in the near distance resembled a colossal stone wall, twenty coordinates wide. Many other lithic formations also protruded up through the trees like rocks sitting in grass. It must have been on these peaks that the thundering waterfalls were born.

Valexs made a mental map of the area as he spoke, "I landed there, so that smaller clearing must be where our ship crashed. We trekked toward—"

"Look, look!" Kiiyeepo blurted. Strands of murky gas had blown in. Most of them appeared to float below the bright colors, though there was no true divide. At that moment, a strand collided with a deep red blotch, causing a chain reaction. The gases rapidly merged and then condensed. Rain cascaded. It must have been a cloud like this that had splashed their ship.

Their mouths hung open. One wouldn't know to dream of such an incredible sight. It wasn't a solo act either. A dozen cloudbursts misted the region, the wind scattering the falling water. They basked in the magic of the display even well after it had ended.

Eventually, they set course in the general direction of their ship. They got close enough, strewn wreckage guiding them the rest of the way. The next mega fragment was spent working hard and wishing for tools. They salvaged any useful parts from the ship: several long wires to use as rope, a pipe for a staff, a seat, and metal panels with which to construct a rudimentary shelter. The shelter itself was small but rugged, with a sturdy branch driven into the ground at each corner. Kiiyeepo's air sail provided more rope, as well as blankets.

Exhausted, they almost wished for night. The sun's position was indiscernible through the radiant sky, making it impossible to gauge the time. Nieyowpon's days could have been entirely different anyway, so they gave in to their fatigue.

Dinner was whatever mash they could scoop out of the food sack. The muddled flavors lingered on their tongues as they crawled inside their makeshift abode and lay down on the soft grass.

Wrapped in the air sail, Valexs was fast asleep in moments. Kiiyeepo wasn't so lucky. With the light and the noise of the forest, he couldn't get comfortable. Instinctively, he would try to roll over only to be painfully reminded of the bruise on the side of his head. Sleep came but was shallow and restless.

CHAPTER 14

Surrounded

Nothing had changed. The sky was just as bright and their surroundings were just as noisy as what they'd slept through, yet they were up in a flash at the sound of howls much too near.

"Regalltees?" Valexs asked.

Kiiyeepo nodded, reaching for the pipe. He'd heard those howls before, while driving iiows north to trade with visiting space gypsies. Regalltees stalked some of Allanoi's largest forests.

Valexs ripped off the air sail and scooted to the shelter's opening. "Of all the other things to eat in these woods, they can't be after us, aye?"

"They're here for us all right." Kiiyeepo touched the clotted cut on his head and sighed, "They can smell blood from several coordinates away."

"Oh... What do we do? Can we scare them off, or do we hang tight?"

"No, they're not afraid of us." Kiiyeepo looked around their shelter, shaking his head. "We have to get out of here. They'll tear this place to shreds."

He racked his brain for anything he could remember from a documentary about the creatures. "We might have a better chance in the trees."

"Aye, I know just the tree! Follow me!" Valexs darted from the opening.

Kiiyeepo struggled to keep up, his heart in his throat. He glanced every which way as he ran, to the point of nearly tripping over roots. In this state, he wouldn't have noticed the creatures if he'd looked right at them. They had perfect camouflage, covered in shadowy green fur and striped with brown bands as wide as tree trunks.

Their destination was a tall tree at the base of the hill. It had several low branches to help them climb. Once up, however, they slid into an adjacent fruit tree with no such limbs to aid their hunters.

Below a giant feline form emerged, too soon and too close, casually circling their roost. Built to devour, it was almost four units wide from shoulder to shoulder and solid muscle, yet it moved with unparalleled grace. Its paws were almost the size of Midek hands, including half unit long claws. Very few creatures could outrun it; fewer still could stand against it.

It gazed up into the branches. Valexs and Kiiyeepo went static, though trembling inside, in hopes that it wouldn't spot them. It circled again and then let out a series of muted howls, calling for its mate.

A reply rumbled from not far enough away. The regalltee turned toward them, shifting its weight to its hind legs, and then sprang. It sank its claws deep into the wood, the whole tree swaying violently from the impact.

Kiiyeepo wrapped his arms around the thick stem and held firm. Valexs was catapulted. By more than a little luck, though, he caught himself on another limb.

They didn't have a chance to get their bearings. Already, the regalltee had clawed its way up. Here, though, the creature's size was a weakness. Only the largest branches could support its weight, and it couldn't squeeze between many of the others.

At first, Valexs and Kiiyeepo managed to stay ahead of it, climbing higher into the canopy. Kiiyeepo suddenly found himself at a dead end when the next branch broke off in his hand. The regalltee was coming straight for him. He swung the pipe, desperately trying to keep the beast at bay.

It paused to time the swing. Then, after a mere moment, it lurched forward and slashed. *Clang!* Kiiyeepo blocked the razor-sharp claws with the pipe but was knocked backward. He had to let the pipe fly, barely able to seize a lower limb. It was to no avail. His attacker pounced down, snapping the branch.

From there, it was a short fall. Kiiyeepo hit the ground and rolled. The regalltee landed right behind him. Before it could strike, Valexs dropped onto its back from above, grabbing it around the neck as tightly as he could. It thrashed but couldn't dislodge the Nilose.

This can only end one way. Something has to die. Kiiyeepo went for the pipe. When he turned back Valexs was on the ground, having been bucked off, and the regalltee's mate was careening towards them.

I can't fight them alone! But I have to. Kiiyeepo jumped in front of his friend, yelling and jabbing at the beasts. They were too fast. One bit the pipe, holding it in its jaws, while the other attacked.

Kiiyeepo stumbled in retreat, tripping over Valexs. Claws and teeth reached for his jugular. *WHAM!* Something huge struck the animal and sent it sprawling onto its side.

A regalltee? Two more! Menacing spiked collars singled out the new pair as they blocked the predators off from the prey. Then streaks zoomed from the undergrowth, mostly purple but fading to yellow along the back. These were Kumors, a species native to Xonero and the fastest land life forms in the known universe. Their four legs were a blur beneath them, and both arms bore weapons.

In an instant one of the original regalltees collapsed, a smoking hole in its side. Its mate fought viciously, without thought for self, but was overpowered moments later.

Valexs scrambled to his feet. Extending a hand to his comrade, he whispered, "Let's get out of here."

There would be no escape. Warriors: Wulvries, Gredwols, Nilose, and the Kumors, surrounded them. There must have been two dozen at the least. Their armor resembled that of Nieyowsue's bodyguards but lacked the pazin emblem. Each warrior wielded a spiked shield and a dual bayoneted blaster.

The company parted for a tall Kumor, obviously of higher rank by the markings engraved in his breastplate. He sheathed a glowing blade and approached the trespassers.

Valexs spoke first, bowing slightly, "Thank you for saving us!"

"Many dangers dwell in these woods." The Kumor had a deep, flat voice that conveyed neither friendliness nor hostility. "What brings you to our land?"

"We crash landed!"

"That much is apparent, but how did it happen? Was coming to Nieyowpon not your intent?"

"Aye, not at all. Everybody says that it's a ball of gas. We were shot down while trying to refuel at one of the space stations."

At the Kumor's command, the soldiers fell swiftly into formation. Some formed a ring around Valexs and Kiiyeepo in the middle of the procession while the officer and trained regalltees went to the front. Then the whole group advanced as one.

Initially, they backtracked on Valexs and Kiiyeepo's route, walking parallel to the very same stream. One of the soldiers shot them a knowing look at the sight of a stick stuck in the ground. The stream slowly veered away, though, as the soldiers maintained a brisk pace and a dead straight course in spite of the obstacles. They snaked through dense clusters of trees and splashed across countless creeks, which were a relief from the heat.

Kiiyeepo panted but simultaneously shivered in fear. *Where are they taking us? Why haven't they told us?*

After a time fragment, he perceived a change in the melody of their environment. The roar of a single waterfall had become distinct from the rest. The first sign of civilization was a wall covered in vines and topped with bladed coils.

Rusted hinges creaked piercingly. The gate opened to a weather-beaten outpost. It comprised several mildewed, log buildings, the largest being a lookout tower. Standing five levels high, the tower was rooted in an enormous boulder at the center of the square perimeter.

The regalltees were corralled in a stable of sorts, and then most of the group was dismissed. Only the officer and three other warriors continued on. They led Valexs and Kiiyeepo to a large land craft with plate armor and sliding gun ports. It rode on six wide, knobby tires: two on each side, one at the nose, and one at the tail.

They ascended the ramp into the main bay. Stacks of wooden crates occupied half of the compartment, thoroughly tied in place. The officer and one soldier disappeared into the cockpit. The engine of the transport coughed twice and then roared.

Valexs immediately opened the gun port by his seat. The soldiers didn't care. They were huddled around a portable data interface, quietly chatting about whatever was on the screen. So, Kiiyeepo popped his open as well.

There was nothing like a bumpy, all-terrain ride in a wheel-based vehicle to make one thankful for hover drives. The path was a collection of ruts, beaten into the ground by many trips. Soon, however, they merged onto a smooth, dirt road, which in turn transitioned to pavement as they passed fenced estates and small orchards.

The road hugged the sheer face of the plateau. Kiiyeepo's gaze panned upward, the plateau looming over him. It seemed to melt into the sky. Shops, inns, and other businesses were carved directly into its stone.

Traffic of bangary drawn carriages and wagons now shared the road with the occasional motor vehicle. Roads coming from four directions funneled into a valley that cut an entry into the plateau.

Turning the corner, the area unfolded before them. The plateau was like an island with a massive bay. Instead of water, a small city filled it. Two to three story buildings of wood and stone crammed the busy streets. The surrounding walls of rock held the equivalent of skyscrapers.

Even so, Kiiyeepo stared straight across the city, drawn to the deep, relentless noise of crashing waters. The falls stood as a ceaseless pillar, simmering white. Most likely, it provided the electricity and water for the whole community.

They kept to a road that rimmed the city, passing through a series of gates. They stopped at the foot of the falls. Waterfront to the sizeable plunge pool, was an elegant, wooden structure. It must have been designed like Veellee's library because the droning roar fell faint the moment the door closed behind them.

The lobby was posh and pristine. Tapestries of tranquil panoramas adorned the walls. A Wulvry sat behind the wide desk, his elongated smile becoming real at the sight of them. He had a broad, oval head that seemed to bulge from the front of his thickset, fuzzy body.

"Ah, captain, how may I be of service?"

The head Kumor stepped forward. "Send word to the palace; we have the extraterrestrials. Those two. We found them near the crash site."

"Of course, of course. The bird does return to its nest, doesn't it? Knowing the king's wishes, I'll be sure they're made presentable."

"Very well, I must be off. I will send Jireck later to escort them."

As the warriors filed out, the Wulvry hopped round the desk to inspect Valexs and Kiiyeepo. He was quite large. His arched back rose like a hump just above the level of his head and then sloped down to a minute point of a tail. "You smell disgraceful. Ew! Follow me. That's easily remedied."

He led them a short ways up a hallway. Doors with pazin plaques, calligraphically numbered, were regularly spaced on one side. On the other, were several entries to an expansive, glass-roofed lounge. He unlocked door number eight and held it for them.

"The room is fully equipped, but don't hesitate to ask should you need anything in the least. The custodial staff would be delighted to assist." It was a dry, rehearsed spiel, and his tone took on an almost threatening tinge.

The guests entered warily while he exhorted, "You will find a menu on the table to order meals. Don't eat too much, though; dinner will be in two and one half time fragments. Until then, prepare yourselves as best you can and rest up! Also, don't lock the door."

Kiiyeepo could bear the ambiguity no longer. "Why were we brought here?"

"To see the king, of course! We don't get many foreigners." As he shut the door gingerly, the Wulvry remarked, "We hope that you'll prove useful."

Once alone, Valexs and Kiiyeepo scanned their new quarters. Neither one could hold back a smile. With two beds, two baths, and a sitting area, the suite was almost as big as Kiiyeepo's house. The accommodations and finery rivaled that of an expensive hotel.

"Wow!" Valexs fell back onto one of the billowy beds. "This might not be so bad after all, aye!"

They forsook exploration for the moment and obeyed the custodian. The warm shower reminded Kiiyeepo of the help Veellee had given him almost a week ago. Was it help he was receiving now, even if forced upon him? *Saved from regalltees but kidnapped at the same time. Given such a nice room yet dragged along like prisoners.*

Their situation was perplexing. He discussed it in detail with Valexs as they munched gourmet snacks. What would the government of Nieyowpon want from them? Information about the other planets was their best guess, but it still didn't make sense. As a colony of Chriyoss and Xonero, they were probably very well informed. One thing did seem clear; they weren't in danger, especially if they could be of use.

They snoozed away the remainder of the break before the Wulvry poked his head in. "It's time to go!"

The soldier called Jireck was waiting for them outside. He greeted them affably and walked ahead, more like a bodyguard than a warden. A polished stone path along the perimeter of the pool brought them to one last gate. Beyond, the ground was tiled in full. A gentle mist sprinkled them. They were so close to the falls now that they could have reached out and touched it.

The tiles rose at intervals to form a wide staircase, which curved behind the waterfall. The next step brought the front of the palace into view. Hidden from all but this one angle, its beauty was exclusive. Vast panes of stained glass and gems inlaid the three story façade.

There was no telling how large the palace truly was or how deep within the plateau its limit lay. Perchance they would find out, though, for Jireck drove the double doors ajar.

CHAPTER 15

Revelry & Authority

Silence screamed after so long of constant noise. Ruddy wood paneled the interior of the palace and imparted a warmth that would be impossible with stone. A grand, crystal chandelier hung from the vaulted ceiling, illuminating the foyer in its golden light.

The hush was broken by a young Zulan, curtsying and greeting, "Welcome, Valexs. Welcome, Kiiyeepo. May I show you to the festivities? Everyone is eager to hear from you."

It was nice to be addressed so respectfully. The more they thought about it, however, the more disturbing it became. How did she know their names? They didn't remembering telling the soldiers. No one had asked.

They trailed after her nervously. While out of anyone's earshot, Valexs questioned, "If it's okay to ask, what's going on?"

"An executive ball, nothing serious. You're the guests of honor!" she answered excitedly. "There's quite a crowd. Rumors spread so fast these days."

"Why? We're nobodies!"

"Don't say that about yourselves! You're the first visitors in orbits. The supply ships really don't count."

"But what about the explorers and scientists?"

"Sorry, I misspoke. I should have said 'the first visitors to *survive* in orbits'. You see, ships do come, but they're always chased down and destroyed. It's been getting busy too lately."

"What do you mean?"

"Last week, a small vessel hit a lake due west of here, and a fighter came after it anyway, shooting lasers like mad." She stopped and faced them. Her voice was hushed but intense, as though telling a secret. "Roughly the same time, a ship managed to land for a while. When the fighter showed up, they battled their way back into space. No ship had ever escaped before that."

Valexs glanced at his partner. With his huge eyes squinted wistfully, he was thinking of something for sure.

Gesturing for them to follow, she resumed walking. They could already hear the music and the rabble. The great hall was teeming with beings of every Chiron and Xonerite species. Whispers rippled through the crowd when they entered, and the clamor quickly ebbed.

Kiiyeepo's skin crawled. Everyone was staring at him. Many faces were smeared with suspicion, disgust, and alarm. His anxious mind omitted the fascination or cordiality of others. He shouldn't have expected better after Nieyowsue's reaction.

Under the direction of several palace workers, the crowd cleared a path. A completely glass wall, forever being painted by the waterfall, backdropped an elevated throne. Respectably sized but flamboyantly colored, the throne had been specifically shaped for the portly Nilose who sat atop wearing a matching crown. Steely eyed and forbidding, his countenance betrayed the joyful choice of colors.

The Zulan brought Valexs and Kiiyeepo before the throne. With a sweep of her arm, she declared, "I present our guests, Your Majesty."

"Thank you, you may go." Once the worker had scuttled off, the king urged, "Please, introduce yourselves."

"Valexs, at your service," he bowed, "and this is—

"Kiiyeepo," the Midek finished, if for nothing else, to make sure the gathering knew he could speak, "at your service."

"Blessings to you! I am Immodin, monarch of all Nieyowpon. Your willingness is greatly appreciated as you may be of some help to me. In the time being, though, we are pleased to have you in our company." He had a singsong but powerful voice. "Do tell us your reason for coming."

A scribe at a diminutive desk jotted down every word of the conversation, so Valexs made sure to get his facts straight. As he spoke, whispers spread like wind rustling through the treetops. They wanted details. He determined not to disappoint, especially when he spotted Nieyowsue in the audience. He barely kept himself from hyperbole, painting a vivid picture with his words of dodging lasers and then piercing the atmosphere.

Kiiyeepo felt so awkward, just standing there before so many eyes, even though he did put in some information about the invaders.

Everyone was enthralled by Valexs's account, except Immodin. He fixed his stare on the Midek and insisted, "Enlighten us further on these invaders. Why are they here? And from where do they come? Tell everything you know!"

Kiiyeepo did, intimidated by the tone of the command, yet the look on the king's face demanded more. On and on he went, talking about the meeting, his experiences with invaders, and the best theories for their coming. His only deliverance was the next question.

"Intriguing. I hope you are sincere. Now what is being done regarding the invaders?"

Valexs answered, "Not enough. The solar system needed to unite to share resources and technology for war production. Aye, that's what should've happened at the meeting. A few countries are preparing for war, but others think this will cause the war or are somewhere in the middle."

"Where do Chriyoss and Xonero stand?"

"They're the ones who insist on making peace with the invaders."

"I understand now..." Immodin said broodingly. Everyone pushed closer, somehow knowing that they were about to hear the latest news from the king's own lips. He raised his voice for all to hear but continued to address the guests of honor, "Recently, an inventor salvaged a device from a destroyed spacecraft. It receives reports and performances from the other planets, which confirm your words. We should like to discuss this further over the coming days. From these shows, we have learned that our mother countries are not protecting us as they would have us believe."

The listeners gasped. They were getting more than they bargained for.

"We have resources valuable to industry. Are these not needed? Or are Chriyoss and Xonero so powerful that they can barricade a whole planet?"

"Like I told the captain," Valexs pointed out the Kumor in the crowd, "most people think that Nieyowpon is a gaseous world."

"We suspect that the Pact has a deal with the rest of the solar system," Kiiyeepo explained. "They don't restrict space traffic across their space stations in exchange for the other nations keeping the secret."

Immodin's eyes shown like fire. He hated the idea as much as Valexs did. Notwithstanding, his anger quickly changed to gloom.

"Go," he said. "Join in the festivities."

The classical music recommenced. It was immediately drowned out as the crowd erupted into conversation. They swarmed the guests of honor.

There was no end to the exuberant greetings. Amidst all the voices, Valexs and Kiiyeepo could only understand, let alone answer, a handful of the questions that bombarded them. The palace workers watched over them attentively, trying to get the crowd to back off. Even so, it was some time before they were able to retrieve a plate of food and then another.

The buffet had a staggering variety of food. Several long tables were piled high. Though lacking their morning meal, they didn't have the appetite even to sample each dish, but they did anyway.

They felt ready to burst. After answering twenty-five more questions about the other planets, though, their stomachs were fairly settled. The attention was mainly directed to Valexs. Of those who approached Kiiyeepo, most wanted to know what he was and where he came from. Eventually, people gave in to the music and pulled away to dance.

"Chriyoss and Xonero have kept them in the dark on so much. Maybe they are after information. What do you think?" Kiiyeepo commented once they had some space. Valexs didn't reply, his eyes darting between the dance and Nieyowsue. She had just stepped out from the group she'd been talking to.

"Well, go on," Kiiyeepo prodded, but Valexs simply pointed to the wall behind them.

There were four round symbols, each set into an ornately framed niche. Pazin plaques displayed their meanings. The first meant king and rested in a significantly larger frame. The second, which was the first symbol upside down, represented prince. The third meant queen and inverted meant princess. It was this last symbol that had been engraved in the armor of Nieyowsue's bodyguards.

Kiiyeepo turned back to his friend, reconsidering, "Maybe you should settle for some punch."

Valexs must've reconsidered as well. He'd approached the princess and now appealed, "Shall we dance?"

Nieyowsue glanced toward the throne for permission, but a small, solemn group now occupied her father. She hesitated, perhaps hoping to catch his eye or deliberating in her own mind. After a long pause, she smiled and took Valexs's hand.

Kiiyeepo watched them sway out to the heart of the room. He poured himself a glass of punch and leaned against the wall. *So, what now? Will we have to work as informants for the king until there's nothing left to explain? We're stranded here if they don't have a spacecraft.*

Though the majority now bobbed and twirled to the rhythm, many still stood along the perimeter conversing or people watching, same as him. Two beings, the Kumor captain and a stalwart, male Gredwol, broke off from Immodin's group. The Gredwol took the long way around, obviously hoping to avoid certain individuals, but eventually made it over to Kiiyeepo.

"You don't want to join in the dancing?" he asked, as he bent down to refill his cup. He was tall, even for a Gredwol, roughly eight and a half units. His species had lateritious flesh, tougher than that of a Nilose. They often seemed expressionless, with small mouths between their prodding eyes.

Kiiyeepo shook his head. "The only dancing on Allanoi was brought in by the other races."

"Was music a foreign concept as well then?"

"Not at all, actually. We have many traditional instruments."

"Interesting. I would have thought dance would be as natural in a society as music." The Gredwol pondered it for a moment before introducing himself, "The name's Zezo by the way, chief of defense. I hear my officer didn't say where he was taking you. That must have given you quite a fright. Not the most tactful, that one."

"I noticed," Kiiyeepo said laughingly but then probed, trying not to be too direct, "So... have you sent space ships to the other planets? Does Nieyowpon have any?"

"A few, very few. Those stations you spoke of probably stopped the ones that we tried to send out. Why?"

"Well, I'm a rancher. Back on Allanoi, I have a lot of animals to take care of. I thought I might be able to do something to earn a ride home."

"I'm afraid that's unlikely." Zezo's flat head recoiled on his sturdy, longish neck. "However, you will be generously compensated for the services you perform for us. Immodin and I shall explain these tomorrow."

Kiiyeepo didn't hide his disheartenment. Several awkward moments passed before Zezo changed the topic. "How did you and Valexs meet?"

"At the meeting. Since we both witnessed an abduction, they had us make a model of an invader for research proposes."

"Could you identify them?"

"Yes..." Kiiyeepo drew out the response leerily.

Zezo quickly explained, "You see, two robotic beings appeared about the time you say the invaders arrived. We've been tracking them ever since."

"Did they show up after a ship that I was told landed for some time, undetected?"

"Yes, they did. The ship you're referring to is a mystery in and of itself. None of my scouts could find it once it landed, and they know those woods like the backs of their hands."

"Then you're definitely dealing with invaders. They have a ship that can go invisible. The robotic beings are probably just drones, though."

The color had drained from Zezo's face. "Excuse me, I should inform the king."

He tipped his head and then hustled straight back to the throne.

A couple of the scattered tables had been vacated, and Kiiyeepo was glad for the chance to rest his legs. His surroundings quickly fell out of focus, replaced by daydreams. He longed for the serenity and security of things familiar, of home. It all seemed infinitely far away now.

He didn't budge when the music changed nor when the dancers cleared the floor for the most skilled duos. Nonetheless, he was on his feet when the smell of freshly baked cake filled his nostrils.

Workers wheeled in the massive desert. It had five cylindrical layers, each a unit tall. Though still quite full, Kiiyeepo was one of the first in line for a piece. Light and creamy, it reminded him of Caltow's sweet cakes. Every bite threatened to shatter his emotionless mask.

Valexs took a seat beside him, but his gaze lingered on Nieyowsue. His smile gradually bent into a frown, though, as another thought took over. He and the Midek remained there, taciturn for the most part, during the last time fragment of the ball.

The crowd had started to dwindle by the time Jireck returned. He escorted them back to the guest building, known as the Royal Gathering. Before leaving them at the door of their room, he advised, "You ought'a get the most sleep you can. It's late."

Saying it was late sounded strange when it wasn't dark out, so Valexs asked, "What time *is* it, aye?"

"Mid-sleep of second light. I don't suppose you'd understand that."

"We'll figure it out."

"Right then. Oh, are either of you missing a black bag?"

"Yes, I am," Kiiyeepo quickly answered.

"Well, we found it. It's on the table there." Jireck pointed to the sitting area. "You'll likely have a different escort in the morn'in."

The moment the soldier had gone, Kiiyeepo checked his bag. He breathed a sigh of relief. It had clearly been rummaged through, but everything was there.

"What a day." Kiiyeepo had already flung himself into bed, and his voice was muffled beneath the pillows.

"Aye, what a second light!"

CHAPTER 16

The Makings of a Plan

Faint sniffles rose to Kiiyeepo's half-asleep ears. He lifted one eyelid to seek out the sound. The room was dark, but the light trickling through a gap in the curtains was enough for him. Across the room, Valexs's sheets were tousled yet empty. The Nilose was sitting on the floor by the foot of the bed. A teardrop glistened on his cheek. With his head hung low, there was no sign of the inexorable fearlessness and optimism that he'd shown throughout their trials. It was heartbreaking to see him like this.

Kiiyeepo sat up on the edge of his bed and softly probed, "What's wrong?"

Valexs didn't respond for the longest time. He wiped his eyes and slowly shook his head. "All this is wrong."

"What do you mean?"

"I haven't contacted my family since we left. It might be impossible to do so from here. They know something happened to me. Aye, they're probably worried sick!" He spoke harshly, but he meant it to himself. "Here I am, stranded in the land of my dreams, living like royalty while what's left of my family waits for deliverance. Linotra will have to drop out of school. Best case scenario, they scrape by one day at a time. Worst case, they can't pay the bills and are thrown out of the apartment. What then? They live on the street? I was supposed to protect my kid sister."

"Stop it! You can't blame yourself. We were shot down."

"Aye, but that's not it. I didn't even think of them, didn't allow them to cross my mind for... how long has it been? Something like three whole days!"

He must feel such a burden to care for them, especially since his father was abducted, Kiiyeepo thought. He'd seen how each member of Valexs's family relied on the others but couldn't think of the right words to say. Before the chance to reply passed, he blurted, "Well, sitting there isn't going to help them."

"Aye," Valexs grumbled almost mockingly. He hopped up and yanked open the curtains so that he could see. He then started pacing the room from end to end but didn't answer when there was the knock at the door.

Kiiyeepo was annoyed at this, and it could be heard in his tone. "Who is it?"

The custodian peered in, knowing precisely how far he could swing the door without it creaking. "Should I bring in your morning meal or will you be having it in the lounge?"

"You better bring it in," Kiiyeepo decided with one glance at his friend, who had completely ignored the Wulvry's intrusion. He had to order for them both off the menu.

Two workers brought in plates and eating utensils, as shiny as could be, and set the table expertly. They left food of glorious presentation. Valexs reluctantly took a seat, putting a hand to his brow to support his downcast head.

"How are we going to get off this planet?"

He stabbed a balloon-like roll on his plate, watching it deflate while Kiiyeepo recounted his talk with Zezo.

"That's it, aye? They've got some ships, but they're not willing to try again."

"Maybe we could try for them," Kiiyeepo schemed. "With all the commotion around the space stations there's an opportunity to get ships through. Some big corporations might be willing to run the blockade if they knew about the resources here. Chriyross and Xonero's hold on Nieyowpon would break down."

"Aye! If we're the only ones here who know a bit about those corporations and have connections on the other worlds, they'll have to send us!" Valexs's smile, though feeble, lightened the mood. "It just might work."

Over breakfast, they formed the idea into a petition and rehearsed their delivery. The inevitable onslaught of questions already rang in their ears. They had to be ready to give answers or else look like fools before the king. They were trying to foresee and work through the hazards of the plan when their escort arrived.

This time, they were shepherded down dim but magnificently excavated tunnels deeper into the plateau. Embroidered carpets kept their feet off the ever colder stone. The soldier halted outside a small foyer but waved them in. It accommodated a handful of chairs and the bolted door to the monarchal conference room.

"We know what to say..." Valexs started but quieted when Kiiyeepo held a finger to his lips.

The Midek explained in a whisper, "I can hear them. I'll tell you what they're saying."

He scooted to the closest seat and angled his ears to the gap below the door.

"...coming up the west side of the plateau." The voice was Zezo's. "If it maintains this course, it will be at our gates in as little as three time fragments."

"It must be destroyed. Meet it in the forest before it endangers the townspeople." Despite sounding like he hadn't slept a wink, this had to be Immodin. "Take the newcomers in your band since they have knowledge of these, so called, 'drones'."

"We will question them before setting out. It's too dangerous for them to accompany us. We don't know what that thing is capable of."

There was a break in the dialog. Kiiyeepo gave Valexs a summary but was cut short by a voice he didn't recognize.

"I have to agree with Zezo. It would not be prudent to take them."

"They are useful to us," Immodin angrily rejoined, "so we will use them!"

"They are our guests, father." The sweet voice of Nieyowsue, though demure, was strained by anxiety.

"Silence, my daughter!" Immodin bellowed. "I have made my decision and it is final! Now get the door."

"Yes, father." Her humiliated tone went unheard as Kiiyeepo relayed the rudiments of what he'd heard. He was surprised when Valexs rattled off a reply, speaking as fast as his sister had, "We'll give the petition later, that way we'll have more leverage..."

They both shot upright as the deadbolt of the door slid heavily. Nieyowsue stepped through with warning eyes. "His Majesty will see you now."

The conference room was larger than they expected. Ten silk-cushioned chairs ringed a broad, oval table. It looked modest centered between the many exhaustive maps on the walls.

Valexs and Kiiyeepo's seats were at one end of the table with Immodin and his daughter at the other. Zezo sat on the right side of the table across from an aged Zulan, no doubt chief of something or other.

He wasn't quite five and half units tall, about the same size as Phendrou, but had brown flesh darker than the taupe of the Decider's lineage. His graying mane and goatee were long but kempt, giving him a formal and astute appearance.

He stood and opened, addressing his words to the foreigners, "This time had been allotted for the description of your tasks, should you be willing to help us, and your payment in doing so. Logically first, we would have discussed your general citizenship. We want to ease the transition into our society for you." Kiiyeepo winced at these words, so contrary to what he had in mind. Luckily, no one was the wiser. "Alas, another matter has taken precedence. We will discuss the items previously mentioned later, assuming that you return. This should be considered a first task of sorts since you will be well paid."

Zezo rotated a map on the table to face them. "As I mentioned to Kiiyeepo, we've been tracking two robotic beings. One of these is advancing on the city nonstop, plausibly drawn by your crash. It will have to be destroyed before it poses a real threat to the people. You will accompany us to verify that it is of invader origin and to give insight about what we are up against."

Immodin nodded, quite pleased. He ignored the pleading glares of his chiefs. "Now go. There is no time to waste!"

Kiiyeepo's opinion of the king was suddenly much lower. *He must be out of his mind! Valexs and I will only get in the way of trained soldiers.* The dark bags under his eyes proved that he indeed was, but his word was law, nonetheless.

It's only one drone and we'll have a whole band of soldiers. Kiiyeepo told himself. It didn't ease his anxiety. He lagged behind Valexs, Zezo, and their escort as they exited the palace. *Will their archaic weapons even mark its armor? If there are drones, the invaders might also have spies here. What if it knows we're coming? We could be the ones walking into an ambush.*

Past the Royal Gathering was the defense headquarters. A tall, barbed fence protected barracks, warehouses, and garages, almost too impressive for their purposes. The important military administration facilities were cut deep into the plateau, all the way up to a walled area on top.

Most of their force was already in the woods. Two more soldiers were assembled, briefed, and equipped alongside them. Of course, Midek armor was unavailable, so Kiiyeepo was wrapped in an oversized, Gredwol style suit. It dragged on the ground more than slightly, like a bizarre metal dress. No helmet would come close to fitting and not for lack of trying to find one, at least on Zezo's part.

They climbed into the very same military land craft for another bumpy ride. Valexs didn't seem to mind as he told of his previous clashes with invaders. It wasn't reassuring for the soldiers, but they were captivated, nonetheless. One seemed to be taking notes in his head.

For Kiiyeepo, however, it was an awful trip. He couldn't stay in his seat thanks to his ridiculous garb. He fell flat on his face when the transport braked hard. Though the soldiers pulled him up immediately, doing their best not to laugh, he was the last to disembark.

"We have to continue on foot from here. The river ahead is too deep for the land craft," Zezo explained.

"Falling Rock isn't far. That's where we'll ambush the drone."

Mighty trees flourished by the river. They staggered down the steep bank to where one such tree had been felled to bridge the current. Still several units above the surface of the water, Kiiyeepo would have liked to crawl across, but Valexs kept a hand on his shoulder, urging him forward and holding him upright.

The ground quickly became too rocky for most vegetation. A cluster of enormous boulders rose from the ground in the small clearing between the forest and the plateau. It was the ideal setting for an ambush.

Soldiers bustled amongst the rocks. Zezo put the two in their company under the command of the captain heading the operation and then took the newcomers up a narrow path cut into the side of the plateau.

It led to the wide ledge known as Falling Rock, named for a projection of the plateau that appeared to be suspended in thin air from this angle. Sand bags piled along the edge formed a low but sturdy wall. At the back of the ledge, was the mouth of a substantial cave.

"You two will get the best view of the drone from here," Zezo said as he handed Valexs a spyglass. "Before we open fire, you are to retreat back into the cave and stay there until I say. Is that clear?"

The words were a relief to Kiiyeepo. Valexs looked disappointed as he straddled the sand bags, one leg dangling over the two story cliff. Kiiyeepo took a step after him and peered over the makeshift wall.

Zezo stepped away to talk to the captain via a multiline transmitter, but that didn't stop Kiiyeepo from listening in as he studied the soldiers' layout. One would lurk in a denser pocket of vegetation on the opposite side of the expanse; three, including the captain, were dispersed throughout the boulders below; and there were two on the ledge, with another hustling up the path. Jireck.

Clipping the transmitter to his armor, Zezo turned his attention to the stocky Nilose, who reported, "That creature can't be more than six micro fragments off, a quarter coordinate I'd say."

"Good. Go to your station." Zezo made sure everyone was in position and then instructed them to get down. Not one could be seen. Crouching behind the sandbags, Kiiyeepo stared anxiously through a minor breach with Valexs. The wait was treacherous, each moment expecting the worst to appear if he even blinked. He nearly choked when it actually did.

CHAPTER 17
Touching Death

Bit by bit, the metallic silhouette emerged from around the bend, first a long arm bearing a pointed apparatus and then a giant, rotund body. It would tower over any of the soldiers but was nothing compared to the mech.

Kiiyeepo snatched the spyglass from Valexs and zoomed in. The drone had come fully into view, revealing a menacing pincer on its left arm. An armored, turret dome was affixed to the slanted top of its body. Scopes, lenses, and alien devices protruded from all sides of the dome, giving it the appearance of a ten eyed monster. The turret rotated gently as the drone glided on a pair of continuous tracks, triangular in shape with the drive sprocket at the peak. A support reached up from its back to a laser cannon, enabling the weapon to tilt and pivot in any direction. He was hard pressed to find a weakness. He returned the spyglass to Valexs with a subtle shake of his head.

"What do you make of it?" Zezo was seated on the edge of a large stone, his foot tapping with mounting pace.

"We can be sure it's a robot," Valexs murmured in response.

"It's definitely an invader drone. Somehow it resembles the mech and the spacecrafts I've seen of theirs. Maybe the materials or the practical design," Kiiyeepo said to his friend. "These are the things we've been hearing about."

"There are more on the other planets?" Zezo asked.

"Aye, they're all over." Valexs glanced at the Midek. "Though I believe the last report we saw said that most, if not all, of them had been found and eliminated."

"What's their purpose?"

"Collecting information, I suppose, or perhaps searching for something. Aye, probably a place to land their ships and..."

He hushed at Jireck's warning, "It's within precautionary range, sir."

Zezo lowered his voice accordingly, probing, "How do we stop it?"

Valexs fingered his relic of a blaster, but Kiiyeepo voiced what was going through their minds, "I don't know how much these guns can do to it. Your best bet is to aim for its sensors or treads. If you can, take out its cannon first."

"Of course. Now into the cave, you two."

They retreated into the cold darkness. Small, slimy critters slunk along the walls of the tunnel. There was no telling how deep it went, yet Valexs insisted that they stay near the mouth, where he could see and watch the soldiers do battle. He paced, eager to fight, while Kiiyeepo sat on a dry spot and counted to himself, keeping a mental tab on the drone's approach.

It's getting close. The Midek fixed his gaze on Zezo, who had taken another look for himself and now spoke quietly into the transmitter. The words were inaudible at this range. Still, they waited.

It must be right below us by now! He picked up on a faint hum of an engine, but Zezo let another moment go. At last, the Gredwol yelled, "Fire!"

The soldiers popped up and unloaded. Lasers flared around the drone, like a prison of light, striking its armor and piercing one of its lenses. Smoke streamed from the seared metal.

The onslaught waned as quickly as it began, the drone returning fire with pinpoint accuracy. When its gun swiveled toward the ledge, the warriors ducked on impulse. Beams, seven times brighter than theirs, flashed exactly where they had been standing and no more than a hair above the wall.

"Keep it spinning! It can't hit everywhere at once," Zezo instructed through the transmitter, and then took a shot for himself. The soldiers spread out and then rose, yet their blasts now looked like little more than the rays cast by a flickering lamp to Kiiyeepo. They ducked again and more radiant beams lit the cave like lightning.

"Increase fire from the boulders!"

Another protocol must have taken over, for the drone's behavior shifted drastically in that instant. It zoomed in reverse for the cover of the trees, keeping its cannon shielded from the boulders and its firepower focused on Falling Rock.

Kiiyeepo watched and listened, trying to make sense of the happenings outside. *It's as if it knows where the orders are coming from and can understand.*

Jireck peeked out and rained down a salvo that punched a hole in the drone's turret. Sparks sprayed and it jolted to a halt. The soldier dropped back to one knee behind the wall, speaking over his shoulder, "Sensors down, sir."

"Good." Zezo raised his transmitter. "Sweep in and knock it—" A loud "No" shrieked from behind, and light flashed before him that splashed against his armor. Reality congealed in his mind, his glazed eyes staring straight through Jireck's body at that diabolical robot. Gradually, as if in gel, the warrior crumbed. He followed him with his gaze and then followed the vapors drifting from his own chest. A hole was burned in the center of his breastplate, leaving only a papery thin sheet of metal. That sliver, however minute, was the difference between himself and Jireck.

The world resumed its fast pace when one of the other two soldiers tackled him out of harm's way. "Are you alright, sir?"

The chief of defense could barely nod. He sat in stunned silence as the soldiers carried Jireck into the cave. There was still life in him. In a moment they had pulled a syringe from the first aid kit, loaded a long tube of yellow fluid, and stuck it into Jireck's arm. Then they looked their fallen comrade in the eyes and saluted him.

One of the soldiers rushed back to battle with Valexs at his heels. The second, a tall Wulvry, yanked Kiiyeepo over and whispered in his ear. His tone was dour yet calm even as a tear slipped from the corner on his eye. "Stay with him. He doesn't have long."

He gave the Midek a firm pat on the shoulder and then departed. Kiiyeepo reluctantly approached the wounded hero. His whole body wanted to look away, but, for the sake of this poor soul, he couldn't. He gulped down the nausea. "It's going to be alright."

What a lie, he thought, but wasn't that what he was supposed to say? Crouching at Jireck's side, he stared into quivering eyes and quivering hands.

Despite the injection, the warrior knew what was going on, and the pain was clearly strangling him.

"I'm so sorry!" Kiiyeepo sobbed. He'd figured out that the drone had located the transmitter's frequency and made that its target. It was he who'd screamed "No" in an attempt to stop that fatal transmission... too late.

Jireck clutched his hand. "When you remember me, Midek..." He gasped desperately for air. "...remember that no hero ever died in vain."

For a moment, nothing stirred. Kiiyeepo repeated the words in his head. He nodded solemnly and then felt the butt of a gun enter into his hand. He took hold of the weapon automatically. The dying Nilose then painstakingly guided its barrel over his own heart. Voicelessly, Jireck cried, *Please!*

Kiiyeepo's jaw fell limply and his eyes dilated in calculation. Torn on what to do, he became petrified by uncertainty. The being at his feet begged to be put out of his misery, but how could he pull that trigger? How could he not? Would he be able to live with himself knowing that he put someone through a long and painful death, or that he ended a life before it was due?

Jireck jerked the gun toward himself, but Kiiyeepo only bit down on his lip so hard that blood flowed. The trigger was forced back by his locked finger and another laser burned through Jireck.

Kiiyeepo couldn't look away fast enough. The edges of the two holes met to form a single gruesome void. The putrid smoke permeated his nostrils. He could have stopped this; instead, he'd tightened his finger and let Jireck kill himself. It had seemed like the right decision, but now his mind silently wailed as he reached out and closed dead, Nilose eyes.

"For Jireck!" Valexs's voice echoed through the cave. Though tears dampened his vision, he hoisted his gun and marched out to the battle cry.

The drone sat stationary within the periphery of the trees. It exchanged fire with the soldiers both at the boulders and deeper in the foliage. Valexs charged from behind a boulder. If its optic and audio sensors had indeed been destroyed, he should be able to deal a terminal blow before the drone knew what hit it. Still, it discerned lasers well enough to shoot back wherever they came from, so he kept his blaster quiet for the time being. Could that same scanner detect him? It was too late for thoughts like that, already half way across the expanse.

A blinding, scathing beam warmed his cheek, and he threw himself to the earth. He continued, crawling on, until his vision clarified. Ahead, the drone's cannon spun madly upon its mount, lasers blazing like a chain reaction of novae in the night sky. Either it had gone haywire, or a final protocol had kicked in.

He looked around; not one soldier had answered his cry. The feeling of aloneness came instantly and intensely. His heart raced. Locking his gaze on the enemy, he noticed that the tilt of the cannon fluctuated as if to a pattern. *It will eventually hit everywhere.*

He steadied himself with long breaths, resolve hardening his countenance. When another blast passed over him, he leaped to his feet, sprinted, and dove below the cannon's aim. The next moment, he repeated the charge, thankful to land in grass.

Up again and pumping hard, he closed in, but this time the cannon pointed to the ground ahead of him. He pushed off with all his might, leaping the beam as it set fire to the undergrowth.

He didn't slow, flames licking at his heels. The drone was nearly in reach. As the cannon faced him once more, he dropped to his knees and skidded beneath the laser. Then, clasping down his blaster's trigger at the same time, he lurched forward and thrust the superheated, duel bayonets into the body of the drone.

Sparks burst from the punctures in its metal hide. Shrill pops and cracks resounded within, an avowal of victory. Valexs grinned and threw a second jab before realizing that the cannon had recoiled straight at him. He closed his eyes, but the bright flash shined through.

A thud forced him to look. The cannon lay at his feet and a burnt hole to his right indicated a miss. Before him, a Kumor stood tall, holding a glowing sword. More soldiers also rushed in, even through the dwindling flames.

What made them come? Why'd they change their minds? He got his answer when he glanced up at Falling Rock. Peering over the sandbags, was Kiiyeepo, with Zezo's transmitter in hand.

There was no celebration or condolence, for the next order of business was a funeral. As prescribed by tradition, not a word was uttered during the ceremony. The silence imparted a tremendous weight of grief and reverence.

They carried the corpse into the forest until they came to a secluded glade. Each person gathered took a turn digging the grave and then another to fill it in. The two soldiers who'd been closest to Jireck of the band performed the rite with tears flowing. Though short, its complexity demonstrated their respect.

Valex had to wipe his eyes, moved by the ceremony. The beings on either side of him, however, stood inert: Zezo, blaming himself over and over, and Kiiyeepo, recalling images of the fallen guards in the meeting chamber.

Another to pay the price of bravery? Everything seemed perfect for the ambush, and still he paid, the Midek thought. A new concept sprang to the forefront of his mind. *No hero ever died in vain.*

He would honor the soldier's dying wish and remember these words, though he failed to see any truth in them. *If ever a hero died in vain, surely Jireck was that one! His death could have so easily been avoided, and the drone would have been destroyed all the same.*

The whole burial took over a time fragment. As the final act, one of the soldiers pressed his hand into the freshly churned earth and softly declared the name of the deceased, "Jireck."

No one there would ever forget that name.

On the return journey, a couple of the soldiers spoke up, trying to figure out exactly what had happened. Since Zezo had gone to the cockpit, Valexs and the Wulvry attempted to answer but had an incomplete understanding themselves. Nonetheless, Kiiyeepo didn't feel like explaining.

He simply stared out of the gun port and tried not to fall out of his chair again. When they reentered town, he focused in on the walled area above the defense headquarters. The roofs of hangars and the peak of a launch tower taunted him. He knew that space worthy ships hid deserted within those confines.

So close but so far... Wait, is that... He squinted at the sky. A trail of smoke rapidly disseminated from the airfield, evidence of a resent landing. He felt hopeful. *An aircraft wouldn't leave a trail like that!*

Did they test run one of their space ships? Or did it come from another planet? He pondered the many potential scenarios until they stopped. Unprepared, he slid right off his seat.

There was no chance to ask about the smoke. He and Valexs were promptly escorted back to the royal gathering, as if in the way of something. Even so, he was content to be free of that misshapen armor and to have new wonderings to busy his mind.

Once washed up, they reclined in their beds. They were to meet the king again later that evening but had ample time to regroup.

Valexs closed his eyes, but Kiiyeepo didn't want to face the nightmares. He traced the wood grain in the ceiling, outlining invisible pictures with his finger. He drew faster as the silence threatened to resummon the gruesome scene, but, before he knew it, he'd drawn a hole in the center of his imaginary Nilose.

This would not do. He looked to Valexs, whose breathing had turned rhythmic, but determined not to wake him. Instead, he grabbed The Unknown Hero from his black bag and read for a long while, afraid to stop.

The protagonist had fought to prevent the fire at the assembly of the dukes, even taking on the saboteurs hand-to-hand. He'd barely escaped with his life. Now, he found himself at a dead end. He had to return to the scene of the original crime where the blood of his family had been spilled. While journeying back west through deserts and woodlands, he stayed in a remote city where a rebel sympathizer was attempting to stir up trouble. In a matter of days, he'd organized a mission to capture the turncoat. One of his cohorts didn't return alive.

Oh, great! Just what I needed. He flipped the book closed, and the next sequestering thought was of Jireck.

CHAPTER 18
The Petition

*O*nce its optical scanner was destroyed, it had only its heat sensor, which was what allowed it to pick up on incoming lasers and accurately return fire, and its receiver to go on. I already knew that the invaders could intercept transmissions since they infiltrated the meeting. How much harder can it be to track the source? On Allanoi, the law enforcement does it all the time! Why couldn't I have put two and two together?

That was it. Kiiyeepo had to spark conversation before he drove himself mad. "Can you believe Immodin sent us out there like that?"

"What!" Valexs aroused with a start. "Oh... I don't think he's too fond of us. Maybe he was right, though. Without us, many more could have died. How you directed the soldiers was crucial. You probably saved my life. Aye!"

The praise was wasted on Kiiyeepo. He frowned, reliving the events and reviving his regret. *There shouldn't have been a tragedy at all.*

"It was a fluke!" Valexs yelled at him. He couldn't stand the Midek's irrational self-blame. "You think you could have stopped it, but that's just hindsight for you. You did the best you knew to. Certainly there's no fault in that!"

Kiiyeepo was taken aback. He couldn't argue, but he wouldn't admit that Valexs was right. Shouldn't he feel guilty? He'd helped the soldier finish himself off!

He ignored the rebuke, reverting to the topic of the king. "He doesn't trust us, which is a problem. I mean, neither would I, but we have to convince him that we can actually strike trade deals with some major corporations."

"We don't know that ourselves. What we have to prove is that there's a real chance. That's all we're offering," Valexs reminded. "Chryioss and Xonero have kept Nieyowpon bottled up on the pretext of protecting them. Immodin knows better now since they salvaged that broadcast receiver. He must be furious with the Pact for their lies. I think he'll accept the petition for the possibility of being free from their grip if he thinks the odds are favorable."

Kiiyeepo nodded. "But how do we get away? They're going to send a whole crew to oversee us. Even if we succeed, I doubt they'll let us go."

"Aye, we will have proven ourselves too 'useful'. I've been thinking about that. I have a plan."

"Oh?"

"I'm going to bring my family here. They'll love Nieyowpon, and we'll have everything we need as long as I'm helping Immodin," Valexs declared. Then he looked at his friend and sighed. "I know that's no help to you. Aye, you have a ranch to get back to."

"Don't worry about me. I'll think of something." Kiiyeepo's glum tone contradicted the smile that he put on. "That works out well for you."

"You could make a good life here. The chiefs said they would pay you generously for your services, and I know my family would love to have someone to fill our empty chair."

That was nice, but Kiiyeepo shook his head. He couldn't stay. There were no Mideks. He'd be like a rare animal at a zoo. People would always be suspicious of him. With each person he met, he would have to answer the same foolhardy questions about what he was and did and ate and knew. It would be too long before he was treated as an equal.

If today is an indication of the sort of tasks they have in mind, remaining here could be fatal. He knew it wasn't a fair charge, but the only life he wanted was the peace and predictability of his little house. He had another motive for leaving, but it was suppressed so deep in his subconscious that he didn't fully grasp it himself.

Vibrations, inaudible to most, seeped into his ears. For once, he was actually glad to hear the custodian hopping toward their room with the evening meal, just in time to interrupt Valexs's attempts to console him. No sooner had they finished their food than their escorts arrived.

The monarchal conference room was vacant as they stepped in, save for a scribe who'd begun adjusting his instruments at a small desk in the corner. Their escorts, two soldiers, showed them to the same pair of seats and then took up their positions on either side of the door.

They waited and waited some more. Half of a time fragment passed, and still no one else had arrived. Valexs was now pacing. The scribe had dozed off after resting his head on a stack of writing sheets. Even the guards had grown slack. They resumed their rigid pose in a flash, however, when the door finally swung.

Nieyowpon's eight chiefs filled the remaining chairs, all recognizable from the group that had diverted Immodin during the ball. They looked weary or perhaps irritated. Nieyowsue sat just off from the table, yet one key constituent was missing, the king.

"Forgive us for the delay; an unforeseen matter arose." The Zulan chief sat where Immodin had. Conceivably, he was next in the chain of power. "Please absolve us from the woes of your misdirected first task. You have shown great bravery and potential. If not for you, this day could have been far worse than it was." His words were addressed to Valexs. "The bonus we have included in your pay is an inadequate expression of our gratitude."

"I don't want your money," Valexs declared. "I shall accept a special kind of payment if you allow us to do something further for you."

Several of the chiefs leaned back in their chairs and crossed their arms. "State your case."

"The Pact perpetuates Nieyowpon's isolation through some kind of deal with the other planetary governments. If there was no secret to protect, that agreement would break down. We're offering to go directly to corporations that would value your resources. War is on the horizon and people can't afford to disregard—"

"Already tried, many a time!" an old Wulvry with a dangling beard cut him off, rolling his eyes. "Each team goes off and is never heard from again."

"You thought Chriyross and Xonero were protecting you. Aye, they're the ones who made sure your ships never returned. Right now, their blockade has a gaping hole in it thanks to the invaders."

Everyone remained silent, expectant, but Valexs had to elbow Kiiyeepo to get him to remember his lines and spew them out. "We know what's out there. We have contacts. We can get an audience with the right people. First, we'll aim to bring in the technologies you'll need to protect yourselves and manage interplanetary commerce."

The chiefs leaned together. Mordant snorts and snickering garbled the words, but the Midek honed in on a couple of the speakers. The bearded Wulvry voiced the general consensus, accusing them of propagating lies in order to abscond. Another chief went as far as to propose that they were scheming to incite some vile nation to overthrow them. Only one openly supported the petition. Present physically but apparently not mentally, Zezo made no utterance whatsoever.

The discussion ended at the head chief's signal. He then folded his hands and questioned the foreigners. "Do you grasp how costly that would be? It would require the last of our enduring fleet and no doubt the bulk of our treasury. Tell us exactly who you would make these trade deals with."

"I don't have names yet..." The chiefs all rolled their eyes, shook their heads, or grumbled in disappointment. Except for Zezo, that is. Valexs quickly explained, "Here's the plan. I know a high official of an interplanetary real estate development company. He would know who would be interested in your resources, and could get us a meeting with them. Aye, once word is out, they'll come to us."

"And what are these technologies that you say we'll need?"

"Better weapons and armor, first of all, to protect yourselves from pirates or the invaders," Kiiyeepo answered. "Obviously, you'll need up-to-date communication systems and equipment to service modern spacecrafts as well. I'm friends with the chief executive of CosmoCon, the largest space transit corporation in the solar system. If anyone knows about that sort of thing, it's him."

Valexs's mouth hung open. Kiiyeepo grinned but got back on script. "We assume that you will send at least a small crew with a wide range of expertise to accompany us. We're not professional pilots or negotiators or anything like that. This crew can also ensure that everything is done to your satisfaction."

The chiefs conferred again, this time in stern whispers. *They've rehearsed their lies... How can they possibly know these people...* Kiiyeepo looked from one chief to the next, imagining what they were saying. *No, I think they actually believe it will work... Fools they are if they believe that... Press them for answers and their own words will rat them out...*

As before, the head chief restarted the dialogue, "You are asking us to take a very big chance. Can you prove that what you say is true?"

Valexs glanced at Kiiyeepo and then back at the Zulan. He almost masked his frustration. "You know we can't. Aye, we're stranded here with no contact to our home planets."

A different chief piped up, "Well, how long do you imagine it would be before these merchant ships arrived?"

Of course, Valexs and Kiiyeepo couldn't give solid answers, which meant that each question led to another. However, the chiefs never asked what sort of special payment Valexs had in mind. By the time the Zulan adjourned the meeting, the interrogation had taken them well into the sleeping portion of the daily cycle. "We must discuss this matter with the king. You have presented us a grievous decision. You'll be brought back here after midday of first dark."

The heavy-eyed scribe led the procession of people filing out. Right behind him, Kiiyeepo got away without an escort. The soldiers couldn't leave without Valexs, but Nieyowsue had fixed a gaze on the Nilose that commanded him to stay a moment longer.

Once everyone else had gone, she softly declared, "I can help you, I can speak to my father, but you must tell me something more."

"Aye, anything you want to know."

"Not here. There is no time." She pursed her lips, calculating. "We can picnic the morning meal. It's the only way I can meet you. One of my guards will be waiting outside the Royal Gathering to escort you in the morning."

She approached the guards at the door and admonished them, "You protect. You do not hear."

"Understood, Your Highness."

She turned to Valxes again. "Go now, and get some rest."

Perhaps it was due to the mist of the waterfall, but it seemed to be a touch darker outside as the soldiers led Valexs back to his room. The short delay had been enough to find Kiiyeepo fast asleep. He should have been easily overcome as well, after such a long day, but was too eager for the morning. He was elated beyond words at Nieyowsue's offer to help and the prospect of a tranquil picnic in her company.

Rest came in spurts until the new day, or whatever they called this time of wakefulness, was upon him. He went out to wait in the lobby. It was in one of those solid wooden chairs, however, that he finally dropped off.

Dreams put him back on the dance floor at the royal ball, except that he and Nieyowsue were the only ones there. Much to his dismay, he couldn't dance at all. He felt like he was constantly falling over. Then a spaceship crashed through the scene, its roaring engines instantly setting the whole room ablaze.

He forced his eyes open. He was slouched sideways in the chair, his neck aching from the awkward position. The door of the Royal Gathering was now wide open, and the thunder of the waterfall gushed through.

A soldier with pazin inlaid armor stood in the doorway. His tone was steeped in antipathy. "Valexs, I presume."

Nonetheless, the Nilose answered enthusiastically and hopped to his feet. "Yes, sir!"

The soldier directed him to follow with a tilt of his head and then started off. The world had lost its radiant glow. The buildings they passed between had a bluish tinge, like in an average dawn on Xonero, though Valexs knew that this was, in fact, dusk. The rich colors of the sky had also dulled, as if gray and black had joined the eddy.

Across the road that encircled the city, stepping stones led to a chiseled archway where the face of the plateau was almost perfectly vertical. Though unpainted and bare, the intricacy of the carving was enough to spellbind. Straight above it, a line of windows, similarly framed, provided light to the stairwell inside. Wide steps spiraled up the hazy passage. The strenuous climb was more than worth it when they emerged atop the plateau.

Life abounded here, far beyond what Valexs had thought possible. Patches of grass grew robustly in the lows of the stone ground and trees sprouted forth from the deepest crags where there was adequate soil.

The majority of the vegetation grew alongside the wide river that fed the falls. They stopped before a small copse of dense bushes. Trimmed by flowers, it displayed the care of a gardener. The soldier waved Valexs toward a well-pruned opening in the hedge.

Through the bushes was a semicircle clearing, bordered by the river. Nieyowsue lounged on a thick quilt, with one foot slung over the edge so that it touched the water ever so slightly. She released her maidservants as they finished laying out breakfast and then bade Valexs to sit.

The two greeted one another and went through the usual how-are-you-doings. They were here to discuss the petition, but neither of them was in a hurry to do so. Instead, they reminisced about their first encounter, and Nieyowsue clarified, "I had thought you were one of the younger males from the woodland villages. Always, a few try to sneak past my guards when I'm out. I find it so amusing when one makes it to me and then can't think of any good words to say.

"You asked for my name, though, and I realized then that I'd misjudged you. You were hardly out of sight when one of my guards informed me that I had to return immediately to the palace. The threat, of course, was potential survivors from the crash that day, your crash. It was quite plain to me that you and Kiiyeepo were those survivors, so we sent a party after you that evening. I'm told they rescued you from regalltees? I warned you about those."

"Aye, a moment later and we would have been goners! That was worse than battling an invader on the top of a skyscraper."

Nieyowsue cocked her head to the side. "Oh, you haven't told me about that."

Valexs dramatized the scene with his gestures and narration but was careful not to embellish it. The princess questioned him here and there and then listened to his prompt answers. She seemed to be all laughs and smiles. Mellifluously, however, she channeled the conversation. By the time Valexs noticed, the topic was utterly divergent. She was now probing his past and inquiring about his family relations. "...That's wonderful. Are you and your sister very close then?"

"Aye, um..." Valexs said, finally catching on. Even so, he wasn't alarmed. He trusted Nieyowsue, perhaps too much.

She continued gracefully, like there was nothing to catch on to, "Aww, how sweet. I presume the 'special payment' you requested is to return to them then with some means to supply their needs."

"Actually, I want to bring them here."

"That would be splendid! It will assure my father that you aren't trying to escape. What about your furry friend? He didn't decline his payment. Does he wish to stay?"

Valexs shook his head. "He wants to go home. It's all he's wanted for quite a while now."

"Indeed. So would I in his place. The poor dear. I will see whether or not I can put a good word in for him too. Tell me about him if you would; my father responds better when I give him the sentimental stories. He's a big softy under it all you know. He just plays tough around other people, especially the chiefs," Nieyowsue mentioned. "Everyone is so strapped for time, more than ever since the coming of the Xonerite ambassador, even small things may help the decision."

"An ambassador is here?"

"As to why, I cannot say, though I feel a major event is at hand. Please now, I do wish to help your friend."

Drawing a blank, Valexs gulped the last of his tea. He didn't know much about Kiiyeepo's background or his relations on Allanoi. He'd inferred that it was a fairly lonely ranch, though. There was the abduction of the Midek's brother, but he couldn't guess what had happened to his other relatives. Mostly, he elaborated on his friend's character and had only good things to say.

Nieyowsue didn't comment, quietly processing the information. After a long pause, Valexs decided to ask a question of his own. "What about your family? I haven't seen any siblings of yours, nor the quee..."

He hadn't finished saying the word before Nieyowsue cringed. He stopped at once and was about to apologize for asking, but she drew a breath and answered, her tone now a dismal lullaby, "She's off with a powerful noble in the west. She was only ever interested in my father for the power and wealth. He knew it too but was much too smitten with her to heed the warnings. For five orbits, they made due. According to Father, neither of them possessed the selflessness that marriage requires. It was no surprise when my mother left us. She didn't have any patience for my father, and he didn't know how to love her. I was very young at the time, but they tell me that Father hasn't ruled the same since. His decrees are often impulsive and driven by emotion, which is why a contingent of the chiefs continually strives to usurp him."

She looked away, blinking to keep from shedding tears. She refused to let out a sob. Between her slow, controlled breaths, she quickly explained, "I've never known the warmth of a family."

Valexs tentatively put his arm around her. She didn't pull away. Shoulder to shoulder, they stared into the river and watched the reflected colors of the sky turn another shade darker.

CHAPTER 19
First Dark

Kiiyeepo had slept in—no need to rush. He too had gone out for breakfast, out to the lounge that is. As he ate, he read up on the many species he'd encountered here. He took it slow, savoring the quiet and the solitude of this leisurely morning. *Where is Valexs anyway? Did he even come here after talking with the chiefs? I haven't seen him since.*

He was finally searching the room's corners and cabinets, when Valexs entered. Or at least that's what he'd assumed by the creak of the door. Not a sound followed. He shot a leery glance across the room. The door was barely open, not enough for the Wulvry to have peeped in.

The wind must have blown it open. A paleness through the scanty gap told him that no natural force had driven the door but a hand and a purpose. He focused in. Red eyes locked with his.

He yelped and sprang backward, a sudden shiver shaking him to the core. However, he rallied for a second look. An empty hall was all he found. *What in the galaxy! Have I lost it? What was that? Why was it watching me?*

He steeled himself and sulked toward the door. *There must be a logical explanation.* His fingers inched for the doorknob. He was all but there when the door flew open.

Shrieking, he slammed against the wall in a frantic attempt to retreat. It was only Valexs that ambled through.

"What has gotten into you? You look like you've seen a ghost!"

Kiiyeepo feigned a laugh and then frowned.

"Nothing. It was nothing," he said while looking up and down the still hallway. He discreetly locked the door. "So, where've you been?"

"Picnicking at the top of the waterfall." Valexs expounded on the pertinent details of his time with Nieyowsue, how it came to be and what she was going to do for them. In passing, he even mentioned the princess's sad upbringing.

Kiiyeepo knew it wasn't the help that had his friend enchanted. The Nilose said otherwise and cast himself dreamily upon the sofa. While they speculated about why an ambassador would be here, Kiiyeepo continued taking inventory of the room's complimentary paraphernalia: extra linens, hygiene products, robes, writing sticks, etc.

It seemed too soon when the custodian crashed into the door, having assumed that it would be unlocked. Though his voice stayed the same volume, it clearly conveyed his fury. "Come on! Your escort is here."

The sky, now a mixture of ink and pitch, loomed like an omen. The night was complete. Lights and torches had been ignited to cope with the sixty time fragments of darkness to come. Even the palace was dim inside, its grand windows only bringing in the night.

They were taken not to the conference room but to the great hall. Immediately, they felt the forbidding stare of the king. He was seated on the edge of his throne. Nieyowsue sat at his side, also on the platform. Before them, stood six of the chiefs. No one smiled. No one moved. The rest of the room, vast and vacant, repeated the night's augury.

At once, Valexs and Kiiyeepo saw the stress that their petition had put on Nieyowpon's leaders. At once, they saw their petition from the chiefs' perspective. They hadn't offered to help this nation advance; no, in the eyes of these people, they had asked to be entrusted with the gates of their world. They felt guilty, ashamed of the brazen attitude they had displayed.

Both winced at their echoing footfalls, as though this tense air could not be churned. They stopped right in front of the throne. Immodin shooed away their escort with a flick of his wrist and then returned his hand to where it perched at his chin.

"You have told us much in these past days. For that we are thankful. Now, however, you dare to present us with a plan that includes powers, events, and technologies beyond Nieyowpon's confines. We cannot verify your words. We cannot communicate with the entities that you speak of. Would you undertake a costly project if everything you knew about it was guesswork? Even the reports we receive from the other planets contradict themselves. Would you endorse a venture built half on truth and half on lies?"

Valexs looked to Kiiyeepo, but found the Midek looking back at him. Neither one an answer. What could they say? Was their plan really this childish? They knew it could work but shouldn't have expected anyone to believe them. They had a motive to lie, there was no proof, and the stakes were so high.

Immodin let them squirm. When he spoke again, it was directly at Valexs. "Then we find out that it is but a scheme for you to get back to your homes and families."

Valexs's heart sank. His talk with Nieyowsue had backfired. The princess pursed her lips guiltily but then winked. Was this what she'd intended all along?

"Aye, it is scheme like you said..." he started to respond.

Several of the chiefs whispered to each other "How dare they!" and "I told you so", loud enough to interrupt.

"Is it wrong that I seek the good of my family first? Those I am responsible for? I think not. Aye, it is my duty!" Valexs declared fervently. "It is a scheme not only for the purposes you cited, though, but also to unshackle you from the Pact and to help defend our solar system. More than even that, it's about saving *you*—"

"How so!" the bearded Wulvry challenged, bellowing.

"As it is, the only factions that have access to Nieyowpon are Chriyoss and Xonero, who are unwilling to stand against the invaders, and the invaders themselves. You're walled in! We know you have no reason to believe us, but I must ask you to acknowledge your peril and see if it's worth taking a chance."

"Enough said!" A smirk broke Immodin's rigid countenance. "It is for those same reasons that I have accepted your petition. As we speak, a crew is being enlisted to accompany you, and our finest vessels are undergoing preparations."

Accepted? That was something Kiiyeepo had lost all hope of hearing. This time, when he glanced at his friend, it wasn't out of anxiety but ecstasy. Valexs appeared to be stunned stiff.

The chiefs were as shocked as them. They flocked around the throne like a pack of blathering birds.

The exasperated inquisitions and demands of the majority drowned out the words of encouragement. Two were visibly pleased, Zezo being one of them.

"Yes... Of course not... Oh, alright..." the king struggled to respond to it all. "I realize that. Now get out."

The chiefs quickly quieted as the elderly Zulan appealed, "Please, Your Majesty. If you would weigh the pros and cons—"

"You too, Malkov. Out! Out! Out!"

The chiefs put on scowls but acquiesced, and he called after them, "Don't you be a hindrance!"

When he could no longer hear their squabbling, the king let out a sigh. It sounded as much like uncertainty as relief. He regarded the foreigners for awhile and then waved a hand at Kiiyeepo. "This... Midek will stay. We need someone to explain the information we gather, to separate truth from error. You, Valexs, should be ample for the first leg of this endeavor, seeing how bold you are!"

Immodin shot a razor-sharp glance at his daughter, who shrank away and avoided Valexs's gaze. "Be prepared to leave tomorrow, for the window of opportunity is propped open by the frailest of twigs."

He turned to the Midek. "You may go."

Kiiyeepo followed the chiefs' trail. He knew why they really wanted him to stay. He'd picked up a few words from the uproar. They were holding him hostage to keep Valexs in line. He wasn't surprised by this imprisoning decree. No, he was mortified.

The chiefs debated fiercely in the foyer just outside yet composed themselves long enough to send him on to the main lobby. It was a lonely space, fitting for the occasion. Kiiyeepo took a seat in the corner by the double doors. Too sad to hope but too angry to cry, he merely listened to his heart beat.

The teleconscious was on. Punctual to the moment for his report to the emperor, Furygon stared at the limited view of the imperial office. The throne was rotated in the opposite direction, its excessive magnitude concealing whoever might be sitting in it along with most of the room.

Exavyir's irritated tone came through loud and clear. Presumably, the emperor was conversing with a being standing before him. "Let's get this timeline behind us now. It's only Furygon. He cannot mind."

Still, the S.O.O. sat vacant-eyed and static, not flinching at his own name.

"But sir, he could divulge information accidently if—" the unseen being argued coolly. Fluid and quick, his voice wasn't remotely Deurtex.

"He knows what we're doing, you ignoramus! Your questions insult me! I could have anyone do your job 'head researcher'. Keep that in mind."

"Yes sir. Pardon me," the being implored. He continued, wanting but not daring to whisper, "We have the pictures of the lifeforms from the other solar system, proof of the fleet's whereabouts. Once we release those to the public, no one will doubt that the epidemic would have been held back. What guilty faction would risk making itself known? The question is, when should this be?"

"It has to be soon. Kallamada 3 is at the tipping point based on General Akwen's report."

"Several important objectives remain undone. We don't know how they've eluded us thus far, though, which means that our time estimates are completely arbitrary."

The throne rotated to a data interface. A few button pushes brought up statistics from the situation on Kallamada 3, updating in real time.

After reading the commentary of the head intelligence officer there, the emperor slouched and closed his eyes, wrestling with the decision. He faced the head researcher again. "Are the images ready for distribution?"

"Yes sir."

"Then do it now." Exavyir hated to say the words. He slammed a fist into the armrest. "Give up on the final targets and reconcile with them at any cost. We have to play it safe."

Their dialogue moved through the results of prevention to successful quarantine. The dates of these events vacillated broadly as they re-evaluated each factor. It was nearly a time fragment later, that timeframes were sufficiently delimited. Whining, Exavyir brought the conversation to a close, "That's good enough for our pressing issues. We can wait on inoculation one season. By then, it may be more crucial. Be gone and do as I've told."

The thud of a shut door echoed, and then the throne spun to face the teleconscious. Exavyir looked vexed and drained, but a smirk shot across his face as he mocked, "A pity isn't it. *I* reap the rewards from *your* victory yet am immune from the main tribulation of your defeat."

"Yes sir, it is a pity," Furygon confirmed, straight and dry.

Letting out a huff, Exavyir ordered, "Status report!"

"The Allanoi invasion will commence in three days, following the negotiation for the Nieyowpon space stations. Orra and Chriyoss have both moved fleets into orbit to protect their trade lines."

"Show no weakness in your dealings with them. If we behave as though we are strong enough to crush them in an afterthought, a few of the rulers will cave and join us in hope of saving themselves. Then we will indeed be able to crush them as the afterthought that they are..." The emperor's declaration fizzled down to a mutter, as though he'd disgusted himself.

"Yes sir."

"What about allies? Did Uryiten respond favorably?"

"Yes, under a tenuous agreement. It is unlikely that he will divulge information about our message. We assured him of his suspicions: that we are not here to wage war against anyone but our true enemies. The Intelligence Department has accused the president of Allanoi, Haazon, of heading the epidemic."

"Keep your First Council focused on conquest rather than on finding the epidemic. It will be costly enough as it is. Tell them that your presence there has stopped it for the time being."

"Yes sir. Vorrnum, king of Krashad on the planet Dasahr, has agreed to meet with us next week. He has shown signs of extreme self-interest and commands a strong military."

"Then go personally. Rallying him is paramount!" the emperor decreed. "Also, send the general strategy for the first invasion when it's finalized. Our next meeting will be delayed a few days."

"Yes sir," Furygon consented, though the screen had already gone black. He summoned his secretary and immediately heard the perennially hurried steps dart to his side. "Alter my schedule. Postpone the next imperial report."

"How many days' delay will this be?"

"Undefined."

"Right away sir!" Such a menial task didn't warrant Myeerp's excitement. He was nearly out the door before Furygon could order, "Take a command to Kallor."

When his secretary turned back, he continued, "Tell him to have the strategists devise a general strategy assuming Vorrnum's allegiance."

Indicating that he understood with a nod, Myeerp departed, his thrill only diminished by a hair.

Kiiyeepo heard when the chiefs were called back in. They must have been relieved since only a couple of micro fragments had gone by without them. Apart from that, he heard nothing but the hushed rumble of the falls. Like white noise, it blocked out anything that tried to penetrate this stillness.

Will this be my life here? Being batted around for information at the convenience of these officials and left for dead in between? What's the bright side? He lifted his head from its downcast low. *At least I have the most beautiful jail anyone ever had.*

Something caught his attention, a muted whiteness. *Oh no, not again!* Instinctively, his gaze jumped to where it had appeared, at the mouth of the hall that he'd taken twice to the conference room. There was nothing to be seen. His grip tightened on the chair's armrests, but he didn't back down. He had to know what was out there. He couldn't allow it to haunt him like this.

Two heartbeats and then it recurred, with scarlet eyes aimed straight at him. Kiiyeepo blinked, and it was gone. He took a breath but was afraid to speak. "I... I know you're there... Show yourself!"

A small, frail being slowly shuffled into the open. Hunched over to the point that its long, thin arms hovered just above the floor and with a face chillingly narrow, this was one sickly Zulan. It halted in the middle of the foyer, keeping a distance between itself and the Midek. Its age, gender, and emotions were all unintelligible, having no mane, not one hair to conceal its pallor flesh, and that blood red stare. Its voice was weak and melancholy. "Me sorry. Me no mean to scare you."

"Okay," Kiiyeepo responded cautiously, quite aghast. "Why were you watching me? Who are you?"

"Me have question," the being answered.

"Well... what is it?"

"You want go home? Yes?"

"Um, sure," Kiiyeepo said distractedly as he made a quick scan of the palace, empty as far as he could see. This didn't seem right. Shouldn't there be a guard to make sure that he didn't wander off? "Are you allowed to be here?"

"Me get you gone."

This demanded greater consideration to make sense of. Kiiyeepo answered doubtfully, "Someone already tried to help me get home if that's what you mean. It only made things worse."

"Me know. Me do different."

"Who are you? How could you help me? Why do you care?"

"Me inventor."

That didn't answer the Midek in any respect, and Kiiyeepo realized that the being had evaded most of his other questions. Bewildered, he probed, "What do you want?"

"You know about ambassador?"

"All I know is that he's here from Xonero. Why?"

The Zulan put a finger to his lips, the chatter of people and the slam of the door to the great hall echoing in. He backed away. "Me go. Talk later. Shhh."

Another question, unanswered, Kiiyeepo thought as the Zulan disappeared down the hallway.

Valexs emerged a moment later, the chiefs trailing behind him. His countenance radiated excitement and sympathy in equal proportions. "I'm sorry about how this turned out for you. I couldn't change his mind."

I'm the one who's sorry. It was my idea in the first place, Kiiyeepo replied in his head but audibly questioned, "What did the king tell you so privately?"

"He outlined his expectations, which I'm supposed to obey regardless of the chiefs' wishes," Valexs whispered double-time. "I'll keep both sets of desires in mind, aye!

"I'm headed to the ship now for some safety and operational training. Immodin wants me to leave as soon as possible. We're mainly waiting for the crew to get here. The ships are almost ready. The king's inventor is just trying to install a way to keep in touch."

The inventor Immodin mentioned during the ball, of course! The one that repaired the broadcast receiver! He happens to be a ghostly Zulan. The fog cleared slightly around the evasive being.

"That's correct," the head chief, Malkov, affirmed. He'd overheard the tail end of the conversation as he approached them. "You, Midek, will be shown to the research area at the defense complex... Your escorts should have been here."

They didn't have to wait much longer. Two soldiers pushed open the palace doors for a Nilose and a Gredwol, the two chiefs who'd been absent. The other six gathered around them to fill them in on the king's spontaneous decision and to sway them to one point of view or another. Before joining the throng himself, Malkov instructed the soldiers where to take the foreigners and sent them off.

CHAPTER 20

Dire Happenings

Valexs and Kiiyeepo finally parted ways at the fifth floor of the defense complex, almost at the top of the plateau. One soldier continued up the steps with Valexs, and one led Kiiyeepo through the somewhat underutilized office space. It seemed like an average workday, but it wasn't busy at all. The most commotion on the whole floor came from the research area, a large room with more than enough desks, filing cabinets, and transcription machines.

The broadcast receiver itself was set up against the wall, roughly centered. There was no denying that it had been ripped out of a space ship's control console. It wasn't pretty, but it worked, currently displaying the news from an Orranian channel.

A scribe sat right in front of the screen, diligently taking notes from the broadcast. Two workers carried stacks of files between desks that were piled high and the filing cabinets, perhaps updating or sorting information. Four were standing around, chatting. The last two workers typed away at a pair of very large, rectangular appliances.

What do those do? Kiiyeepo wondered. He could tell they were old just from the look of them but never figured out that they were simply pre-Separation data interfaces. Nieyowpon's technological scarcity had led to the usage of a strange blend of tech from all eras.

"Juyoo, deal with this!" a Kumor at one of the desks ordered as soon as he looked up from his work. He plopped his stack of files into the arms of the dawdling Nilose and then walked over to greet their visitor.

"Ah, you must be Kiiyeepo! I was told you might be coming in today! We really appreciate your help!" The Kumor pointed to himself with both thumbs and grinned as he added, "I'm Nim, the supervisor here!"

Kiiyeepo was momentarily dumbstruck, "...It's a pleasure to meet you, Sa—Nim!" He'd almost said the name of his math teacher back at the orphanage. Never again had he expected to encounter such hyperenthusiasm.

"I've been sorting out any information that you might be able to shine some light on. It's all stacked according to its urgency—generally—so we can jump into the most important stuff first!" Nim grabbed an extra chair and showed Kiiyeepo to a desk buried under five towers of files and a transcription machine.

Kiiyeepo was undaunted. If he was to be stuck here doing this, he might as well have plenty of it to do. Some of the files contained new technologies that had been mentioned in broadcasts, like hyper cells and space lanes. He explained what each one did as far as he knew.

The bulk of the job, however, was in verifying details or providing context for the latest happenings. As they worked, Nim put each file into the transcription machine to edit it and, if he deemed it significant, to make copies for the chiefs.

Much of the information was news even to Kiiyeepo. Orra had a fleet just outside the atmosphere to maintain space lanes to Zanquin and Dasahr. *Perhaps that will ensure a safe exit for Valexs.*

Tensions were high around the Nieyowpon space stations, and the invaders had agreed to a negotiation. They would be hosting. According to the report, it would take place in two days' time.

This was big news: the first formal meeting or dialogue of any kind between the officials of their solar system and the invaders. Kiiyeepo tried to describe just how important this negotiation could be.

"Listen to this!" the scribe called. He cranked up the volume on the broadcast receiver as everyone crowded around.

"Breaking news!" the reporter exclaimed. She sounded surprised herself or perhaps scared. "Moments ago, Vorrnum, king of Krashad, announced that he has a scheduled meeting with the leader of the invaders to discuss terms of allegiance."

"Nooo..." Kiiyeepo quietly moaned. The news hit like a bombshell. Vorrnum was wicked, but he was also infamously nationalistic. Would he really join the enemy even after the dropping of the Krashad tariff? How could the solar system's strongest military force turn against them? *Praxus would be doomed.*

He didn't know what to say. Thankfully, the reporter did most of the explaining and speculation for him. The team still had many good questions, though, and he did his best to answer.

"Wow, this is huge!" Nim's unfaltering excitement was an encouragement to Kiiyeepo. "I'll make sure it gets right to the chiefs!"

They worked until it came time for the evening meal, at which point most of the team headed home. Kiiyeepo had to wait on his escort. Packing up to leave, Nim thanked him again, "It's been a pleasure. Thank you."

"It was a pleasure working with you too," Kiiyeepo replied. "You seem really happy here."

"I'm very thankful to have this job, this..." the Kumor pulled Kiiyeepo aside, "...opportunity to influence my government for good! I determine what information the chiefs see from these broadcasts and thus the issues they think about. Now... don't help anyone figure that out."

Kiiyeepo nodded. "I won't. I think you're the right guy for the job."

Nim beamed.

They'd descended to the ground floor before bumping into Kiiyeepo's tardy escort. The soldier directed Kiiyeepo out of the defense complex but then let him walk to the Royal Gathering by himself.

The Midek ate dinner alone and read the next chapter of the Unknown Hero. The turncoat in the forest village had been captured but at no small cost. On the second page, however, the rebel committed suicide rather than disclose his information. Had the trail gone cold again? For three days the loyalists of the village, including the protagonist, searched for clues about the rebels' plans. Their reward: a coded document.

Almost two time fragments later, Valexs finally showed up. They exchanged summaries of their evenings before washing up and crashing into bed.

Haazon listened to the quiet. For the first time since he got back, he could see all four walls of his office. Usually, they were obscured by a cacophonous mob of advisers and officials. He knew every last one of them stood impatiently outside the door. It was his own doing; he'd decided that this would be more efficient than individual appointments for less important matters. There simply wasn't enough time to keep up with everything.

He hefted a vocal transmitter and dialed a convoluted twenty digit number. A whiny, stressed voice came through, "Oh Haazon, give me good news." Cueyo III.

"No terrestrial military contact. The invaders have landed in three areas. They continue to test our air force and have begun limited bombing raids. They've targeted two refineries and two air fields. All our space stations are either abandoned or controlled by the enemy." Haazon's tone was perfectly matter-of-fact. "They could attack at any moment. Everything they do is fast but methodical."

Cueyo sighed. "So much for good news."

"What's been happening over there lately?"

"More than a solar system could handle! War production started large scale yesterday in accordance to the Cueyo III doctrine of defense. My military is presently the third or fourth strongest after Vorrnum, Thirasmasoaric, and maybe Phendrou. Why are the invaders allowing me to build up my defenses? If they're here for conquest, why would they go after your world first? It doesn't make sense, Haazon. It's like they've come specifically to fight you. Can't you think of any reason why?"

Haazon didn't answer.

"Anyway, though, this has brought Orra's financial problems to the forefront. Each party in the assembly has proposed a budget. The argument is still fierce, but I am already tormented by what might arrive at my desk."

"What about your Nieyowpon fleet?"

"Oh, that's the most taxing of all!" Haazon could almost see the Orranian rubbing his temple. "Who can guess what will transpire at that meeting? I'm sure you know that the negotiation will be at one of the captured Nieyowpon space stations. The invaders have offered full accommodations to our delegations, all via text transmission. No actual conversation.

"My diplomatic party is already on the way. There will also be representatives from Zanquin, Krashad, Praxus, and the Pact, of course. They will be the first beings to converse with an invader face to face. They are very brave."

"Indeed. It's fascinating to think what they might learn just from interacting with the staff."

"On top of everything else, I have a meeting with an ambassador from Praxus this evening. If Vorrnum joins the enemy, Orra will have to get its ore from Zras. That makes everything more expensive. The whole solar system is falling apart!"

"Then it looks like they were quite calculated in blockading Allanoi. They further divided us. The connection between our planets and Rodeous is severed, forcing Nighdra to shift her ties to Zanquin. We know Thirasmasoaric has lower morals than Vorrnum when it isn't politically detrimental to show it."

"Oh my! Maybe Phendrou was right from the start. We can't win."

"This war has only just begun. We haven't even seen their army to determine its strength. There is still time. We can still be united."

"How? Everyone is doing what's best for them alone. Do you really believe that it's possible?"

There was a pause, long and grim, before Haazon answered honestly, "No... But I'm doing everything in my power to prove myself wrong!"

After another long quiet, Haazon asked, "How are you holding up?"

"Frankly, I could use a substantial glass of fermented, fruit cider right about now." Cueyo tittered halfheartedly. "I'll be okay. I have to go. Zras's ambassador is here."

It was a lie. The emissary would arrive at any moment now, though, as Cueyo hung up the transmitter. He rose and strolled into the hall. On one side was his office, the conference chamber, and other presidential amenities, but his gaze was turned to the thick, tinted glass opposite.

A riot raged outside, exactly one hundred levels below him. The people's twisted scowls and hate filled cries were too far to perceive. Even their huge, red-lettered signs were unintelligible, but he knew what they displayed: slanderous insults beyond repeat, insults meant for him. The crowd was here because he'd signed legislation that decentralized the wellness system.

He looked away, teary eyed. *How can they do this? Can't they see I'm trying to save them? No, they don't understand or even care to learn.*

It had been a hard decision. Cueyo I and II had spent orbits putting it into place, to take control of health away from the people. *Don't you know you that nothing is free? You sold a portion of your freedom to make someone else pay for your problems! Don't you remember...*

At the latch of a door, he stopped and composed himself. His assistant hovered over. "The Praxus emissary awaits you in the chamber. Shall I escort you?"

"Thank you but no." Cueyo III glanced down at the rioters. "You tell the enforcers to put an end to this."

The hallway network of the Sovereignty felt infinite. Where one passage stopped an identical perpendicular one began. If Prodek didn't have a map of the dreadnaught downloaded on his headset, even he would get lost in this sector.

Behind him, people hurried between offices, but the path ahead was stagnant. He turned down the thirty-fourth side hall and sped up, matching Myeerp's usual pace. The corridor was eerily empty, and his data said that it would remain so for the next fifteen micro fragments. He checked the time. *Fourteen.*

He stopped abruptly at a door imperceptibly shorter than the rest, that of a janitorial closet. A swiveling camera monitored the corridor. Concealed in a surveillance node, there should have been no way to tell where it was pointed. He, however, knew its rotation timing. He waited two moments, glanced over his shoulder, and then slipped silently into the room.

Chemicals, brushes, a floor cleaning machine, touch-up supplies, and tools for light repairs stocked the small space. Nonetheless, he found what he was looking for immediately. "So what are we doing in a dark closet, Myeerp?"

Furygon's secretary stood from the vat of floor cleaner that he'd been sitting on. "Keeping secrets isn't easy around here, and some things can't be phrased in code."

"Let's have it. Time is never in the favor of secrecy."

"I wanted to wait until the first invasion was underway, but it looks like our chance is now! Furygon talked to the emperor yesterday and was told to postpone the next imperial report for an open-ended period. I'm thinking that gives us three days for sure, though I wouldn't hope for more," Myeerp explained. "You're on break tomorrow and there's a gap in Furygon's schedule. We're never going to get a better opportunity."

"What about the council session tomorrow and the negotiation? Furygon is needed for both!"

"So what if he isn't able to make it. He hit his head pretty hard when he fell," Myeerp said leadingly. "There are plenty of good excuses, and by then he'll be able to participate remotely."

"If it goes as we expect." Prodek found himself a makeshift seat. "I can't believe we're really going to do it."

"We've been dreaming about this for so long."

"Since twenty days before the fleet's departure," Prodek reminded, "but it does seem like longer than that. With the truth about Furygon, came the truth about the Epidemic and our, dare I say, daring plan to take advantage of it."

"We'll be heroes in a matter of time fragments, even if Furygon is the only one who knows!"

"What if I can't perform the operation? I mean, I've studied everything there is to know about... devices like that. I don't have any real training, though, and what we're about to face is likely far more complex than any of the ones I've seen. Maybe we should get a technician involved."

"You know we can't do that. He'd never keep his mouth shut! Besides, the medics will be right there when we're done, totally oblivious." Myeerp's tone was exasperated but confident. "Look, I'm going to summon you from Furygon's office in the morning. You better be ready."

Prodek gulped. "Yeah, okay."

"Now let's get out of here while we can."

Prodek stopped Myeerp at the door, but only for a moment, timing the camera. He wouldn't follow too close. Before setting out, he put soothing ambient music on loud in his headset.

CHAPTER 21
Departure

The trip to the launch pads was filled with anxious talk about Vorrnum's meeting with the invaders. Kiiyeepo had recounted the news report in detail.

"...It would mean losing our greatest land force and handing it to the enemy."

"It's not as scary as it seems, though," Valexs said, "since his army is stuck on Dasahr. Even with the invader's fleet, it would be extremely costly in time and resources to move any significant force."

"I'm afraid for Praxus," Kiiyeepo explained. "Zras is a great ally. Losing Praxus would be a hard hit on the solar system."

Valexs grimaced. "Aye, they wouldn't stand a chance."

"But why would this Vorrnum do that?" Zezo questioned. "He may be meeting with them, but that doesn't mean he'll switch sides, surely?"

"The reporter said 'to discuss terms of allegiance'. He's considering it at least," Kiiyeepo reminded.

"Couldn't he be bluffing? If these intruders are as mysterious and dangerous as you have described, why would anyone join them?"

"Vorrnum is a wicked Dragon, dead set on destroying Praxus and ruling all of Dasahr."

"Aye!" Valexs agreed. "Even if it takes shaking hands with the devil himself!"

Marching down the stairwell was a group of soldiers clad in dark blue armor. The armor looked familiar to Valexs and Kiiyeepo, though very different from anything they had seen here on Nieyowpon. The soldiers stopped and shifted formally to one side, according to their sergeant's signal.

Zezo questioned the officer, "How did you fair with the blasters."

"Fine, sir. It's just getting a feel for 'em that's tricky."

"And the armor?"

"It's good," the sergeant knocked on his breastplate, "very good, sir."

"Hm." Zezo turned and continued up the steps with the foreigners. He resumed their previous conversation. "About the Vorrnum situation, is there nothing that can be done?"

"Perhaps is!" a fragile voice called down. The inventor stood at the top step. "What us doing?"

"Never mind." Zezo stopped three steps short of the Zulan so that they were eye to eye. "How is the communication system coming?"

"It set. Me testing now."

When they were sufficiently past the Zulan, Valexs quietly asked, "What happened to him?"

"I don't have a clue. It's only coming on two weeks that he's been working here," Zezo answered as he typed a code into the keypad on the door. They stepped out onto the plateau, enclosed by the wall Kiiyeepo had observed from below.

A row of five hangars was built along the left side. At the back of the walled area was a wide gate used to move vessels out to the runway, a long, leveled strip across the plateau. The launch tower stood at the head of the large gap between the hangars and the other buildings.

One hangar was open, and a long tube-shaped ship had been wheeled out. Several beings hurried around it, lugging tools of every kind. Kiiyeepo couldn't tell what they were actually doing, however, until he saw the supervisors with their checklists.

Valexs's twelve-strong crew, not counting the soldiers who would accompany them, was studying information about the solar system's current circumstances in the briefing center. They were a diverse group, chosen for their knowledge and aptitudes. Together they had almost every relevant field of expertise covered, except the one that Valexs gladly offered: experience and connections on the outside worlds.

Most of them introduced themselves cordially but only to Valexs. Even so, Kiiyeepo helped his friend answer their questions and talked about Allanoi, though it was no obligation of his. As soon as he was no longer vital to the discussion, he headed back into the ever cooler night.

He watched the workers testing each component of the tubular spacecraft. He circled the ship. It was smaller than the space jet by a third but had an identical twin still in the hangar that would fly with it.

He couldn't help but wonder what sort of ships resided in the other hangars and casually made his way to the last one in the row. Its door was raised only a few units, enough to furtively peek under. One large vessel took up the whole space. High-tech and immaculate, it had to be a century ahead of anything on Nieyowpon. Was it this that had created the smoke trail he'd seen two days ago? He made sure no one was watching and then ducked inside.

Both sides of the ship were printed with enormous symbols, insignias of the Xonerite government if he remembered correctly. Equipped with the latest hyper cell, this could only be the ship of the ambassador who he kept hearing about. Having seen enough, Kiiyeepo slipped back out and continued monitoring the workers. He even ventured aboard at a supervisor's invitation.

Thrusters took up the bulk of the tubular ship. The rest was utilitarian to the extreme. It would be a tight fit for everyone, especially with Valexs's mother and sister. Controls filled the cockpit, far more complex than those in the tiny craft that had gotten him here, which was both alarming and comforting at the same time.

"Test one, three, two... one, two, three!" the inventor's voice came suddenly through the ship's intercom. A worker declared, "I hear ya, loud and clear."

"See signal strength!"

The worker ambled out, leaving Kiiyeepo alone in the cockpit. A camera swiveled toward him, and then the intercom spewed, "Ah, Midek, me tell plan to get home?"

"Right now?"

"Can't hear you. Speak into mic on control console."

Kiiyeepo found the black dot that the worker had been standing by. "I guess so."

"Good. Ambassador going to negotiation. You know about that?"

"The negotiation with the invaders?"

"That the one. Us go with him."

"How? Why would they let us leave?" Kiiyeepo didn't know whether to face the intercom or camera. It felt wrong to speak to someone like this, knowing he could be seen without having a similar privilege.

"Me got junk on head chief. Him want me gone. Them need us on that ship to keep ambassador honest. If king think worthwhile, him send us. You want go Krashad?"

"What! No. I want to go home, to Allanoi."

"You go from there. Might need you. Tell Zezo you do anything and must be way."

"Well, okay... I guess. What do you mean by junk on—"

"You talk Zezo. Me be up in moment."

The worker returned. "Signal strength, ninety-eight. We have limited variations. Approximate fluctuation range, seventy to one ten..."

The numbers waned behind Kiiyeepo. Outside, Zezo had just emerged from the briefing center, but the Midek wasn't about to talk. What was the inventor's plan? He tried to piece together the things he'd been told. *The ambassador must have stopped here on his way to the negotiation. The inventor is blackmailing the head chief to send us with him. Why is he so desperate to leave? Why would the king send us to Krashad?* His lips went from pursed in thought to a deep frown as it all clicked at once. *Oh no, he's going to send us to stop Vorrnum from making a truce with the invaders! That's all they know about Krashad... Speaking of the devil.*

The sickly Zulan hobbled out of the door to the stairwell. Zezo met him halfway. "How's it coming?"

"All done," the inventor answered. Kiiyeepo could hear them clearly since the bustle of the workers had died down. "Us get clear from Dasahr—Orra! Him be sending from Orra."

"Right. And the rest of the ship?"

"Just inspecting."

Zezo nodded and started toward the door, but the Zulan beckoned, "Wait! Me talk Midek. Us join negotiation if him get home." When Zezo turned around yet failed to reply, he added, "Him do anything."

"I'm heading to the palace now, but I'll keep that in mind."

Kiiyeepo shook with rage as the pale Zulan strolled up to him, and griped, "How could you tell him that? I never said I'd 'do anything'!"

"You say 'okay'."

"It's an impossible mission! What do they think we can do to stop Vorrnum? They don't know how things work out there..." It was worse than walking into a brick wall. "*You* don't know either."

The tiny being looked down, shifting from one foot to the other. There was a long, tense pause, each waiting for the other. Kiiyeepo finally parked himself on a bench close by. What could he do? Chase after Zezo? He wouldn't make it past the first door without authorization and an escort.

I'm overreacting. I must be missing something, Kiiyeepo hoped. "If we're going to be working together, then I need to know something about you. What's your name?"

"Me Sufralycoo."

That was quite a name. Finding it difficult to process, Kiiyeepo asked, "Can I call you Suf for short?"

"Me no like Suf! You know what Suf is?"

"Oh, uh, no. I had no idea it meant anything. Sorry!" The Zulan didn't respond, so Kiiyeepo continued questioning, "If you don't mind me asking, what happened to you?"

"Me sick. From birth." Sufralycoo climbed up on the bench beside him. "No have good treatment."

"Oh. I'm sorry to hear that." Kiiyeepo did his best to sound sympathetic. They sat there quietly for a while. Apparently, he would have to drive the conversation unaided. "Is that why you want to leave so badly: to find better treatment?"

"No... well maybe. It be adventure," Sufralycoo answered quickly as the supervisor walked over with a checklist.

"Inspection complete, sir. We're all set."

"Me look. You get word to chiefs," Sufralycoo ordered and then scurried to the ship.

Watching him do the final evaluation, Kiiyeepo continued mulling over the situation. *How will we get to Dasahr from the negotiation? How does any of this help me get home? I'm being used, played for a fool.*

A wind kicked up. Pebbles clanked against the side of the briefing center, forcing him to hurry in. Valexs and his team sat around two tables, finishing their midday meal and chatting about anything of little consequence. He noticed his own grumbling stomach and stole an open seat but was too far from his friend to solicit his advice. The conversation died awkwardly around him, like a Buladuke land-whale had stomped into the room. He ate quickly and then cleared out. The whirling winds were better than this embarrassment.

As soon as the door shut behind him, it flew open again. Valexs emerged. "Hey, wait! Sorry about them. I'm sure they'll come around eventually."

"Yeah, eventually."

As they moved to the side of the building, where they would be shielded from the elements, Valexs probed, "There's something else, isn't there?"

Kiiyeepo collected his thoughts and answered, "The inventor says that he has a way for me to go home—"

"Really!"

"I'm not so sure. I haven't heard Allanoi anywhere in his plan. I think he's trying to get him and me sent to Dasahr to stop Vorrnum from making an alliance with the invaders."

"The chiefs won't go for that."

"He's blackmailing the head chief, maybe others too, and you've seen Immodin in action. He seems to make decisions by a coin toss!"

"Aye, but that's crazy," Valexs mused. "It's probably a misunderstanding. It's hard to understand anything that Zulan says!"

"Let's hope, but why else would he be talking about Dasahr?"

"I don't know, and I don't think he's a trustworthy source."

"We will find out soon."

"You will." Valexs sighed. "As soon as word comes from the chiefs, I'm off. I can't watch your back on this one."

"I'll be fine. I'll sort out the misunderstanding. You have enough to worry about."

"Here," Valexs stuffed a writing sheet into the Midek's hand, "it's the transmission code of my ship. Maybe, when you get a chance, you can call me and tell me how things are going. Aye, if you do get off Nieyowpon then this goodbye might be forever."

"Don't say that. I'm sure..." Kiiyeepo froze. The only thing he was sure of at this point was that, without this Nilose, he had no one. He wasn't willing to admit it, though, not even to himself.

"However the winds blow, you were the best friend I could have asked for through these wild days," Valexs said with sincerity. "I can't thank you enough. You saved my life. Aye, more than once! I wouldn't have had this opportunity to rescue my family if it wasn't for your clever scheme."

One of the crew members rounded the corner, a middle-aged Gredwol. "There you are. I've been looking all over! We got the okay for launch. We're loading up now. I say we shove off before the severity of our operation dawns on the rest of the crew. Not to call them cowards, but you never know."

"Aye! I'll only be a moment."

"As you wish. We'll be waiting on you, captain." The Gredwol left faster than he came.

Turning back, Valexs laid a hand on Kiiyeepo's big, furry shoulder. "I better see you again one day."

"You will, somehow. We'll find a way," Kiiyeepo promised. They started toward the ship. "I've been meaning to ask you something: how are you so fearless? Even now, you don't seem anxious at all." Since Caltow's abduction, fear of what might lay ahead had become his way of life.

Valexs shrugged. "I can only think of a few things that I'm really scared of, losing my family for one. I do know this: courage is not a lack of fear but the ability to see beyond it, to keep your eye on the prize that is victory. We're not here to sit around and be comfortable. Aye! We're here to fight for that which is good and true! That's my motto."

Kiiyeepo stored the words away in his memory. He would never forgive himself if he forgot them, especially if this was the last time he spoke to Valexs. He hastened to catch up.

Around the corner Nieyowsue had pulled Valexs aside. He gave them space but eavesdropped between gusts.

"I shall miss you... such a blessing to us..." the princess's tender song was lost easily to the wind. "...filled my heart with hope..."

"I will think of you every day," Valexs replied, gently yet quickly.

"...the day you return. Godspeed to you!"

"Thank you." Valexs kissed her hand and then turned toward the ship.

Such mush! Kiiyeepo helped his friend load and secure the last of the crates. A bag had been thoughtfully assembled for Valexs with all the personal items he would need.

Once everything was set, Kiiyeepo descended and the boarding ramp retracted behind him. He joined the throng, gathered to send off the voyagers. Valexs and a couple of the other crew members stood in the doorway, waving to anyone they knew who had authorization to be there.

"Goodbye," Kiiyeepo called, yet his voice mixed with that of Nieyowsue, Sufralycoo, and everyone else on the premises, "and farewell."

The thick door sealed with unyielding solidity, severing all contact to those beyond. It was like they had stepped into an alternate dimension whose portal now closed forever. Valexs was gone.

The nose of the ship was raised halfway to vertical on the launch tower. The ailerons at the ends of its narrow wings tilted to hold the vessel on course. As great pillars of fire exploded from the engines, everyone stepped back and shielded their faces from the wave of heat and light, everyone except Kiiyeepo. His thoughts were too deep to be upset by a slight discomfort. *So this is what it's like to be alone. I'm a pariah among these people with no one I can truly call a friend.*

The ship began to lift, and then mechanisms in the launch tower swiftly accelerated it. It darted heavenward, leaving the onlookers momentarily blind and deaf as the dark of the night charged back in. When their eyes readjusted to the lantern light, the ship was already receding into the blacks and grays of Nieyowpon's slumbering sky.

Still, Kiiyeepo didn't stir as the twin vessel was hoisted to the equivalent takeoff angle. It went through the same procedure as Valexs's ship, blinding him and blasting him with the same scorching heat. He finally turned away but not until every last speck of light from its thrusters was long buried behind the atmosphere's gaseous shroud.

Surrounded by her bodyguards, Nieyowsue stood an excessively safe distance from the launch tower but slowly moseyed up to him with her hands folded in front of her. She asked sympathetically, "Are you alright?"

"Yeah, I'm fine. Thinking that's all."

"He will not be gone so long."

"For you," Kiiyeepo corrected. "Depending on what happens to me, I might never see him again."

Nieyowsue pursed her lips. She knew something. "About that—"

"I think I just want to be alone right now."

He began to leave, but the young, Nilose woman quietly persuaded, "It might put your mind at ease."

Kiiyeepo stopped. After a moment, he found his manners. "That would be good. Thank you."

"I don't know how much you have gathered, so let me start from the onset of our current affairs."

Nieyowsue led him to the bench now that the winds had ebbed. "Ambassador Falair of the Chriyoss-Xonero Pact arrived the other day. He requested information on any anomalies and on all the recent crashes. When we questioned him, he told us the same old story that the traders always use, saying that the rest of the planets are malicious and that only Chriyoss and Xonero are protecting us. Both what you've told us and what we've seen on the broadcast receiver, as you call it, refute his claims. So far, he persists in denying this evidence.

"He and his team are currently in custody at the palace. Tomorrow, he is supposed to be at the armistice negotiation regarding the space stations around Nieyowpon. From there, he would go to Dasahr for a talk with Vorrnum."

"I don't follow," Kiiyeepo said. "How am I involved?"

"We are sending our most stubborn chief, Ordmin, to lobby Nieyowpon's best interests. Since Falair continues to spew lies about the solar system, however, we hope you will help detect those lies. The inventor will also be going."

Kiiyeepo was skeptical. "Why is the inventor going? Don't you need him here?"

"He will maintain communication with us and prevent Falair from sending a distress transmission. The Pact cannot find out what we're doing. The prime chief insists that the pitiful Zulan should go," the princess answered.

She got back on topic, nearly pleading. "It seems like a simple task and I'm certain that you will be perfectly safe. Afterward, you are welcomed and encouraged to return to Nieyowpon, but you will be supplied with enough pazin to go wherever you wish."

The Midek pictured his ranch and smiled unconsciously. "Okay, I can do that."

He walked away contented. Valexs had been right about it being a misunderstanding. To think he would be sent to stop Vorrnum now sounded as absurd as it was. When he reached the door that would lead him off the plateau, he gestured a guard over and commanded, "Take me to my room."

CHAPTER 22

Facts & Redemption

Kiiyeepo had locked himself away in his room for the rest of the day. He needed to sort out his muddled emotions. First, he discarded the residue of his confusion and anger. He owed Sufralycoo an apology for assuming the worst of him and some gratitude. Would he even be going on this trip if it wasn't for him? Despite the terrifying fact that he would be in a space station full of invaders, he was happy to help the chief represent Nieyowpon.

The sorrow of Valexs's departure was harder to ignore. It looked like their paths wouldn't cross in an eon. Overshadowing even his sadness, though, was excitement. He became more excited by the moment to finally go home. *And to wake up from this crazy dream.*

From wishful thoughts of Allanoi, his mind inevitably fell into the asphyxiating pit of all things related to Caltow. Worries and memories gushed from the masked recesses where he'd kept them bottled up, zipping faster than he could make sense of. He didn't try to stop them. On every surface, a thousand Caltows relived both the joyous, vernal holidays of their youth and the dreadful nights after their parents' deaths.

He pulled the thick bed sheets over his head, though it technically wasn't late. Not a sniffle left him, not even a heavy breath, but tears slithered through his fur unrestricted.

Something crashed against the roof, and a light penetrated his squeezed shut eyelids. *Nieyowpon's powerful rain and transport headlights?* Any excuse would do as long as he didn't have to get up. All of his drowsiness was sucked away, however, when a wheezing laugh echoed around him.

He sat up on impulse. The room's lamp had been lit, and a ghost stood at the foot of his bed. His fright was short lived. It was only Sufralycoo. Irritated to the point of anger, he demanded, "What are you doing here? How did you get in?"

"Come look!" Sufralycoo pointed enthusiastically to a hand-held digital screen. "See what be happening!"

Kiiyeepo grudgingly slid out from his covers but approached fast when he caught the king's voice, faint as it was. "...where the law mentions any jurisdiction of yours!"

Sufralycoo held out the device for them both to see. It showed a side view of the throne, though it was small in the wide picture. Immodin and six of the chiefs faced an unfamiliar, male Kumor.

The being had blue on its underside, rather than the purple tones of the Kumors from Nieyowpon; a lighter red on his sides; and a much lighter yellow, almost white, over his spine. Two soldiers stood on either side of him, but the positions of their weapons proclaimed that they weren't here as bodyguards. This was ambassador Falair.

"You put a camera in the great hall?" Kiiyeepo questioned in disbelief.

Sufralycoo put a finger to his lips and nodded.

The camera must have been hidden among the pictures and decorations on the walls of the huge room. The distance would explain the view and the weak audio as Immodin spoke again to the Kumor. "Your silence is an admission. You have no power to tell me what you will or will not do. How can you continue a centuries old lie while outsiders bring us the truth and a new technology gives us knowledge of how the solar system actually is?"

Falair didn't answer. Instead, he retorted, "Trust the governments that founded Nieyowpon and fortified it with space stations. You are a fool to heed testimonies from self-interested spies! You don't know where their loyalties—"

One of the soldiers slapped the Xonerite at Immodin's signal. Sufralycoo laughed, choppy and chaotic, yet snapped his mouth shut as the king bellowed, "How dare you refer to me with such wayward disrespect! You are the fool, calling it unwise to listen to those who have no incentive to lie—"

"You cannot treat me this way! I am a representative of your motherlands. Nieyowpon is a colony, subject to the rule of the Pact."

"Never in my reign has the Pact ruled Nieyowpon. Never have they tried to deal with our problems. They don't care as long as we don't overstep their guidelines, which were established centuries ago. All they care is that they can steal our goods and raw materials. The so called traders pay us in a bygone currency. We now know that it's nearly worthless anywhere but here."

Falair gulped. He had no counter.

"You have lied enough for the Pact. It's time you lied to them. You shall carry on with the course of action already planned but will lobby for Nieyowpon's best as my chief instructs. Ordmin has agreed to go and oversee the voyage." When Immodin gestured to the chief, Kiiyeepo was more than a little disappointed. It was the bearded Wulvry who'd opposed Valex and him from the very beginning.

The king continued, "It will be my soldiers and crew aboard your ship. Only your pilots will remain. Do you understand?"

"My guards are trained with higher caliber blasters and armor—"

"I think not," Immodin answered his own question. "Do you think me so stupid that I would let you mutiny? It will be *my* soldier's in *your* gear. The squad that will be on your ship, monitoring your every move, is training with the advanced weapons presently."

Falair's jaw was clenched tight. He was seething inside. It took him a long, long while to finally reply, "I have one condition: I do all the talking at the negotiation and with Vorrnum. This is necessary because I am required to record the proceedings for the Pact. Therefore, I have to know exactly what your expectations are before we leave."

The king called together the chiefs, but the two eavesdroppers couldn't hear what they were saying. It gave Kiiyeepo a chance to ask, "Why are you showing me this?"

"Us partners..." Sufralycoo reminded, "...and me need place to hide."

"From what?"

"Me not supposed be around."

"How'd you get in my room?" Kiiyeepo had learned to ask Sufralycoo one question at a time if he ever wanted answers.

"Custodian unlock door. Him bring dinner."

Kiiyeepo knew the Wulvry wouldn't have brought dinner unless he'd ordered it, but, finding the table set for two, it was apparent that someone had ordered for him. Nonetheless, the meal was a welcomed sight.

Sufralycoo grinned impishly, and then froze as the voice of a chief came through the device. Zezo addressed the guards, "Take the ambassador to the conference room."

The soldiers escorted the Kumor out of sight. The chiefs followed at a leisurely pace, talking among themselves, but Immodin headed in the reverse direction. Soon there was nothing to see or hear in the great hall.

"Us eat now," Sufralycoo said. He powered down the device and then took a seat.

Kiiyeepo joined him. They ate quickly and quietly as the gale picked up outside. Lightning made the whole sky flash red, but no bolts came down. He shuddered at the thunderclap, longer and louder than any he'd heard. Only after his plate was spotless, did he attempt another question. "So, why did you plant the camera? They didn't say anything about us."

"Could have if went differently. Still good info. You no think?"

"Oh, definitely. I can't believe how the traders defrauded Nieyowpon."

"It tribute. Never was trade." Sufralycoo had impeccable table manners, holding his utensils just so. "That why me request be paid in pazin, hazin, and gems."

"Why are you helping me?"

"If you go, me go."

"What do you mean?"

"If them think ambassador so delinquent to need *you*, then also need me to control transmitter contact," Sufralycoo said condescendingly, as though Kiiyeepo should have know. It did make sense with enough thought. He gloated over his achievement, "That why me laugh. Them play into me hand! Us going for sure."

He's more determined to get off Nieyowpon than I am! Kiiyeepo thought. He couldn't reply through the next peal of thunder.

Unable to finish the generous helping of food, Sufralycoo slid off his chair and scurried for the door.

"Bye," he uttered as it latched behind him.

"Bye..." Kiiyeepo called weakly and then said to himself, "Odd little fellow."

The custodial staff came in promptly. As they cleared the table, they remarked that a restless sleep was in store for them this second dark. It would take several time fragments for the storm to run its course, cascades splashing down on the very roof over their heads.

Kiiyeepo crawled back into his bed, nonetheless. He buried his head under a heap of pillows but knew he wouldn't be getting much sleep with his sensitive ears. It was like rain treatment all over again, complete with the tortured screams.

Screams. He threw off the pillows to listen, but ice-cold water splashed on his face. A hole, small but perfectly round, was burnt through the steep A-frame of the roof, and the water stampeding down the slope poured in. *A laser hole... In my room!*

He flung himself from the bed flat on the floor and then crawled up below the window. Taking a deep breath, he peered over the sill. Two Nilose were collapsed on the wet stone ground, but only one struggled for a transmitter or struggled at all. Lightning illuminated the scene. A large form glistened bright as a white flame before disappearing between two buildings. *The other drone.*

"Valexs, you sure knew when to get out of town," Kiiyeepo thought aloud and then yanked open the window. With a sheet bundled under his arm, he climbed out into the dense mist that filled the city. He sprinted to the transmitter, which had fallen just outside the reach of the conscious Nilose, and scooped it up. Finding the right buttons, he shouted as more thunder rumbled like an avalanche, "Two soldiers down! Send a medic squad immediately!"

"Where?" The voice returning was equally strained and harshly stern.

"Outside the right flank of the Royal Gathering. Hurry!" Kiiyeepo released the device and crouched beside the soldier. He tried to sound caring despite the conditions. "Where were you hit?"

The Nilose opened his mouth to speak but grimaced. He instead pointed to his thigh. It wasn't a direct hit, but the laser had cut bone-deep. Only black, charred flesh was visible. Kiiyeepo dunked the blanket into a puddle, letting it soak up the frigid water. He then pressed it onto the hot wound and began to wrap it. The soldier cried through clenched teeth and jerked as the pain shot up his spine. He forced himself to sit up, helped half of the way by the Midek.

"I'll do it," he said with heavy breaths. "Please... check my mate."

Kiiyeepo nodded, gave him the rest of the sheet, and then hurried through the mist. Laser battles made for atrocious sights. He knew that better than most but wasn't prepared to see an inert being with its right arm lying beside it, severed. He gagged yet managed to hold onto most of his dinner. Averting his gaze from the arm, he knelt down and put his ear on the being's breastplate.

Bump-bump. The sound of pure relief, a heartbeat. He looked at the being's face, pale and feminine. Her wide eyes were locked in a frozen stare. Nieyowpon didn't use women soldiers, so he scanned the surrounding area for clues. Sure enough, no gun lay nearby, only a shock dagger and a metal first-aid box flipped on its side. This couple had been a medic team themselves. *On their way to someone else.*

Kiiyeepo pulled the strap of the box over his shoulder and returned with the good news, "She'll make it."

He didn't give details, but the medic had a knowing look on his face. Opening the first-aid box, Kiiyeepo asked, "Is there anything in here that can help—"

The Nilose snapped it closed. "I'll be okay. There's a Gredwol critical. Get to him. Follow that street to the first corner and turn left." His hand motions said more than his words, as he explained, "Give him the large yellow injection and then half of the reddish vial right in the heart."

Fear gripped Kiiyeepo. *Jireck got a large yellow injection!* The medic handed back the transmitter and shoved him forward at the same time. Kiiyeepo didn't resist; he couldn't let someone else die. Running as fast as he could without slipping, his world was soon condensed to a narrow street parallel to where the drone had gone.

A gust blew through the street, pelting him with a fusillade of droplets. He shielded his eyes and shivered but didn't slow down. The next cloudburst came down right on top of him. He had to move sideways along the walls of the buildings for a bit of shelter. Waves of water poured off the roofs, over the gutters, and splashed up from the street. He was drenched. His teeth chattered, yet he kept running. He owed it to Jireck to save that soldier.

If I'd only called out sooner... He shoved that thought deeper as he turned the corner. His gaze locked on a shivering Gredwol. He sprinted to him, sloshing through the puddles. The soldier was propped up against the side of the alley. No wounds were visible from this angle, but his heartbeat was barely audible.

All emotion drained from Kiiyeepo's mind as he searched the first-aid box. He found the monstrous injector among other tools in the main cavity. Eight vials of colored fluid were strapped to the lid, their needles already attached. The long yellow tube slipped into the back of the syringe with a faithful click. He located a small break in the upper arm of the soldier's armor, where Jireck had received his shot, and then had to force the needle through thick Gredwol flesh.

He sent the chemical surging up the vein as fast as he dared, but the being didn't flinch. The push of a button ejected the empty tube, and he immediately loaded the reddest vial in the box. Peeling back the breastplate, he rammed the needle into the center of the soldier's chest. He squeezed, a little more than half getting in before he pulled out the injector. This situation seemed like it could use the extra bit. Still, his efforts yielded no response.

Too late... again? There was one way to be sure. Kiiyeepo hesitated. Was he standing over another corpse? He pushed aside his fear and laid an ear over the being's heart. *Bump-bump.* The sound was strong, alive.

Resuming a crouch position, he found the soldier's eyes opened and blinking. They stared at him with gratitude, unspoken yet unspeakable, and he smiled back. The soldier seemed to be telling him to go on with subtle motions of his hand, but Kiiyeepo couldn't leave him like this. He raised the transmitter to his lips. "Soldier down, badly injured..." he glanced about for a landmark, "...behind a blacksmith's shop."

"We're on our way."

He stayed until soldiers and medics rounded the bend. Only the electric lamps continued to light the dark, deserted streets. At the intersections, he could see soldiers headed every which way. Apparently, the drone was still at large in the city, but they didn't seem to have a clue where.

He quickened his pace. There were no sounds of combat or flashes of lasers anywhere, and he realized that there hadn't been since he'd come out. Nonetheless, it was spine-chilling to walk alone while a foe roamed unchecked. Each shadow began to resemble the drone. Any noise he heard sounded like its engine. He looked back every couple of paces as he ran for his room.

He burst from the street into the now empty clearing where the two Nilose had lain and shot one last fleeting glance rearward. All his fears were embodied by the monster at his heels. It had been a moment's glance as the corner separated them, but a flash of lightning had burned every detail into his mind: the mangled cannon, the metal body battered black and riddled with holes, and the spike-shaped gadget on its right arm that gleamed in spite of it all.

Never in his life had he run so fast, pushing off the ground with his long arms to keep himself upright. He charged into the Royal Gathering and slammed the thick door. Not a moment later, he had both locks fastened.

No noises came from outside. He sighed with relief and put his hands on his knees, steadying himself. The custodian hopped hastily into the foyer, roused by the commotion. When he saw Kiiyeepo standing there, sopping and muddy, on the solid wood floor, the look on his face changed instantly from surprise to loathing. He shook his head scoldingly.

"Drone... out there... I'm okay... Sorry about the water," Kiiyeepo explained, panting heavily.

"Don't give it another thought. It is our pleasure to assist." Those were the custodian's words, but his tone said something entirely different.

"Thanks," Kiiyeepo said warily and then walked to his room a touch quicker than usual. He wrapped a towel around himself before plopping down on the edge of his bed. It felt so wrong to sort the events of this night, because, for many brave souls, the battle wasn't over. He'd done what he could. It was up to the soldiers now.

Its canon is destroyed. The drone won't survive but a few more shots. It's just a matter of time. He tried to debrief and his small world complied... for a time.

The wall creaked sharply. He gulped. *A hum!* The subtle noise grew loader. *CRUNCH!* He shielded his face with his hands as the wall ruptured inward. Boards crashed to the floor between the two beds and then snapped beneath the treads of the drone.

It reached for Kiiyeepo, catching his ankle as he tried to retreat. He screamed when the claw tightened and lifted him upside-down into the air. It lowered swiftly, pinning him to the debris covered floor. The Midek writhed and called out, unable to pull free. He became frantic when the drone moved in its spike apparatus. Once the spike's thin tip pierced his skin, though, he went stiff, every muscle as tense as raw gortal. Struggling now would tear his flesh.

A ring at the base of the spike, bearing metal cylinders, spun to a different mode. The next moment icy syrup inundated his bloodstream. *Such irony. I was just administering shots to save lives, and now I...* Suddenly, his thoughts scattered, and a void of false euphoria took their place. His body relaxed against his will, but Kiiyeepo fought to keep his mind. *...I get one... an injunction?... Cake?*

CHAPTER 23

One Way Out

"Cake," the drone said again. The tight, resisting eyes of its hostage loosened this time.

"The cake is good, isn't it?" It was a test to ensure that the drug had taken hold. The chemical annulled the victim's rationale, rendering deliberate action impossible. His understanding of his surroundings would become extremely vague and suggestible. He could do only what he was told and would do anything commanded of him.

"Yummy," the Midek quietly replied.

This was the kind of answer hoped for. It proved that they'd administered a proper dosage. Too much and the victim could lose access to his memories. The drone then began its interrogation. "What is the epidemic?"

"I don't know." The Midek's voice remained slight. "I was hoping you could tell me."

Apparently, this being had a vivid imagination. Most victims answered in as few words as possible by this point. Too bad it was the *wrong* answer. The drone continued to pry, "Why are the invaders here?"

"To takeover and ruin us all."

This Midek had been involved in too much to know so little. Wasn't this the same being who'd been at the natives' meeting? Hadn't he been part of the team that destroyed the other Nieyowpon drone? Yet he was saying what he thought to be true. Surely, it would come down to asking the right question. "What are you doing to stop them?"

"Nothing. I am going to a negotiation and then to Krashad to tell Vorrnum not to join you."

Puzzling response. It seemed like a contradiction, but that was impossible under the drug's influence. Prodek rolled his chair away from the large screen, seeking out Hajrius from the many intelligence officers who surrounded him. For the moment, this was the most active division of the control room.

"Hmm... Perhaps he isn't doing either of the tasks he mentioned of his own will. Whatever the case, stopping us isn't his motive. That would cause the disconnect in his answer," Hajrius explained. "Get his name."

Prodek nodded and rotated to face the screen. He spoke into an encoded vocal transmitter, his words being reconstructed and played by the battered drone. "Who are you?"

"Kiiyeepo."

"Tell me about yourself."

"I'm sixteen orbits old, a Midek, and a rancher from Allanoi. I want to go home. I do better one-on-one than in a crowd. I worry too much... I am alone."

"Anything else?"

"No."

Another startling answer. People usually didn't run out of things to say about themselves. At one time, he must have tried to isolate his identity from his superfluous desires and past, now drawing on that memory.

Hajrius stepped closer. "Ask him who we are."

Prodek adjusted the words to yield a more informative response. "What are the invaders?"

"Monsters from the lost worlds, maybe."

Hajrius leaned toward the vocal transmitter and probed for himself, "Why do you say that?"

"You took my brother!" Kiiyeepo's tone spiked for just an instant, a sign of extreme emotion.

"Who is he?"

"Caltow... Caltow."

How strong was this Midek's sentiment that it could surface even through the overwhelming force of the drug coursing through his brain? It was heartbreaking to hear, but war was a tragic thing. *Some have to suffer so that many might be saved*, Hajrius reminded himself. He pointed at a lower ranked officer. "You heard the name. Find him and see what you can learn from him."

"Yes sir."

When Hajrius turned back, Prodek was on to another subject. "Do you think Vorrnum will join the invaders?"

"Yes."

"Why—" the question was drowned by a shout.

"Fire!"

The screen flashed a blinding red, the red of weak lasers, but Hajrius was already facing the agent at the drone's controls. He yelled, "Hostage-shield, now!"

The world tipped sideways. Pain shot from Kiiyeepo's ankle, leg, and back as he was yanked upside-down in front of the drone, but none of it registered in his brain. His thoughts consisted of a muddled happiness, though his soul didn't feel a hint joyful. He couldn't feel his soul at all, and that would have scared him if he'd had the ability to be scared.

"Don't move," the drone commanded, speeding in reverse.

Kiiyeepo wilted in response, arms dangling and hands dragging as he watched a squad of soldiers emerge from the gaping hole in his room. They were following him, fear and uncertainty written on their faces. The rest of the Royal Gathering soon shrank into view. More soldiers hurried around the sides but slowed when the drone aimed its spike at Kiiyeepo and demanded, "Get back, or he dies!"

It hissed at the Midek next, who was obediently trying to pull away. "Not you! Stop moving."

Kiiyeepo again went limp. After crossing the main road that encircled the city, they bounced over stepping stones and then through an archway carved into the plateau. The drone tilted precariously and drastically decelerated as it started up the spiral stairwell. They'd bobbled high enough that the entry was half obscured, when Zezo's voice echoed in. "Free yourself!"

Kiiyeepo's muscles reacted to the command as if by reflex. He reached up with both hands, each seizing one finger of the drone's claw, and then wrenched them apart. His feet were down on a step before the beast could spew more orders from wherever they were being sent. "Stop. Freeze!"

Zezo appeared in the archway. Apparently, he'd caught on to the fact that the Midek would obey anything as long as the drug was in his system. "Pull it down!"

Kiiyeepo tightened his grip on the fingers, but the drone prevented him from doing more, crying, "No!"

Zezo's voice returned in the same moment. "Do it!"

Leaning back, Kiiyeepo yanked down on the metal arm. The heavy drone tipped slowly forward above him, and then another order was screamed from below, "Get out of the way!"

He dove. The hulking mass of metal slammed against the stone steps, so close that his own bones shook at the impact. The drone slid and tumbled. The stairs that had been its escape route now transformed into a crash course of destruction. Shrill cracks and crunches reverberated off the solid walls, a noise worse than being inside of a thundercloud.

Zezo took a few point blank shots at the mangled drone, just to be safe, and then ran up the stairs to the unmoving Midek. "Are you okay?"

The answer was driven by the drug's influence. "No."

"The drone is gone. No one died thanks to you. You're a hero," Zezo declared. He sighed when there wasn't the faintest reply. "And we're going to get you back. Come on."

A command, it jerked Kiiyeepo to his feet. Zezo carefully guided him around the sharp shards. Most of the soldiers had gathered at the archway, celebrating at the sight of their felled foe or brainstorming about what to do with it. Nonetheless, they immediately cleared out of the way for Zezo and Kiiyeepo.

"Hey, Midek, roll over!" someone called with a sardonic laugh.

Kiiyeepo moved to obey, but Zezo stopped him. The chief of defense would not tolerate this. He scanned the faces around them. It could have been anyone until the crowd parted, exposing the culprit. Zezo marched up to the Nilose. He got in his face and hissed too low for Kiiyeepo to hear, "What was that?"

"I, um, I don't know."

"One lap, private, around the *plateau*! That should give you time to figure out what it was."

"Uh..." the private stammered at the order, wide eyed, but then hurried to the road.

Another soldier laughed as the first jogged past him, and Zezo quietly directed, "You can join him."

There were no jokes after that. When they reached the Royal Gathering, Zezo instructed the custodian to put Kiiyeepo in their best room. He also stationed a team of medics and guards close by. Not even the ambassador's medics had heard of a substance like this, able to take complete control of a being, so any treatment would be guesswork.

Perhaps sleep was what the Midek needed. Zezo pulled a blanket over Kiiyeepo, like a father would for his child, and then commanded, "Sleep."

Kiiyeepo stared blankly at the bandages that wrapped his hands. His sleep had lasted longer than the drug. It was past midday, he supposed. Traces of blue bled into the darkness outside, the first sign of dawn.

He'd fared well, considering what could have, statistically should have, happened. No permanent harm had been done. His ankle, however, was severely swollen and bruised under its wrapping of icepacks. What was worse, he had the headache to end all headaches. It felt like his brain was being squeezed by the paws of a regalltee, and it flared up at any sound.

He'd sent away the medics, which in and of itself had been a source of great cheer for everyone. It demonstrated that the drug had lost its hold. Alone, his physical ailments paled in comparison to the emotional toll of the night. He remembered every detail: having no say over his own body, no volition to think or act except when an order was given, and no way to hide. Even his secrets and memories had lain bare before the drone.

He was humiliated. The soldiers had seen him at his very lowest. Some, he now knew, regarded him as little more than an animal.

An experience like this stabbed at the core of a person. He'd taken a blow to the soul. What hurt most was what he didn't say about himself. When asked who he was, he'd offered only a handful of phrases. What about his friends, the challenges he'd faced, and his beliefs about life and its Creator? Were none of these things part of who he was? Those thoughts piled into the same dark crevice as Caltow, and Jireck, and the truth of his existence when the bedroom door opened.

He slid off the end of the bed onto his good foot as the prime chief, Malkov, entered. He was accompanied by Zezo and Ordmin. They set a handful of writing sheets on the low table in the sitting area and then took seats, except for Zezo, who hastened to the limping Midek. "How do you feel?"

Kiiyeepo huffed, "Don't ask."

"That bad?" Zezo questioned anyway as he helped him to a chair.

"Has your unawareness completely passed?" Malkov probed louder. Once in the cushions, Kiiyeepo nodded to both inquires, but the Zulan pressed, "We should not have you make the decision we are here to present unless you are fully conscious and deliberate of your faculties."

With his headache flaring, Kiiyeepo couldn't take this discourtesy for more than one reason. "I'm fine, as far you're concerned, which obviously isn't that far."

"Very good." Malkov cleared his throat to conceal a scowl. "Let us begin. Due to the appearance of an ambassador of the Chriyoss-Xonero Pact an opportunity for you to leave this planet has arisen..."

No apology for what happened? No gratitude for stopping the drone or saving at least one life? Valexs was showered in praise when he fought a drone. They even offered him a bonus as a reward! Kiiyeepo knew the prime chief didn't like him, probably on the sole basis that he was a Midek. It had become increasingly plain since the ball.

He tuned out the conversation. It was everything he'd learned beforehand about going to the negotiation. He had already made up his mind to accept, since this was his one way out of here. Nonetheless, he let the prime chief ramble on. There was a mischievous pleasure in making this prominent official repeat it all.

When the other chiefs began to explain what was in it for him, freedom and a chest full of pazin, he quickly agreed. His quarrel was with the prime chief alone. The writing sheets were a sort of contract for him to sign, but he merely scanned them until he got to the dotted line.

The invaders are hosting the negotiation. We'll be in their domain, in their clutches... They can't do anything to me there. I'll be part of a diplomatic delegation! They will have to pretend to be civilized. He suppressed the tide of apprehension. He couldn't back out now, so close to getting off this planet.

It's just a meeting. We go, we talk, we leave, and, possibly, we find out how to beat these monsters in the process. With that, he plotted his name on the line.

"Fine," Ordmin said. "Now get yourself ready. We were supposed to leave at midday!"

As the chiefs rose, the Wulvry mentioned, "A soldier is waiting in the hall to escort you. Don't be late."

You just told me that we're already late. Kiiyeepo thought, but he restrained himself from mocking.

Zezo put in one last statement. "We'll send someone in on our way out."

True to promise, a medic arrived only a few moments later. First, she removed the dressings from his hands and the icepacks from his finally numbed ankle. After cleaning the wounds, she treated them with a variety of herbs and medications. She then wrapped them in fresh bandages.

As she took a blood sample, she informed him that a larger one had been taken while he was asleep in an attempt to identify the drug. No wonder he'd dreamt about a flying drone that was sucking his blood. Falair was going to send the sample to advanced labs on Chriyoss.

The medic left a staff to help him get around but at the same time encouraged, "You shouldn't need it by tomorrow."

If only a set of crutches would have been the right size. That was hoping for too much on this planet. The staff worked well enough, though, as Kiiyeepo grabbed his black bag and made his way down the hall. It was a painstaking journey to the launch area in the worst sense of the word.

Not surprisingly, trying to hustle up the steps in the defense headquarters took the greatest effort. The soldier did his very best to help, and, eventually, another being on the busy stairwell stopped to lend a hand. By the time they broke into open air, the officials were checking their time keepers and impatiently tapping their feet.

"What's the rush? The negotiation is just outside the atmosphere," Kiiyeepo asked Zezo.

"The invaders invited the representatives to come as early as they wished, probably for P.R." the Gredwol answered. "Falair wanted to spend some time snooping around in an invader controlled space station. He just talked to the Pact and had to concoct an explanation for the delay. Thankfully, they believed it."

Kiiyeepo pushed off a little harder with his staff. He would have liked to snoop around himself. That space station could be a jackpot of information about the enemy. Because of him, they'd most likely lost their chance at some of it. It wasn't his fault, he knew that, but he was the cause, nonetheless.

The gate at the back of the walled area was open. He could see the tail fin of the ambassador's ship sticking up above the wall. It was too big for the launch tower, so they'd wheeled it out to the runway.

Once past the gate, Kiiyeepo got a full view of the ship. With two interior levels, a hyper cell, and a design meant to impress, it had to be the same class as Haazon's, though noticeably longer. It resembled a futuristic version of Valexs's vessel, somewhat cylindrical. Of course, that's exactly what it was, a space jet that exemplified Xonerite design.

The soldier pulled Kiiyeepo to the top of the boarding ramp. Similar to Haazon's space jet, it led to a relatively small room, this one packed with multiple rows of g-force seats. Because of the large screen on its front wall, though, it could double as a briefing or theater room.

A worker directed Kiiyeepo to the second row. The cook and the maid were seated beside him. Both were struggling to fasten their straps with shaking hands. Kiiyeepo pretended not to notice. He knew he'd been just as scared on his first flight.

Only Falair, the soldiers guarding him, and Ordmin had yet to board. They received a few final instructions from Zezo and Malkov before ascending. While the workers seated everyone and secured the straps for them, one of Falair's pilots explained to all the first timers what to expect and how not to faint during takeoff.

The boarding ramp was also the hatch, folding up to seal the entry. A tremor rippled through the ship.

The mighty engines had started. Immediately, they began to roll forward.

The pilot's eager voice came through the intercom, "Three, two, one..." The thrusters roared. Several passengers yelped as they were slammed back by the acceleration.

Dizziness and nausea were instantly added to Kiiyeepo's list of aliments. His stomach clenched when the ship rocketed off the side of the plateau and then curved vertical. *Will I ever get used to space travel?*

The heat of the atmosphere penetrated even these walls. Suddenly, he could hear the chorus of heavy breaths around him. The engines had cut out, though the world was still red and orange beyond the porthole. He gulped down anxiety; their speed was dropping fast.

They passed into the speckled blackness of the cosmos relatively slow. Minor side thrusters ignited to rotate the ship to the same angle as the space station. Kiiyeepo listened to the comforting rumble. *Cutting the engines early was just a freakishly effective means of deceleration,* he figured, *since we'll be landing so soon.*

While the ship was still unaligned, he could see part of the space station. Of course, it was the same one that he and Valexs had been headed to when they were shot down. It soon shifted out of sight, and his view through the window passed over a space naval standoff. The force nearest the station was undoubtedly a portion of the invader's fleet. Most of their vessels looked tiny, surrounding a cruiser big enough to swallow the whole space station. An Orranian fleet, or so he deduced, floated in opposition.

His observation didn't last long as they drifted between the twin parking towers of the station and then turned into one. The structure had no wall on this internal side, exposing many levels, greatly varying in size. Each was marked for a different class of spacecraft. On their level, one of the first docks had been set aside for them.

They hovered above the pad, and then thrusters on the top of the ship gently pressed them down. Landing legs absorbed the minute impact and magnetized to the floor. Automatically, long lights on the roof illuminated red and walls dropped down on all sides. The ship was boxed in without even a seam between the walls.

Next, vents jetted gas into the new room, the dock, letting the muffled wine of a siren reach the ship. They'd waited only four micro fragments before everything stopped in unison and the lights transitioned to pale white. At last, the boarding ramp fell open.

CHAPTER 24

Den of the Alien

Furygon lay face down, unconscious, on the floor of his office. Two metal panels were stacked nearby. The black sphere that encased his head had been opened up. Exposed was a mess of wires and tubes.

There were two separate motherboards, three audio receivers, and various sensors. The main hardware was installed along the right side of his head and into the massive gouge in his skull. It replicated the functions of the lost brain tissue. On the left side, was a pump connected to two small tanks: one of blood to maintain natural circulation and one of an opaque, light green fluid. Some of these parts worked together, day in and day out, to keep him alive despite his injury, only some.

"Grip claw, now!" Prodek held his hand out, and Myeerp supplied the tool. He then plunged the grip claw into the wires.

He was kneeling beside Furygon, bent over the breach in the black sphere. Every other moment, he glanced down at diagrams spread out on the floor. They showed the inner working of two vaguely similar devices. He compared them to what he saw in the helmet, double checking everything he did.

One mistake could foil their plan or even kill Furygon. On top of that, he was up against the clock. If exposed to untreated air too long, the flesh of Furygon's head would suffer permanent damage.

The music blaring in his headset was all that kept Prodek from locking up under the pressure. He set the motors in his suit to give resistance, enough to steady his shaking hands, and then surgically removed one of the audio receivers: one that didn't aid in hearing.

Tossing it in Myeerp's general direction, he turned his attention to a portable data interface. It was hooked up to one of the motherboards to reprogram the apparatus. For the most part, it did the job autonomously. When it couldn't determine whether to keep, discard, or change a line of code, it would tag it for the operator to edit.

He extended a hand without looking up. "Laser needle!"

Myeerp found and handed over the tool in an instant. He didn't know how to write code or how to deconstruct electronics, but he did his best to follow his friend's instructions. For fear of distracting Prodek, he didn't make a peep. Never had he seen him so stressed or so stern.

The laser needle easily melted away tiny pieces on the smaller motherboard. As he leaned in close to make the precise incisions, Prodek ordered, "Tag anything in the code that says 'audio', 'sound', or 'stimulus thirty one'. There shouldn't be any left but double check."

Using the grip claw again, he removed several wires and two sensors. He could have removed so much more. No one should have had this kind of power at his fingertips. His body went static, stilled by the thoughts warring in his mind. Here and now, he could put an end to the madness. He wanted to, but he told himself that there was peace in control.

It's there in case of an emergency. We don't know what Furygon might do without it.

The last thing he did was install a new audio receiver in the place of the one that he'd taken out. *New but just as evil. We won't use it... I won't use it.* He had to amend his mental vow because he knew that Myeerp wouldn't leave such power untapped.

He switched off the music for the final inspection. Before unplugging the data interface, he ran several tests as quickly as he could. Everything seemed to be working with the new programming, but only time would truly tell.

"Call the medics," he said and reached for the panels to close up the helmet.

Myeerp grabbed them first. "I'll take it from here. You have to go now."

After a moment, Prodek nodded, got to his feet, and made his way to the door. Each step was faster than the previous one. He had to get away, had to create his alibi. No one could know that he was here at this time.

A wide, stark corridor led to the service kiosk. Normally, this was where travelers would purchase fuel or pay for maintenance on their ship, but now all the screens were black. From there, the Nieyowpon delegation took a heavy-duty level interchanger down from the parking tower and into the central disc of the space station.

They had to walk briskly to keep up with their guide, an invader almost nine units tall measuring to the tips of his straight, narrow ears. That wasn't an issue for the Falair or the bodyguards, all strong Kumors, or even for the Wulvry hopping beside them, Ordmin, but Kiiyeepo fell behind a few strides. He tried to ignore his aching ankle and pull a little faster with his staff. *Good thing we left Sufrallycoo at the ship. That sickly Zulan could never have kept up.*

He remained within earshot of the guide, who was explaining how they took over with a "lightning charge" to "limit bloodshed". Altogether, there had been only one death and seven injuries for both stations. Most of those had been due to people trying to fight back, or so he claimed. Just hearing the guide talk made Kiiyeepo's skin crawl. *Smooth-tongued and perfectly polite, it's like an evil version of Agent Taatus!*

He interested himself in the sights around him, more to watch his own back than to see anything in particular. He couldn't help but feel nervous; it was like walking through a ghost town. They passed vacant check-in desks and disabled security posts and then plunged into an echoing expanse.

The grand room marked the center of the space station. This was the principal locale for travelers, commonly known as the hub, and most stations had one. The dome-shaped ceiling was riddled with windows overlooking the hub from suites and studios. Small stores were built into the walls, ready to offer travelers food, lodging, or knickknacks that they didn't know they wanted. The usual crowd, however, had been replaced by a three member team of invaders who were rolling away the vending stands that once filled this marketplace.

Ordmin lagged back, next to Kiiyeepo. He obviously had something to say, but eventually the Midek had to take the initiative. "Need something?"

Ordmin huffed in disdain. A few steps further he began, nonetheless. Speaking quickly, quietly, and without making eye contact, his gruff voice was even harder to understand. "Assuming that we can make an agreement with these metal beings, Falair says that it would be more in our interest to limit trade than to fully restore commerce around Nieyowpon. Why might he say that?"

"I'm not sure. What were his reasons?"

"The Pact knows ships left Nieyowpon without their authorization. Our ships, I'm sure. Others may have picked up on them as well. Our secret may be out. We're not prepared. Limiting traffic may be a necessary safeguard."

"The planetary governments already know, they must, and it wasn't going to be a secret much longer anyway. Hoping for the best from the rest of the solar system is safer than trusting Chriyoss and Xonero," Kiiyeepo said, evaluating the whole situation. "Forcing their ambassador to do what we want here and at the meeting with Vorrnum is going to really tick off the Pact! We have to consider them opposition now."

"He claimed the other planets were desperate for resources due to the invasion and would ravage Nieyowpon. What of that?"

They wouldn't do that... Well, maybe a little, but they need the materials to fight the invaders, Kiiyeepo thought, glancing at their guide. Although he didn't fully believe his own words, he answered,

"The Pact and the invaders control the space stations. They're the only ones who can do major damage to Nieyowpon. Having the traffic there is our only way to keep them in check, the Pact at least."

"Yes, yes, I know," the Wulvry spat and then bounded ahead to catch Falair and the guide.

That was hardly true, and Kiiyeepo knew it. *He just doesn't want me to know how much power I have over him. He's going to make the ambassador push for exactly what I just told him.*

They circled a hundred and twelve degrees around the perimeter of the hub to another wide corridor, stylish compared to those of the docking bay. A second level interchanger then carried them up into a sector that had the air of an office building.

In spite of that, they stopped in a depressingly bare room. It was large by Kiiyeepo's standard or looked that way while devoid of furniture. Nothing but paint decorated the walls and ceiling, and the floor was tiled in a boring, checkered pattern.

Their guide turned on his heel and addressed Falair, "Are the three of you all representatives of the Chriyoss-Xonero Pact?"

Ordmin didn't give the ambassador a chance to answer, waving a hand toward Kiiyeepo. "No. This

Midek is a guest in transit." He glared at Kiiyeepo, commanding him not to argue more clearly than his words ever could.

"I see," the guide replied. Two servers emerged but only brought chairs in for the 'representatives'.

As Falair lounged on his seat, specifically designed for Kumors, he asked, "Have the other diplomats arrived?"

"Yes, every one of them. They were touring the more active regions of the station." The guide checked his time keeper, built into the back of his hand. "I'm sure they're hurrying back now. We are set to begin shortly."

He gestured one of the servers over and instructed, "Escort this guest to the sitting area. You may attend to him."

"Come with me, please," the server invited. Kiiyeepo bit his lip to keep his frustration from bursting out and followed. Behind him, the second server offered the Wulvry and Kumor a drink or entertainment. Kiiyeepo heard them graciously accept both before he was out the door.

The intelligence officers at work in the control room had to jump to their feet to show respect when Hajrius stormed in. He carried a small folder and a large attitude of annoyance. After signing for everyone to return to their tasks, he demanded, "How long until the negotiation?"

The answer was prompt. "Five micro fragments, sir, and counting."

"All the assassins and reaper spies are in position then?"

"AP10, Tesha, is making her way to the last post presently," Prodek explained. Both he and the Chief of Intelligence had made the agent's acquaintance previously.

"Good. Get Rekiph on the screen and link the audio. I need a word with him."

"Right away, sir."

The commodore appeared life-size on the huge display. An assistant moved about him, equipping his formal attire. Magnetized to his chest, a large, pazin disc bore the symbol of his rank. The next piece was a red pauldron, boxy but complementary to the panels of the exoskeleton.

Rekiph noticed Hajrius on the small screen in the room and faced him. "I assume we're all set."

"Yes, but there's been a change of plans," Hajrius declared. "The council session was dismissed. Furygon has reportedly taken ill."

"What!" Rekiph's tone was half shock and half skepticism. No Deurtex ever got sick outside of the most extreme circumstances; their suits were too well sealed. "What do you mean, taken ill?"

"It seems to be related to his combat injury, perhaps a malfunction in his helmet. The medical staff says that he'll be fine, but they're keeping an eye on him." Hajrius spoke fast, stressed and tired. "Myeerp delivered his orders for the negotiation."

"New orders? Furygon has never gone against the emperor's decrees in his life, even before he gave up the authority to do so." While Rekiph spoke, his assistant unfurled a black cape, trimmed in red. The left corner clipped to the pauldron. The right draped over Rekiph's opposite shoulder and attached to the pazin disc by a ring of the same shining metal.

"Yes. Consider all previous orders null and void. This is directly from the S.O.O." Hajrius flipped open the folder and read off a sheet within, "Compromise. Keep all that is necessary to ensure that the Allanoi blockade is impenetrable. Allow the resistance to have their trade routes, except to

Allanoi, in exchange for the displacement of their fleet. Be as courteous as possible in your dealings for the sake of the acquisition of allies."

"The emperor said to 'show no weakness', to never back down. His orders were to act as though we have more than enough power to destroy the planets of this solar system and some of the leaders would join us in order to protect their interests. Once they did, we would have every bit of the power we claimed."

"But if we failed to scare them into submission and their space forces came against us, our fleet would be spread thin."

There was a pause as Rekiph placed his scarlet crest on the top of his head. The ridge of fibers stood a unit in height but narrowed as it came down in the back over the upper portion of his cape.

Securing it by its pazin mount, he replied, "That was my point in the beginning, but it was silenced."

"I know. Apparently the emperor changed his mind," Hajrius concluded. "You'll be the first to know if anything else is adjusted. Furygon will try to observe the proceedings from where he rests in his chamber."

"Very well." Rekiph repeated the orders to himself. They were simple, and he would obey. *Obey and show no weakness.*

He touched the lens over his right eye and then slid his finger at a diagonal, switching the glow of both lenses from blue to blazing crimson. A regalltee would have cowered at the sight.

The door slid away silently. He stepped out behind the consuls awaiting him, who stood facing the prominent set of doors on the far wall. They were oblivious to his entrance and to the fact that the seating had been removed.

They went staggering, expecting to fall over their chairs, when he welcomed, "Greetings, envoys of the solar system! I am Rekiph, Aerospace Commodore of the Pazarin Empire. You have chosen wisely to accept our invitation. This meeting is to establish an agreement for the space stations and our respective fleets around Nieyowpon. Let us not digress from that purpose and thereby waste one another's time."

"Oh, but we must digress a little if we are to get anywhere in this meeting." A large Velphan, one of the diplomats from Zanquin, stepped forward and stood tall. He spoke with drawn out vowels, seemingly emphasizing words at random. "We have to know two things: why you have come to our solar system and what your end goal is."

"To declare our mission would be to jeopardize it, which is why we didn't attempt communication up to now. Nonetheless, I will say what I can. We have not come to make war against you. War is your choice as it was Haazon's. If you strike us, we will strike back."

"How can we believe anything you say unless we know your motives?" The demand came from the Prax Ambassador. He growled, "Moreover, how can we trust any agreement we reach today?"

"Why do you trust any of your treaties? You know these nations have lied to you. You know they have spies in your government, ready to sabotage you at the slightest provocation," Rekiph reminded, looking from one emissary to the next. "I will tell you. You trust your treaties because they are mutually beneficial, neither party wants to break them. So shall this agreement be."

The Prax thumped his heavy tail on the ground. "How can we know what is beneficial if we do not know your intent?"

"When do you ever know the full intent of a nation? You listen to their lies, trust the information gathered by your spies, and then hope you've bargained well. What more do you expect from us?"

There was silence. The representatives seemed to think that they were entitled to an answer. Rekiph made sure to relieve them of that misconception. "We called this assembly for your sake. We do not need a treaty. However, to show that we do not wish to destroy you, we are willing to bear some limitation as to our infringement upon your trade routes."

"How charitable," Falair commented sarcastically. "There would be no meeting if it was for our sakes alone. What's in it for you?"

"A more secure blockade. That, of course, is why we took these space stations."

The head emissary of the Orranian delegation floated higher on his hover disc and squealed, "Do you expect us to just sit back and let you invade Allanoi?"

"If invasion proves necessary, yes."

No one knew what to say to that. Each delegation glanced at the others, waiting to see who would speak up. None did. The planets and countries they represented could do very little for Allanoi unless they wanted to engage the invader's fleet, which they certainly did not.

Eventually, the Orranian replied. He didn't rise even a micro unit this time. "Well... What do you want with Allanoi?... Or are you not permitted to say?"

Rekiph let the silence answer.

The large Zanquinite stepped forward again. "How can we know that you're not going to do the same thing to us, picking us off one by one."

"I think you will find that scenario most implausible. In this solar system, Nieyowpon is the beating heart of interplanetary trade. If we were here as conquerors, we would have captured or destroyed every space station around Nieyowpon immediately."

The next pause was broken by the Prax ambassador. His gaze shifted from Rekiph to the single Dragon envoy as he probed, "What arrangement do you have with Vorrnum?"

"We will meet with him. Nothing is set," Rekiph allowed a hint of frustration into his tone. "Now can we get to what we came for."

CHAPTER 25
The Face of Evil

K iiyeepo dabbed his face with a wet drying cloth. He'd gone to relieve himself, to check his bandages, and, most of all, to have a moment unto himself. *Without me, will Ordmin be able to control the ambassador? He certainly has the personality to do it. Why'd he kick me out?... Because he doesn't trust me. He thinks I'll say too much.*

Kiiyeepo balled up the cloth and slammed it into the trash bin. His supposed colleagues had sidelined him, and now he had to wait in a room with two invaders. He took his sweet time on the way back to the lounge.

"Are you sure I can't get you anything? Perhaps entertainment or a drink," one of the servers reoffered cordially while steering him to a seat. The second invader stood patiently by the wall, just inside Kiiyeepo's field of vision.

What do these monsters consider entertainment? Perhaps mind controlling some random person like they did to me, Kiiyeepo wondered. When he asked what the options were, the server seemed a bit unsure too.

"I could play a film for you or some music."

I want to learn about them, don't I? Yeah, but that doesn't mean watching propaganda! Kiiyeepo answered callously, "No, I don't want anything."

"Very well. If you change your mind, just let us know." The attendant withdrew, disappearing through a doorway.

Kiiyeepo felt discarded and exposed. That he was, but no one cared. Ordmin seemed to have the same view of Mideks as the prime chief. Then again, he didn't seem to like anyone at all. Falair had a one track mind to get this whole thing over with and maybe salvage his career. Kiiyeepo understood that, though, his own sights set on Allanoi.

He didn't want their sympathy, just his fair share of respect. He'd earned it, hadn't he? *One more stop and then I'm home free. I shouldn't have to put up with this for any more than a week.*

"Please, don't look so upset. You're in no danger, and we're ready to get you anything you need." A chair had appeared beside his, and the second server leaned over the armrest toward him. "What's wrong?"

Startled, he recoiled and faced her. He'd guessed that both attendants were female by their voices and figures, differing slightly from that of the guide, the spy on Orra, and the mech pilot. Next to any of the other invaders he'd seen, however, this server would have looked like a child. At full height, she'd barely be eye to eye with him. Also, her face and ears were far less blade-like in shape.

"Sorry for startling you." She had a faint accent, as though she were humming as she spoke. Anything she said sounded somewhat dry because of it. "Would you like to talk? My name is Tesha, what's yours?"

"Kiiyeepo," he replied, just as plain. As much as he did want to talk to her, to learn about his foe, or—*maybe just maybe*—to find out if Caltow was alive, how could he? Not one aspect of this creature felt genuine. Between the crystal, blue eyes glowing artificially and the hard, black metal encasing her body, there was no telling what truly dwelt within. As he eased back to the middle of his seat, he could even hear the subtlest of motors at work in her false hide. *They must support the extra weight of the armor, or, beyond that, they might make the wearer stronger and faster.*

"Perhaps I could answer a question for you?" Tesha suggested, still hopeful.

"What are you?" Kiiyeepo finally let the question off his tongue and then added, "Do you always wear that armor?"

"I'm a Deurtex, and yes. If I didn't have this suit, the world would be a painful place."

"Why? What would happen to you?" Kiiyeepo interrogated strictly. The server looked discouraged. *What did she expect? Friendly small talk? Not after what they did to me.*

She sighed and answered, "Normal air would burn my skin. If I had to breathe it, I would eventually die. On the way here, I often daydreamed that one of your planets would have an atmosphere safe for us... Not to be."

"Oh..." Kiiyeepo almost felt sorry for her but fired off another question, "What happened to the people you abducted?"

"I don't know. I'm just a laborer. I'm sure they are taken care of. Our protocol is to avoid hurting innocents at all cost."

Oh, I bet! That's why your drones go rampaging through cities! Why don't you tell the medic whose arm was sliced off all about your protocol. Anger formed the reply in Kiiyeepo's mind. Before it could escape his lips, though, he tensed at Tesha's icy touch.

Her small hand stroked his shoulder so tenderly, like his adoptive mother use to whenever he was upset, and that made matters worse as she probed, "Tell me about you and your family."

"I don't have one anymore."

"Oh... I'm very sorry to hear that... Though I can't say I sympathize. I wish I didn't have my family, but at least they're worlds away now."

"You wouldn't say that if *you* were an orphan."

"Maybe, maybe not," Tesha shrugged. "My parents are rotten. They despise me. I wasn't anything like what they'd wanted, but I guess that's what they get for trying to have their own child. I'm a minikin Deurtex, and my features are round instead of the model sharp appearance! They didn't care to have me around, so I left the first chance I got. That was five orbits ago. I was twelve obits old." Her voice faded dreamily. "Eventually that led to coming here with the fleet."

Kiiyeepo looked at her. She had slouched against the armrest of her chair, as if pulled down by the weight of the memories. Nonetheless, she turned back to him wearing a smile. This was not the face of evil. Behind that mask of metal was a soul, and a life, and a yearning for acceptance. He couldn't think of her as a warmongering invader, but isn't that what she was? What was her side of the story? He decided to ask, "So, why *are* you here then?"

Tesha's eyes dulled. She seemed afraid to answer. In reality she had received a transmission in her headset. "Stall. We're reformatting the 'official' report."

Another voice spoke up in the background, but she could only make out the first two words, "But sir..."

Whatever the objection was, Hajrius promptly reminded, "Falair has that taken care of."

While she listened, Tesha obediently bought time. She made a show of glancing around the room and then whispered to the Midek, "I'm not sure if I'm allowed to tell you that... You have to promise me that you won't tell anyone."

"Why would you take that chance?" Kiiyeepo was already skeptical.

"I see the way you look at me. I see your fear and anger. You think we're evil, but we're not."

"Okay, I promise," Kiiyeepo consented without a second thought. He was not deceived. He knew the answer he was about to hear would be a half-truth at best.

Right on cue, Tesha received the command in her headset, "Repeat after me and don't be overheard."

She got up on her knees and leaned close to the Midek's ear, her metal cheek brushing his fur. As quietly as she could, she relayed the message as it came through, "One of the governments of this solar system, or a group of them most likely, unleashed a disease epidemic in my solar system. It has killed thousands, but we're here to stop it and get the cure."

The words of the invader spy suddenly rang clear in Kiiyeepo's mind, *You will never be able to continue your epidemic. Our vindication will be absolute.* Could it be true? Might the invaders only be seeking to save people in another solar system? He needed a moment to mull it over and so requested, "You know, I think I would like a glass of water after all."

"Oh!" Tesha sprang from her chair. "I'll only be a moment!"

It's a lie. It has to be. There's no way she would have divulged sensitive information like that if it were real, Kiiyeepo thought. For the claim to be true, it had to make sense of the invaders' every action since their arrival. *From the get-go, they've been gathering information, first through the abductions and then by sending out the drones. It's possible that they've been searching for something, perhaps the source of this 'epidemic'. That does explain why they forsook the element of surprise and didn't attack immediately.*

If it were true, though, why wouldn't they have told everyone about the epidemic? The nations that aren't involved could help pinpoint the offender... No, that wouldn't work. If all of them are in on it, they could lead the invaders—I mean Deurtex—on a wild iiow chase. If it were a coalition, one could take the fall while the others continued their scheme, or they could work together to incriminate an innocent faction as their scapegoat. If the invaders stay quiet, then the offenders have to stay quiet or else expose themselves. Only then would a confession be meaningful.

He winced at the thoughts buzzing through his brain. It was the best explanation he'd heard yet and the most disturbing one at that. *There must be an easier way to stop the epidemic than to invade the whole solar system... They must be desperate! If all of this is true, then I might have helped the bad guys!*

Images of the solar system's political leaders in the enormous chairs of the Orra meeting flashed by. Not one of these beings would he trust. *...except for Haazon.*

"Here you are." Tesha presented him a generous, precisely rectangular glass.

"Thank you." Kiiyeepo took a sip. Though it contained no ice, the water was so cold that he wondered how it hadn't frozen. Placing the cup on the low table, he declared, "I should apologize. I've been kind of rude to you." It was contrived but contrite.

"It's fine. I should have expected it."

He didn't want to sound like he was still interrogating her, but he had more questions now than when he got here. "If you knew who was responsible for the epidemic, would you stop trying to take over everything?"

"If we knew for certain, then of course. Our intelligence team is working tirelessly to determine the guilty parties. All we want is to make sure the disease can never be disseminated again." Her eyes flashed a touch brighter as she asked longingly, "Do you have any clues as to who they may be?"

Kiiyeepo shook his head. Whoever was behind it had to have found the lost worlds. He knew Chriyoss had attempted deep space exploration, but they were the ones arguing to make peace with the invaders. *Maybe they were right after all.*

"Why would they want to do this to your people?"

"Not just to us. There are several species in our solar system. Deurtex are actually the least susceptible," Tesha clarified, unconsciously caressing two, narrow cylinders on the bottom of her jaw. She then answered, "I don't know."

Not even Vorrnum would launch such a diabolical attack without a reason. Who has something to gain from the epidemic? Answer that and you'll know who the culprits are. At this point, Kiiyeepo believed her about the epidemic. Logically, he had to in lieu of a better explanation, but it still didn't sit right with him.

He wished he could hear what was being said just up the hall in the negotiation. *The ambassadors had questions already prepared. How the Deurtex officials answer could clear the fog. They must know more than this server, but they also wouldn't be as open.*

Lost in thought, Kiiyeepo never responded. Nonetheless, Tesha seemed perfectly content just to sit there at his side, so that's exactly what they did for ten micro fragments.

Kiiyeepo yawned and asked, "What time is it?"

Unlike the guide, Tesha didn't appear to have any sort of time keeper, yet she answered immediately, "Eight point one six. I'm not sure how that translates into your time. Maybe early evening. Oh, are you hungry? There will be a banquet after the meeting, but I could bring you a meal now or a snack."

"No, I'll wait."

"We found tons of really interesting looking food on this station, which we have little use for. A transport is coming to take it and supposedly distribute it to the poor. That's what I'll be doing tomorrow, helping load it up."

"Do you not eat?"

Tesha opened her mouth to show that there was, of course, no opening. She then pointed to a tiny hatch on her side. "That goes right to my stomach. We have to make a special slurry."

Kiiyeepo was more sad for her than he was disturbed. "You don't get to taste anything?"

"I don't think I'd want to taste that stuff. It's meant to be nutritious, nothing more," Tesha said, looking on the bright side. She changed the topic anyway, "What would you normally be doing at this time?"

"Back at the ranch? It depends. On a bad day, I might be shoveling iiow manure. On a good day, I might be taking a nap." Kiiyeepo closed his eyes for a moment and smiled at the thought.

"You're welcome to lie down on the sofa until dinner. There no telling how long the meeting will be."

It didn't take much deliberation. Resting was the best thing he could do for his numerous aches and pains. "I think I will."

He reached for his staff, but she took his hand. "Let me help you."

She pulled him to his feet. She was strong for being so petite, or at least her suit made it seem that way. Putting her arms around him, she bore his weight as he walked across the room and then gently lowered him onto the long sofa. "I'll just be in the next room. Do you want the light on or off?"

"You can leave it on." Kiiyeepo knew he wouldn't be falling asleep. He reclined and closed his eyes, but his mind was hard at work. Repeating and sorting, he tried to remember everything Tesha had told him down to the letter.

CHAPTER 26
A Setup for Tragedy

"The threat is too great, and the treaty is too easily broken," Falair proclaimed. "You must agree not to bring heavy weaponry to your space stations. No bombers, ordinances, long range artillery, etc."

"The risk for both sides must be limited proportionally. Each of us would have to shoulder the same restraints, or I would have no way to defend these stations," Rekiph countered. "The clause must be universal: no heavy weaponry may be moved to the Nieyowpon space stations, to the planet's surface, or anywhere within the jurisdiction of this agreement. Is that acceptable?"

The delegations immediately began deliberating among themselves, except for two. The Dragon ambassador looked genuinely surprised to hear that Nieyowpon had a surface, and Ordmin waggled a finger at Falair, silently commanding him to wait.

The Wulvry had a decision to make. He and the other chiefs wanted Valexs to bring back weapons and artillery. However, this clause would mean that the invaders couldn't attack Nieyowpon without first breaking the treaty. Not even the Pact could respond with force if Nieyowpon declared its independence. The artillery wouldn't be as necessary, and they could still bring in new handguns and armor for their soldiers. He gave his verdict with a slow nod.

The Orranians remained apprehensive. "How would this be enforced?"

Rekiph didn't take long to answer, which meant he'd prepared the solution beforehand. "Each of you: Chriyoss, Xonero, Orra, Krashad, Praxus, and Zanquin, may have one designated inspection ship, and I will have two. With probable cause, these ships may intercept vessels suspected of carrying cargo in violation to our agreement."

"What isn't probable cause when tensions are running so high?" the Zanquinite ambassador asked rhetorically. "That could lead to an oppressive number of searches."

"What do you propose?"

"Each party may have two search rights plus an additional right at the beginning of each month, according to the interplanetary calendar, to a maximum of three. If a search finds a violation, then the search right is refunded."

"You're asking for twelve of these 'search rights' to our two. Be reasonable!" Rekiph scolded. For a moment his crimson stare darkened, almost to black. "You may each have one and we will require three. Even then you will have twice as many as us."

Again, the representatives conferred with their companies. The Orranians, however, quickly probed, "What will be the punishment if someone violates the treaty?"

"Their ship will be seized by the searching party, but the crew may not be imprisoned or harassed unless they resist. If a nation in any way authorized, paid for, or permitted the illegal shipment, then that nation will be barred from Nieyowpon and the space stations surrounding it."

"To be barred from Nieyowpon for a designated period is enough. Shall we say two months or a season? The ship must be allowed to return the way it came. Private vessels violating the treaty completely independently will have their cargo confiscated."

"Very well. Do the rest of you agree to these terms?" Rekiph noticed Falair's scowl and amended, "The punishment will be different for Chriyoss and Xonero as they own the space stations. They will have a choice to either surrender their sensitive cargo or pay a weighty fine."

Falair was appeased. "Fair enough."

Indeed, the terms did seem amicable to the parties present. A time fragment had been spent getting to this point. It took another to choose specific numbers and answer questions. The emissaries did their job, double checking everything. If they missed something or left a loophole, it could easily come back to bite them.

By the time the call for final concerns came, the Orranians had noticeably drooped on their hover discs. Notwithstanding, their head diplomat floated up to assert himself. "We are worried that this treaty doesn't provide enough protection. The situation could implode as easily as before, and we'd be worse off than we started. We want more certainty. We want to leave a portion of our fleet in its present position."

"Your point is valid," Rekiph agreed but then went quiet and still. He was listening to the voices in his headset: orders from Furygon and calculations from the control room.

The emissaries didn't know whether to wait or to make a proposal of their own. The Zanquinites had begun to speak, but Rekiph quickly cut them off, "I will allow two destroyer-class warships and their associated vessels to act as a vanguard for your space stations, and I will leave my battle cruiser to guard mine. The movement of these ships without consent will be considered an immediate violation of the treaty and may be responded to with unrestricted warfare."

"That is acceptable," the Velphan ambassador consented.

When several others nodded to show their approval, Rekiph asked, "Which of you will provide these vessels?"

"Chriyoss will supply," Falair immediately declared.

"Orra as well," the Orranians said.

There were no objections. Either the other nations weren't willing to send a destroyer or their diplomats didn't have the power to offer.

Rekiph glanced at the delegation from Zanquin. They'd been chatty earlier and effective in prolonging the negotiation. Nonetheless, they were finally contented.

Seemingly to no one, he commanded, "Draw up the armistice."

A table was rolled in. On top, were a writing stick and a large document titled The Nieyo-space Ceasefire. Each representative gave it a tedious scan, especially Ordmin, before signing their names.

Falair additionally stamped it with the seal of Xonero. The Orranians did likewise. Everyone else would have to wait for the treaty to be voted on by a special commission or signed by their executive, depending on the procedure of their governments.

"It has been a pleasure, sirs," Rekiph concluded. As he turned away, his heavy cape generated a sound like a gust of wind. He exited through the double doors, and then two workers entered.

While one handed out copies of The Nieyo-space Ceasefire in sealed cases, the other addressed the group, "Thank you all for your presence and prudence. A banquet has been prepared for you. Please enjoy it. For those who wish to remain for the night, accommodations will be provided. Our guides can show you to wherever you need to go."

The pair released everyone back into the hall. Half the emissaries nodded, satisfied with the outcome of the previous time fragments; the rest sighed in relief that it was over. Their bodyguards trailed after them. These sentinels had stood around the room like columns, unnoticed for the duration of the meeting.

Down the passage, a guide directed Ordmin and Falair into the sitting area to rejoin their "guest". Kiiyeepo and a petite Deurtex were seated at opposite ends of the long sofa.

This Deurtex didn't have the posture of a server, sitting casually with her legs tucked to one side, yet she instantly popped up at Kiiyeepo's request, "Can I have a writing stick and something to write on? For keeps."

"Oh, of course!" She smiled and thoughtfully retrieved his staff for him before speeding off.

Kiiyeepo took another gulp of his water, lukewarm now, and then questioned his colleagues. "How'd it go?"

"Fine, different but fine." Falair's tone was pleasant, yet his small ears were set forward. He was anxious. "They wanted to expedite the negotiation and forced us to stand to encourage that. Either that or standing for such occasions is a kind of tradition or custom in their culture."

Ordmin, on the other hand, wore a huge grin like he'd accomplished some great victory. He was eagerly describing the terms of the ceasefire when the server returned.

Kiiyeepo took the writing stick and blank page, but his ears perked up when Ordmin mentioned "Allanoi's sequestration". It was the first he'd heard in connection to the blockade, but, without details, he didn't make too much of it. He purposed to ask about it later, though, and went to work jotting down what he'd learned about the epidemic.

"Will you be needing rooms?" Tesha inquired of the ambassador.

"That won't be necessary. Please excuse us." Falair waited for her to be far out of earshot and then explained, "We are leaving at once."

"Why?" Ordmin demanded. "I thought we were here to learn. We wanted to look around!"

"I think we really should go too, really," Kiiyeepo pled. Having awoken from his nap to find Tesha stroking his ears, he was very much perturbed that the young Deurtex had become infatuated with him. Perhaps it was simply a difference of customs.

"Give me some reasons!"

Both Ordmin and Falair looked to Kiiyeepo, who stammered, "Well, um, I think that server has, uh, taken an interest in me."

Ordmin laughed, actually laughed, and it was a terrifying noise. "I don't think *you* need to worry about *that!*"

Falair answered dryly, "The sooner we get to Vorrnum the better. There's no telling what he has already put into the works."

The chief wasn't convinced, but Kiiyeepo was prompt to second the notion, "Yeah, he might lead another campaign against Praxus!"

The expression on Falair's face said that the statement was an utter absurdity, but the Kumor had no reason to correct it. He merely urged, "Come on. It's best if we get out first."

Chrion and Deurtex workers alike were servicing the ambassador's ship when they reentered the dock.

"That company currently holds the contract to do the repairs for Chrion and Xonerite government vessels," Falair mentioned. He told Kiiyeepo and Ordmin to go on ahead, which they didn't, and then called out to the supervisor of the Chrion crew, "What is the meaning of this?"

"The pilot reported a hesitation in the stabilizers. We're running a diagnostic now and doing general maintenance," the Gredwol explained as he strolled over. He extended a folder to Falair. "We were authorized by your boss, the Chief of Foreign Affairs. Here's the official documentation and your receipt."

While Falair flipped through the paperwork, Kiiyeepo and Ordmin finally headed up the boarding ramp. Both of them made a beeline for the kitchen, but Ordmin got there first. He pulled a stack of cans and boxes from the cabinets, mostly snack food, and then carried it off to his quarters. It was a wonder how he didn't drop any of it while hopping down the hall.

Scrounging through foreign delicacies with names he couldn't begin to pronounce, Kiiyeepo was about to summon the cook when he spied a few fruits and vegetables from Allanoi. He fixed himself a plate and tossed in familiar meats. It was the stuff of home, or pretty close at least. The flavors brought his ranch strongly to mind, and he vowed to return to it if it was the last thing he did.

He was in good cheer as he scraped his plate clean. However, they were still grounded and he wanted to know why. He sought out Sufralycoo in the bridge. "Why haven't we left yet?"

"All me know, them take forever to refuel," the pale Zulan replied but kept typing away at one of the data interfaces. He was preparing the treaty to be transmitted down to the palace.

"It looked like they were making some repairs."

Sufralycoo shrugged, mentioning parenthetically, "Me think there be funny business going down."

"Like what?"

"Me not know, but ambassador have crowded sleeves... How it go?"

"They said it went fine. Ordmin kicked me out... You have the treaty there; what do you make of it?"

"It okay, too okay. Looks more like taken offer than a product of debate. Me think invaders got exactly what they bargained for, and me wonder why them bargain for it," Sufralycoo said, reviewing the digital document. He spoke low and muddled, as if rambling to himself, despite that there was deep meaning in what he was saying. As soon as he'd finished his appraisal, he questioned, "What you think of invaders?"

"They're... just people I guess. They aren't all bad." *The real bad guys are the monsters behind the epidemic,* Kiiyeepo mentally added. Nonetheless, he would keep his talk with Tesha to himself.

"Me knew that whole time."

Kiiyeepo continued, "What we would call normal air is caustic to them. They have to wear special suits that encase them completely. It makes living a bit more complicated for them."

"Even on their planet them need suit?"

"I didn't ask. Their home world must have an atmosphere safe for them, right?"

"Hmm..."

Kiiyeepo shuffled closer to the data interface, looking over Surfalycoo's head to see the screen. "Does the treaty say anything about Allanoi?"

"Directly? No. Some implications."

"What do you mean?"

Sufralycoo didn't answer. From his hand gestures, he seemed to be imagining the conversation in his head. What he eventually came up with was, "Ask Falair. Me not know all the facts."

He glanced back after a few moments of quiet. Kiiyeepo was just standing there, worrying about his home world. The Zulan rolled his eyes and invited annoyedly, "You want help me?"

"Yeah, sure!" Kiiyeepo stayed up with him to finish the transmission. They also sent some of the information they'd collected about the Deurtex and the present naval situation around Nieyowpon.

At last, the siren blared and the dock lights switched red. Kiiyeepo instinctively searched for a g-force seat, though they were unnecessary in space. Sufralycoo didn't even look up from his work, as if he couldn't hear the shrill noise. This seemed strange for someone who'd never ridden on a spacecraft before today.

Falair was in no mood for questions when he entered the bridge. Weary and agitated, his expression was a command. The pilot and copilot immediately took their seats and prepared to depart.

Once everyone had evacuated the dock, the vacuums siphoned out the air. Next, the dock walls rose away. The pilot retracted the landing gear, guiding the ship free from the massive structure with small engine thrusts. They emerged from between the two parking towers and then set course on a space lane to Dasahr.

The drive engines steadily accelerated the ship. After several micro fragments, the copilot announced, "We have reached cruising speed."

"And me all done!" Sufralycoo declared. Only then, did he step away from the data interface. Did the cosmos not interest him? Anyone else would have been glued to the windshield for his first extraterrestrial voyage, but this Zulan clearly wasn't just anyone.

He pointed a bony finger at the ambassador, who had turned to leave, and interrogated, "Why them take so long refuel?"

"Technical difficulties," Falair answered as he walked away. "Everything is operational now though."

"Liar! Me'd see alert here."

Falair stopped in the doorway. "Unfortunately not. It was an issue with the stabilizers. Apparently, there wouldn't have been an alert unless they were active. Raym, our pilot, noticed it when we landed and requested an inspection."

"It's nothing serious right?" Kiiyeepo interjected.

Falair hesitated. "No... but we're keeping an eye on it."

After the Kumor had gone, Raym waited a couple of micro fragments and then stood and yawned. "Time for me to hit the sack!"

He left the copilot at the controls. Kiiyeepo and Sufralycoo followed him out. Except for the guards, everyone on board had private quarters. Small screens on the doors designated each room by the passenger's name. As it turned out, theirs were side by side.

They wished each other a good night before going in. The rooms were tiny, furnished with a bed, a chair, and a low cabinet that doubled as a desk. Kiiyecpo was glad to see that the maid had brought up his black bag. He tucked his notes about the epidemic inside.

I have to get this information to Haazon. If only the good guys of our solar system knew the truth. If only we knew who the good guys are... Just stop worrying about it for a moment! he commanded himself.

It wasn't terribly late, so he passed the next time fragment in the world of The Unknown Hero. An elderly mystic in the forest village did what no one else could; he deciphered the coded document. It contained the time and place of a secret meeting between the heads of the rebellion and the most powerful dukes. Immediately, the protagonist, mystic, and another loyalist set out to infiltrate that meeting. Only one was successful, but he reported everything he'd heard. The rebels had played on the dukes' animosity for one another. In the end, the dukes conceded a large tract of land to the rebellion.

Does anything good happen in this story? Kiiyeepo thought, though he was happy to have his mind distracted from the stresses of the real world. He killed the lights and pulled up the blanket. *I wonder if I'll ever see Tesha again...*

CHAPTER 27
The Battle of Wills

Kiiyeepo slipped out of his room bright and early into a slumbering vessel. He left his staff behind today, as the medic had predicted, in hopes of moving more quietly through the ship. Only the cook was up, ready to fix an exotic breakfast, and maybe a few of the soldiers, but they kept to themselves.

The food was bland, despite the elaborate recipe. It was a Chrion delicacy, and evidently that's how they liked it. For the cook's sake, he pretended to enjoy the meal.

He ended up having a very long conversation with the cook, who was dying to know more about the great solar system he'd launched himself into. The maid joined in as soon as she overheard the dialogue. Neither of them knew who else they could approach with their questions. Kiiyeepo didn't mind. They proved to be very interesting and understanding people in their own ways, but eventually they had to get back to work.

The subsequent time fragments would be blander than the food. Falair didn't come out of his quarters until midday and then hid away on the bridge. Ordmin hogged the broadcast receiver for most of the day, watching who knows what. Other than transmitting the cyclic positional update, Sufralycoo busied himself with personal matters.

A transmission came in from the palace that afternoon, congratulating Ordmin and stating their agreement with his decision. It also mentioned Valexs's crew. When they last checked in, they were preparing to dock at an Orra space station. Since their old vessels were unregistered and they didn't have flight plans on file, they would have to undergo an inspection and screening. Of course, Valexs already had a plan to ease the process.

Another new development was that the overseer of the Chrion mechanics back at the space station had come aboard. The reason, though not surprising, was quite unnerving. The Gredwol claimed that they hadn't been able to confirm the cause of the stabilizers' delay, and he'd offered to monitor the system first hand. Presently, he suspected that it was a minor electrical issue, like a weak power cell or loose wire.

Kiiyeepo, however, was worried about a different matter. They had one full day before their meeting with Vorrnum. *Vorrnum! The infamous, Dragon king! What will we say to him?*

In preparation, he read the whole section of his pocket guide devoted to Dasahr with a particular interest in the Dragons. Three distinct types of Dragons existed: Common Dragons, Serpentine, and Wyvern. Each type had many subgroups, varying broadly in size and coloration.

As the name implied, Common Dragons comprised the vast majority of the population. They stood upright with thick muscular bodies to anchor their long, powerful necks and tails. Vorrnum was a prime example of such a Dragon, though capable of emitting an electrified gas rather than the usual flame or frost.

Never had Kiiyeepo encountered a Dragon on Allanoi; it seemed that the people of Krashad had no escape from Vorrnum's cruel reign. Nonetheless, he felt feeble at the mere description of the beings.

Rather improbably, the travelers' separate ways converged in the dining compartment. Falair and the Gredwol overseer chatted about their favorite Tactball teams for the entire meal, leaving the rest of them scratching their heads. Kiiyeepo had been meaning to ask the ambassador about Allanoi's present state of affairs, but apparently that would have to wait once again.

Afterwards, Falair did accompany Ordmin and Kiiyeepo when the copilot took them on the mandatory emergency drill. It was obvious that this had more than a little to do with the 'technical difficulties'.

The ship's layout was based around the two central hallways, one on each floor. The passengers' rooms, the lounge, and two store rooms occupied the upper deck. The soldiers bunked on the lower level, which also housed the kitchen, dining hall, launch room, and sanitation area. Capping off the hallways at either end were the bridge and the engine room.

The drill taught them how to reach the escape pod safely and quickly, as well as how to pilot the tiny craft. It was mounted to the rear of the ship below the hyper cell and was accessible from the engine room. One would enter the pod through an airlock and then a hatch mounted between its two thrusters. There were ten tight seats inside and the bare minimum controls.

Kiiyeepo started getting antsy by the end of it. Despite the copilot's assurances, his stuttering proved that the drill wasn't a normal occurrence. This was not a good sign.

When the opportunity finally arose, part of him was afraid to question Falair. Odds were that he wouldn't like the answer. Nonetheless, that didn't stop him. "What's going on with Allanoi?"

Falair answered tersely, "It's blockaded."

"The whole planet!" Kiiyeepo probed. It was the answer he'd expected, but also the one he was most unwilling to accept. "A ship could still get through, right?"

"The aliens aren't letting anything in or out. No exceptions. That's why they took over the two space stations, to prevent blockade running via Nieyowpon."

No exceptions. The phrase reverberated in Kiiyeepo's mind, and his hope shattered. *Why? All I want is to go home. Is that too much to ask?*

He retreated to his quarters but stopped in the hall. The more he thought about the information the more his emotions shifted from sadness to anger, and he had a good idea of who to be mad at. He knocked on Sufralycoo's door.

"Who it?" the Zulan squealed.

"You knew didn't you?"

The door opened just a little. Sufralycoo peered through the crack, askance.

Kiiyeepo clarified, "You knew about the blockade."

"Nooo..." Sufarlycoo drew out the answer, gauging the Midek's reaction. "Me hear something but not really."

"I don't believe you. You deceived me! You and the chiefs! They told me I would be free to go but conveniently neglected to tell me that Allanoi wasn't an option!" Kiiyeepo fumed.

I guess that's why Nieyowsue was so quick to invite me back to Nieyowpon. Did she think I knew about the blockade? Or did she know that I wouldn't have agreed to come on this trip if I hadn't thought it would get me home? There's someone on this ship who was most certainly deliberate in leaving out information! Kiiyeepo realized. "I have to talk to Ordmin."

"That no help," Sufralycoo admonished.

"There's something I need to make clear to him!"

"Him not care what you say. It only make you look bad."

"Argh!" Kiiyeepo growled and stamped his foot in frustration. Of course, he knew it was true.

"Go to bed. You think clearer tomorrow."

Kiiyeepo heeded the advice, slamming the door to his room. He went straight to the porthole, but the dusky green sphere in the distance was Xonero. He was on the wrong side of the ship to see his home world.

How long will the blockade last? Why would they blockade Allanoi? What do I do now? I worked so hard to get off Nieyowpon. I have to get home. I have to. I'll run the blockade if that's what it takes.

Maybe I can make a deal with the aliens. I'll let them search my ship. I'll prove that I just want to get home! If there are others like Tesha, why wouldn't they let me through?

There was a glimmer of hope, but then a bleaker thought took over. *If they lock me up, at least I might see Caltow again.*

He flopped into bed. For a while, he thought only about his lost brother. Despair eventually gave way to boredom, however, and boredom put him to sleep. He tossed and turned, the best time fragments of rest coming in the early morning.

When he got up, Dasahr looked big and imperious through the porthole. Dense gray clouds enshrouded the planet. Where they parted, he could see various hues of brown evidencing the mountainous topography. They would be landing in just a few time fragments. While they waited to be seen, they would explore the capital city.

He wandered to the lounge half awake and plopped down before the broadcast receiver. Snippets of information regarding The Nieyo-space Ceasefire had already gotten out, and the media was cheering.

"Why else would the aliens yield to any restrictions? Our representatives stood together and showed who's boss in our solar system!" the news anchor declared. Kiiyeepo knew what a wild hyperbole this was, but it still put a smile on his face.

Too soon, it bent into a frown as Tesha came to mind. Both sides got what they wanted, so shouldn't he be happy? He wasn't sure of anything now. He just wanted to go home and forget all this, to leave it in someone else's hands.

"...which means the invaders realized that they didn't have the upper hand at the Nieyowpon space stations. They might not be as powerful as we feared," journalists on another broadcast hypothesized. *They're so desperate for hope, so naive, and still they could be on the wrong side.*

Kiiyeepo flipped to a third news channel. The reporter was just as excited, but she checked herself. "I can't stress this enough. Until we see the actual content of the treaty, we cannot jump to conclusions. All we have are a handful of comments from officials who weren't even there. I want to hear it from the lips of our ambassador and—"

The lights flickered and the receiver automatically switched off. Kiiyeepo jumped to his feet. Right away, the voice of the copilot rang over the intercom, "Attention all personnel—"

The voice crackled and warped into a piercing screech. It stopped when the room's power cut off altogether. Yells echoed up the dark corridors as

Kiiyeepo rose off the floor in the absence of a gravity field. *This can't be happening!*

He was brought down a moment later, but only a third of the lights relit, just enough to see by. Another screech and then the copilot's voice broke through. "Backup power active. All personnel evacuate the ship. This is not a drill!"

Kiiyeepo hustled to the escape pod, the route fresh in his mind, but veered off to get his bag. He heard commotion in some of the rooms as he passed, yet the halls remained inexplicably vacant. When he reached the airlock, Sufralycoo was somehow already there with a bulging travel case in tow.

"What going on? You seen Falair?" the frail Zulan queried.

"No, I haven't. The power went out. Technical difficulties!"

"Duh. You know nothing," Sufralycoo muttered. He pulled his case into the pod and took a seat by the controls. Kiiyeepo rushed in after him. They waited a moment, the lights flickered again, and then Sufralycoo commanded, "Go get ambassador." His tone was quiet but extremely stern.

"The ship is shutting down and you want me to go back in there? Falair will come."

Ordmin emerged, bounding toward them with three soldiers, half of the force, and the copilot, but this seemed to further upset Sufralycoo. He demanded again, "Go! If ambassador not here, this be very bad!"

"But..." Kiiyeepo stammered, only to have Sufralycoo yank the black bag out of his hand and scream, "Go!"

The Midek gulped and then charged up the passageway. He took the upper corridor to bypass Ordmin, glancing in rooms and nooks in the slim hope that the ambassador would be there. *If Falair will be anywhere, it will be the bridge... On the other side of the ship!*

The overseer stepped out into the corridor ahead of him and questioned, "Where are you going? We have to be on that escape pod ASAP!"

"I have to get Falair," Kiiyeepo said, not slowing down. He attempted to run past, but the Gredwol caught him by the arm and hauled him to a stop.

"There's no time. We have to go!"

"No! We can't leave him!" Kiiyeepo shouted, jerking away.

Before he could move, the Gredwol pulled a gun on him. "I can't let you do that. It's suicide. Falair insists on going down with the—"

He spat as Kiiyeepo slugged him in the gut and wrenched the blaster from his hand. The Midek didn't stop to watch him double-over; he had to get to the bridge. *There's no time for debate!*

He was there in a few moments but slammed against its locked door. It didn't budge, try as he might to force it open, so he called in, "Falair! If you're there, open up!"

It was too long before the bolt slid mechanically, but the ambassador shouted back at the same time, "I thought I could save it... It was a last ditch effort to get the systems on line."

Kiiyeepo flew into the room as soon as the door swung. Nonetheless, Falair was still at the controls. "Give up. Didn't you hear the pilot? We need to get out of here now!"

"Yes, yes, you're right." The Kumor pressed two more buttons before finally hopping up. He started for the door. "Let's go."

As only a Kumor could, he instantly accelerated to four times his original speed. Lowering his shoulder to ram, he shifted his trajectory straight at the Midek.

The wall hit first and then the metal floor as Kiiyeepo toppled. The blaster soared from his hand. His fury, however, roared stronger than the pain. He lunged when Falair galloped toward the blaster and swept the Kumor's hind legs out from under him. Falair was sent sprawling to the ground. Up first, Kiiyeepo tackled him and pinned him down.

"What are you doing? Are you mad!"

"Perfectly calculated if it wasn't for you!" Falair yelled, thrashing beneath the firm hold. He waited for Kiiyeepo's pupils to widen, proof that he was considering what he'd just heard, and then thrust a knee into the Midek's chest and rolled on top of him.

Blocking a jab, Kiiyeepo grabbed the Kumor's arm before he could jump away and landed a punch of his own. He yanked him down on his side and they rolled, Falair trying to break loose and snag the blaster while Kiiyeepo did anything in his power to stop him.

Eventually, Falair kicked free. When they both got to their feet, the Midek still stood between him and the blaster. They faced off with locked stares and labored breaths.

Kiiyeepo probed fiercely, "You mean this was all a ploy? The ship is just fine, isn't it?"

"Do I look scared? Of course it is."

"Then where'd you get the mechanics at the space station? They couldn't have been a real company."

"The Pact sent them. They set this up!" Falair answered. "I have to get rid of the Nieyowpean pests; the Pact demands it. If I'm not able to properly represent Xonero to Vorrnum, then I'm through. I'll never represent anything again."

"Can't you see how wrong this is? You can't just launch three people into space!"

"Just Ordmin and that diseased Zulan..." Falair shot forward, fists flying. "You don't matter!"

Kiiyeepo caught both fists, grunted, and then shoved back as hard as he could. The plan backfired. Falair didn't even stagger to find his balance. Instead, he reared up on his hind legs and kicked with the front pair.

Kiiyeepo was floored. For a moment, he couldn't move at all. It took great effort, but he rose, futile though it was. Falair already stood over him, gun in hand, and softy hissed, "Let's go."

They rushed down the corridor. He pressed the gun barrel against Kiiyeepo's back, demanding a pace that the Midek couldn't offer. He let up a little, however, when they heard anguished yells ahead and ground to a halt when they entered the engine room.

The copilot and overseer lay breathing but unconscious in front of the airlock. Their somnial states evidenced some kind of tranquilizer or powerful stun. Advancing further, they could see Sufralycoo and Ordmin inside the escape pod plus the laser-pierced corpse of a guard.

Falair thrust Kiiyeepo into the pod as two soldiers appeared behind them. Charging with raised blasters, the soldiers shouted, "Ambassador, stop right there! Drop the weapon!"

The blaster clanged to the floor. Falair put his hands in the air, but it was too late. He'd already swung the hatch shut.

The airlock immediately sealed, a thick panel cutting off the escape pod from the ship. Gases hissed, metal clamps released, and then the pod ejected into silent space and Dasahr's gravitational field.

What did you think of
The Unknown Hero?
Review it on **Amazon**
or **Goodreads**!

Find more
information on the
official website
www.IsaacPhilips.com

Follow Isaac Philips
on social media
for the latest news.
@fictionbyisaac